Praise for Graeme Macrae Burnet's *His Bloody Project*

SHORTLISTED FOR THE MAN BOOKER PRIZE 2016

FINALIST, *LOS ANGELES TIMES* BOOK AWARDS 2016

WINNER, SALTIRE SOCIETY FICTION BOOK OF THE YEAR 2016

WINNER, *VRIJ NEDERLAND* THRILLER OF THE YEAR 2016

'A spellbinding piece of serious new fiction...Riveting, dark and ingeniously constructed.' EDMUND GORDON, *Sunday Times*

'A smart amalgam of legal thriller and literary game that reads as if Umberto Eco has been resurrected in the 19th-century Scottish Highlands.' MARK LAWSON, *Guardian*

'An astonishing piece of writing ... a voice that sounds startlingly authentic.' JAKE KERRIDGE, *Telegraph*

'Compelling and entirely true to its setting ... as good as historical fiction gets.' Critics' Choice, *Times*

'Brings an extraordinary historical period into focus ... This is a fiendishly readable tale that richly deserves the wider attention the Man Booker has brought it.' JUSTINE JORDAN, *Guardian*

'Gripping, blackly playful and intelligent ... one of the few [Man Booker longlist titles] that may set the heather – and imagination – ablaze.' ROBBIE MILLEN, *Times*

'*His Bloody Project* has a feel for authentic-seeming time and geography that transports readers into the moment ... but its overarching themes are timeless.' *New Statesman*

'Sucked me in from the very first page with compelling narratives ... A series of convincing but unreliable voices circles the central event and left me breathless.' VAL MCDERMID, *Guardian*

'A brilliantly written story of rural hardship, fractured community and eventual, inescapable bloodshed.' IAN RANKIN, *Guardian*

'Burnet proves that the undeniable pleasures of the crime novel can be combined with real literary value and an experimental narrative structure ... Few readers will be able to put down *His Bloody Project* as it speeds towards a surprising (and ultimately puzzling) conclusion.' BARRY FORSHAW, *Financial Times*

'One of the most convincing and engrossing novels of the year.' DAVID ROBINSON, *Scotsman*

'The dark intimacy of Graeme Macrae Burnet's *His Bloody Project* – a rich, brooding book ... is difficult to classify, and utterly compelling from the first page.' JON DAY, MAN BOOKER PRIZE JUDGE

'Grabs you by the throat and doesn't let you go. This multilayered novel about a 19th-century murder near Applecross is as heartbreaking as it is desperate.' KIRSTY WARK, *Guardian*

'Darkly engaging.' SALLY MAGNUSSON, Books of the Year, *Herald*

'The overwhelming appeal of this excellent novel is its authenticity: Macrae Burnet marshals a wide variety of Victorian styles and voices and every single one of them rings true.' *Times Literary Supplement*

'A gripping story, a deeply imagined historical novel, and glorious writing ... a tour-de-force.' CHRIS DOLAN, Book of the Year, *Herald*

'Compelling ... a fine achievement from an ambitious and accomplished writer.' *National*

'This is a novel on which Robert Louis Stevenson might have bestowed an envious blessing.' ROBERT MCCRUM, *Observer*

'A real box of tricks ... a truly ingenious thriller as confusingly multilayered as an Escher staircase.' *Daily Express*

'Riveting.' *Mail on Sunday*

'Wonderfully vivid and moving ... a love letter to Scottish literature ... a terrific psychological thriller.' ALISTAIR BRAIDWOOD, *Scots Whay Hae*

'Such an engrossing plot that I couldn't put it down.' – NICOLA STURGEON, Books of the Year, *Herald*

'Graeme Macrae Burnet makes such masterly use of the narrative form that the horrifying tale he tells in *His Bloody Project* ... seems plucked straight out of Scotland's sanguinary historical archives.' *New York Times*

'Halfway between a thriller and a sociological study of an exploitive economic system with eerie echoes to our own time, *His Bloody Project* is a gripping and relevant read.' *Newsweek*

'Offers an intricate, interactive puzzle, a crime novel written, excuse my British, bloody well.' *Los Angeles Times*

'Burnet has created an eloquent character who will stick with you long after the book is read.' *Seattle Review of Books*

'Maddeningly brilliant... A cunning and unreliable tale that still bloody nags at me.' HANNAH KENT, *Sydney Morning Herald*

'Genius ... *His Bloody Project* is provocative, rewarding reading for its deeply observed explorations of repression, loyalty, justice and truth.' SUMANA MUKERJEE, *Livemint*

Praise for *The Disappearance of Adèle Bedeau*

'Burnet skilfully knits together a solid detective story and a compelling character study to make a captivating psychological thriller.' *Herald*

'One of the best debuts from a Scottish writer in some time.' *National*

'A character-driven plot that is incredibly engaging ... the writing is evocative and the characters intriguing.' *Bookseller*

'A strikingly singular talent, Burnet blends a gripping story with compelling characters and surprising sweeps of the imagination. This is an accomplished, elegantly written and exciting first novel.' *Booktrust*

'Clever, playful and bleakly funny, *The Disappearance of Adèle Bedeau* has all the makings of a cult classic.' *A Novel Bookblog*

'Imagine *Crime and Punishment* filtered through the sensibilities of Simenon and Beckett and distilled into a novel ... Gripping and mysterious, *The Disappearance of Adele Bedeau* lingers in the reader's mind long after the late nights of reading it has inspired.' JOHN LANGAN, author of *The Fisherman*

'This is a crime novel but it is so much more than that, and whilst it owes a lot to Simenon, it is in no way diminished by that comparison.' *Crime Review UK*

'A deeply atmospheric read ... in Graeme Macrae Burnet, we have a refreshing new storyteller, one who presents his morbidly interestingly tales in a most assured and riveting fashion.' *Scottish Books*

LONGLISTED FOR THE WAVERTON GOOD READ AWARD

SELECTED AMONGST SCOTLAND'S BEST 2014 TITLES BY *THE LIST* MAGAZINE

THE Accident ON THE A35

RAYMOND BRUNET

Translated and introduced by
Graeme Macrae Burnet

CONTRABAND

Contraband is an imprint of Saraband

Published by Saraband
Digital World Centre, 1 Lowry Plaza,
The Quays, Salford, M50 3UB, United Kingdom
www.saraband.net

ISBN: 9781910192870
ISBNe: 9781910192887

Editor: Craig Hillsley. Cover artist: Scott Smyth.

Printed and bound in Great Britain by Clays Ltd, St Ives plc.

10 9 8 7 6 5 4 3 2 1

Contents

Foreword

On the 20th of November 2014, a package addressed to Raymond Brunet's former editor, Georges Pires, was delivered by courier to the offices of Éditions Gaspard-Moreau on Rue Mouffetard in Paris. Pires had died of cancer nine years earlier, and the parcel was instead opened by a young trainee. It contained two manuscripts and a letter from a Mulhouse-based firm of solicitors stating that they had been instructed to dispatch the enclosed documents to the publishing house on the occasion of the death of Brunet's mother, Marie.

Brunet, the author of a single previous novel, *The Disappearance of Adèle Bedeau*, had thrown himself in front of a train at Saint-Louis railway station in 1992. Marie Brunet, having outlived her son by some twenty-two years, died in her sleep at the age of eighty-four, two days before the dispatch of the package.

Despite (or perhaps even because of) the anachronistic nature of the submission, the trainee, who had not been born when Brunet's earlier book appeared in 1982, did not grasp the significance of the contents. The manuscripts were logged in the usual way and consigned to the firm's slush pile. It was not until four months later that a more senior member of staff at Gaspard-Moreau realised what they had in their possession. It is the first of these manuscripts, *L'Accident sur l'A35*, which you now hold in your hands.

The decision to publish was not taken in haste. It had first to be ascertained that Gaspard-Moreau was not the victim of a hoax. It was, however, a simple matter to confirm that Brunet had indeed lodged the manuscripts with a lawyer shortly before his suicide. The solicitor in question, Jean-Claude Lussac, was long retired, but he remembered the incident well and, as the only accessory to the scheme, had observed the rumours about the existence of unpublished works that followed Brunet's suicide with a mixture of amusement and guilt. A simple test also showed that the manuscripts had been written on the typewriter that still sat on the desk of what had once been Brunet's father's study at the family home in Saint-Louis. Such proofs, however, are entirely redundant. Even to the casual reader, it is obvious that the style, milieu and thematic concerns of *The Accident on the A35* are indistinguishable from those of Brunet's earlier novel. And for those inclined to interpret the work as a *roman-à-clef*, it was quite obvious why Brunet did not want the novel to be published in his mother's lifetime.

GMB, April 2017

The Accident on the A35

What I have just written is false. True. Neither true nor false.

Jean-Paul Sartre, *Words*

One

THERE DID NOT APPEAR to be anything remarkable about the accident on the A35. It occurred on a perfectly ordinary stretch of the trunk road that runs between Strasbourg and Saint-Louis. A dark green Mercedes saloon left the southbound carriageway, careered down a slope and collided with a tree on the edge of a copse. The vehicle was not immediately visible from the road, so although it was spotted by a passer-by at around 10:45pm, it was not possible to say with any certainty when the crash had occurred. In any case, when the car was discovered, the sole occupant was dead.

Georges Gorski of the Saint-Louis police was standing on the grass verge of the road. It was November. Drizzle glazed the road surface. There were no tyre marks. The most likely explanation was that the driver had simply fallen asleep at the wheel. Even in cases of cardiac arrest, drivers usually managed to apply the brakes or make some attempt to bring the vehicle under control. Nevertheless, Gorski resolved to keep an open mind. His predecessor, Jules Ribéry, had always urged him to follow his instincts. *You solve cases with this, not this*, he would say, pointing first to his considerable gut and then to his forehead. Gorski was sceptical about such an approach. It encouraged an investigator to disregard evidence that did not support the initial hypothesis. Instead, Gorski believed, each potential piece of evidence should be given due and equal consideration.

Ribéry's methodology had more to do with ensuring that he was comfortably ensconced in one of Saint-Louis' bars by mid-afternoon. Still, Gorski's initial impression of the scene before him suggested that in this case there would not be much call for alternative theories.

The area had been cordoned off by the time he arrived. A photographer was taking pictures of the crumpled vehicle. The flash intermittently illuminated the surrounding trees. An ambulance and a number of police vehicles with flashing lights occupied the southbound lane of the carriageway. A pair of bored *gendarmes* directed the sparse traffic.

Gorski ground out his cigarette on the shingle at the side of the road and made his way down the embankment. If he did so, it was less because he thought his inspection of the scene would offer up any insights into the cause of the accident than because it was expected of him. Those gathered around the vehicle awaited his verdict. The body could not be removed from the car until the investigating officer was satisfied. If the accident had occurred just a few kilometres north, it would have fallen under the jurisdiction of the Mulhouse station, but it had not. Gorski was conscious of the eyes of those gathered on the edge of the copse upon him as he scrambled down the slope. The grass was greasy from the evening's rain and his leather-soled slip-ons were ill suited to such conditions. He had to break into a run to prevent himself losing his balance and collided with a young *gendarme* holding a flashlight. There were suppressed titters.

Gorski took a slow turn around the vehicle. The photographer ceased his activity and stood back to allow him an unencumbered view. The victim had been propelled, head and shoulders, through the windscreen. His arms remained by his sides, suggesting he had made no attempt to shield himself from the impact. His head slumped on the concertinaed bonnet of the car. The man had a full greying beard, but Gorski could ascertain little more about his appearance, as his face, or at least the part that was visible, was entirely smashed in. The drizzle had plastered his hair to what was left of his forehead. Gorski continued his tour around the Mercedes. The paintwork on the driver's side of the vehicle was deeply scratched, indicating that the car might have travelled down the slope on its side before righting itself. Gorski paused and ran his fingers over the crumpled bodywork, as if expecting it to communicate something to him. It did not. And if he now took his notebook from the inside pocket of his jacket and scribbled a few perfunctory notes, it was only to satisfy those observing him. The Road Accident Investigation Unit would determine the cause of the accident in due course. No flashes of intuition were required from Gorski or anyone else.

The offside door had been forced ajar by the impact. Gorski wrenched it further open and reached inside the overcoat of the victim. He indicated to the sergeant in charge of the scene that he had concluded his inspection and made his way up the slope to his car. Once inside he lit another cigarette and opened the wallet he had retrieved. The dead man's name was Bertrand Barthelme, of 14 Rue des Bois, Saint-Louis.

THE PROPERTY WAS ONE of a handful of grand family homes on the northern outskirts of the town. Saint-Louis is a place of little note, situated at the Dreyeckland, the junction of Germany, Switzerland and eastern France. The municipality's twenty thousand inhabitants can be divided into three groups: those who have no aspiration to live somewhere less dreary; those who lack the wherewithal to leave; and those who, for reasons best known to themselves, like it. Despite the modest nature of the town, there are still a few families who have, in one way or another, built up what passes for a fortune in these parts. Their properties never come up for sale. They are passed down through the generations in the way that wedding rings and items of furniture are passed down among the poor.

Gorski pulled up at the kerb and lit a cigarette. The house was shielded from view by a screen of sycamores. It was the sort of street where an unfamiliar vehicle parked late at night swiftly elicited a call to the police. Gorski could quite legitimately have delegated the disagreeable task of informing the family to a junior officer, but he did not wish it to appear that he was not up to the job. There was a second, more insidious, reason, however; one that Gorki had difficulty admitting even to himself. He was here in person because of the address of the deceased. Would he have had the same misgivings about sending a lower-ranking officer to a home in one of the less salubrious quarters of the town? He would not. The truth was that he believed that the people who lived on Rue des Bois were entitled to the attention of the town's highest officer of the law. They expected it, and were Gorski not to carry out the task in person, it would later be whispered about.

He contemplated postponing the task until morning—it was close to midnight—but the lateness of the hour provided no excuse. Gorski would have had no qualms about disturbing a family in the shabby apartment blocks around Place de la Gare at any hour of his choosing. It was, furthermore, possible that in the interim the Barthelme family might hear the news from another source.

Gorski walked up the drive, his feet crunching on the gravel. He felt, as he always did when approaching such houses, like he was trespassing. If challenged, he would no doubt make some apologetic remark before bringing out the ID card that authorised his intrusion. He recalled the panic that ensued in his childhood home when a visitor called unannounced. His parents would exchange alarmed glances. His mother would cast her eyes around the room and hastily straighten the cushions and antimacassars before opening the door. His father would put on his jacket and stand to attention, as if ashamed to be caught relaxing in his own home. One evening when Gorski was seven or eight years old, two young Mormons who had recently taken up residence in the town called at the apartment above his father's pawnshop. Gorski heard them explain the nature of their visit in broken French. His mother invited them into the little parlour. Albert Gorski stood behind his chair as if awaiting the appearance of the mayor himself. Gorski was sitting beneath the window, turning the pages of an illustrated book. To his child's eyes, the two Americans were identical; tall and blond, with closely cropped hair and wearing tight-fitting navy blue suits. They stood in the doorway until Mme Gorski directed them to the chairs around the table at which the family took their meals. They did not appear in the least ill at ease. Mme Gorski offered them coffee, which they accepted enthusiastically. While she busied herself in the kitchenette, they introduced themselves to M. Gorski, who merely nodded and resumed his seat. The two men then made some remarks about how pleasant they found Saint-Louis. As Gorski's father made no response, a silence ensued, which lasted until Mme Gorski returned from the kitchen with a tray bearing a pot, the good china cups and a plate of madeleines. She wittered away while serving the visitors, but it was apparent that they understood little of her monologue. The Gorskis did not normally take coffee in the evening. Once these formalities were complete, the young man on the left, after casting his eyes meaningfully around the room, gestured towards the mezuzah fixed to the doorpost.

'I see you are of the Jewish persuasion,' he said, 'but my colleague and I would very much like to share with you the message of our faith.'

It was the first time Gorski had heard his parents referred to in this way. Religion was never mentioned in the Gorski household, far less practised. The little box on the doorpost was merely one of the many knick-knacks arrayed around the room that his mother dusted on a weekly basis. It held no particular significance, or if it did, Gorski was not aware of it. He was not even sure what the phrase 'of the Jewish persuasion' meant, other than signifying that they—the Gorskis—were different. Gorski was affronted that these strangers would talk to his father in this way. He remembered little else of the conversation, only that when the Americans had drunk their coffee and eaten his mother's biscuits, his father had accepted the literature they pressed into his hands and assured them that he would give it careful consideration. The young men seemed delighted by this response and said that they would be happy to call again. They then thanked Mme Gorski for her hospitality and left. Mme Gorski made a remark to the effect that they seemed like pleasant young men. M. Gorski perused the leaflets the Americans had left for half an hour or so, as if it would have been discourteous to immediately cast them aside. After his father's death, Gorski found them in the wooden box under the window sill in which papers deemed to be of a certain importance were kept.

Gorski was about to ring the bell of the house on Rue des Bois for a second time when a light went on in the vestibule and he heard the rattling of keys in the lock. The door was opened by a stout woman in her early sixties. Her grey hair was tied in a bun at the back of her head. She was wearing a dark blue serge dress, tight around her figure. Around her neck she wore a pair of spectacles on a leather string, and a small cross, which nestled in the cleft of her bosom. She had thick, manly ankles and wore brown brogues. She did not appear to have hurriedly dressed to answer the door. Perhaps her duties did not end until the master of the house had returned. Gorski imagined her sitting in her quarters, slowly turning the cards of a game of patience and letting a cigarette burn out in an ashtray by her elbow. She looked at Gorski with the expression of vague distaste to which he was quite accustomed and which he no longer allowed to offend him.

'Madame,' he began, 'Chief Inspector Georges Gorski of the Saint-Louis police.' He proffered the ID he had been holding in readiness.

'Madame Barthelme has retired for the night,' the woman replied. 'Perhaps you would be so good as to call at a more sociable hour.'

Gorski resisted the urge to apologise for the imposition. 'This is not a social call,' he said.

The woman widened her eyes and shook her head a little,

drawing in her breath as she did so. Then she raised her glasses to her eyes and asked to see Gorski's identification. 'What sort of time is this to be calling on a decent household?'

Gorski already felt a healthy loathing for this self-important busybody. She clearly believed that her status as gatekeeper to the household endowed her with great authority. He reminded himself that she was no more than a servant.

'It's the sort of time,' he said, 'which would suggest that I have called on a matter of some importance. Now, if you would be so good as to—'

The housekeeper stepped back from the door and grudgingly invited him into a cavernous wood-panelled hallway. The oak doors of the rooms on the first floor opened onto a landing, bounded by a carved balustrade. She ascended the stairs, leaning heavily on the banister, and entered a doorway on the left. Gorski waited in the semi-darkness of the hallway. The house was silent. A pale sliver of light emanated from a closed door on the right of the landing. A few moments later the housekeeper reappeared and made her way back down the stairs. She moved with an uneven gait, throwing her right leg out to the side as if troubled by her hip.

Mme Barthelme, she told him, would receive him in her room. Gorski had assumed that the mistress of the house would receive him downstairs. The idea of informing a woman of her husband's death in her bedroom struck him as vaguely indecent. But there was nothing else for it. He followed the housekeeper upstairs. She gestured towards the door and followed him in.

On account of the age of the victim, Gorski had expected to find a more elderly woman propped up on a pile of embroidered pillows. According to his driving licence, Barthelme was fifty-nine years old, but even from the cursory inspection Gorski had made, he had seemed older. His beard was thick and grey, and the cut and fabric of his three-piece suit old-fashioned. Mme Barthelme, by contrast, could not have been much more than forty, perhaps even younger. A mass of light brown hair was piled haphazardly on her head, as if it had been hastily arranged. Ringlets framed her heart-shaped face. On her shoulders was a light shawl, which she had likely donned for the sake of modesty, but her nightdress hung loosely around her chest and Gorski had to consciously avert his eyes. The room was entirely feminine. There was an ornate dressing table and a chaise longue strewn with clothes. The bedside table was arrayed with little brown bottles of pills. There was an absence of masculine articles or garments. The couple, clearly, kept separate rooms. Mme Barthelme smiled sweetly and apologised for receiving Gorski in bed.

'I'm afraid I was feeling rather—' She allowed her sentence to trail off with a vague gesture of her hand, which caused her breasts to shift beneath the linen of her nightdress.

For a moment Gorski forgot the purpose of his visit.

'Madame Thérèse did not tell me your name,' she said.

'Gorski,' he said, 'Chief Inspector Gorski.' He almost added that his forename was Georges.

'Is there enough crime in Saint-Louis to merit a Chief Inspector?' she said.

'Just about.' Normally, Gorski would have been offended by such a remark, but Mme Barthelme managed to make it sound like flattery.

He was standing midway between the door and the bed. There was a chair by the dressing table, but it was not appropriate to sit to deliver such grave news. The housekeeper loitered by the doorway. There was no reason she should not be present, so it was only to assert his authority that Gorski turned to her and said: 'If you wouldn't mind giving us some privacy, Thérèse.'

The housekeeper made no attempt to conceal her affront, but after making a show of straightening the cushions on the chaise longue, she complied.

'And close the door behind you,' Gorski added.

He paused for a few moments, adopting the solemn expression he wore for such occasions. 'I'm afraid I have some bad news, Madame Barthelme.'

'Please call me Lucette. You make me feel like an old maid,' she said. The first part of his statement seemed to have made no impression on her.

Gorski nodded. 'There has been an accident,' he said. He never saw any sense in dragging things out. 'Your husband is dead.'

'Dead?'

They all said that. Gorski did not read anything into people's reactions on hearing such news. Were he to receive a visit from a policeman at an unsociable hour, it would be clear that he was to receive bad news. But such thoughts did not seem to occur to civilians, and their first response was generally one of disbelief.

'His car left the A35 and hit a tree. He was killed instantly. It happened an hour or so ago.'

Mme Barthelme emitted a listless sigh.

'It appears from the initial inspection that the most likely scenario is that he fell asleep at the wheel. Naturally, a full investigation will be carried out.'

Mme Barthelme's expression barely changed. Her eyes drifted away from Gorski. They were pale blue, almost grey. Her reaction was not unusual. People did not cry out in anguish, faint or fly into a rage. Still, there was something curious in her subdued response. His eyes wandered to the array of bottles by the bedside. Perhaps she had taken a Valium or some other tranquiliser. Gorski allowed a few moments to pass. Then she started slightly, as if she had forgotten he was there.

'I see,' she said. She raised her hands to her head and started to tidy the ringlets around her face. She was quite charming.

'Would you like a glass of water?' he asked. 'Or perhaps some brandy?'

She smiled, exactly as she had when he entered the room. Gorski began to wonder if she had understood what he had told her.

'No, thank you. You've been very kind.'

Gorski nodded. 'Is there anyone else at home, besides the housekeeper?'

'Just our son, Raymond,' she said. 'He's in his room.'

'Would you like me to inform him?'

Mme Barthelme looked surprised at this offer. 'Yes,' she said, 'that would be very kind.'

Gorski nodded. He had not expected to have to go through the business twice. His mind had already drifted to the beer he planned to drink in Le Pot. He resisted the urge to glance at his watch. He hoped Yves would not have closed up by the time he got there. He bowed his head slightly and explained the need for a formal identification of the body. 'We'll send a car in the morning,' he said.

Mme Barthelme nodded. She directed him to her son's room. And that was that.

The housekeeper was sitting on an ottoman outside the door. Gorski assumed she had heard every word.

Two

Raymond Barthelme was sitting on a straight-backed chair in the middle of his bedroom reading *The Age of Reason*. The only light in the room came from the anglepoise lamp on the desk by the window. Aside from the bed, there was a worn velvet sofa, but Raymond preferred the wooden chair. If he tried to read somewhere more comfortable, he found his attention drifting from the words on the page. Besides, his friend Stéphane had told him that Sartre himself always sat on a straight-backed chair to read. He had returned to the chapter in which Ivich and Mathieu slash their hands at the Sumatra nightclub. Raymond was enthralled by the idea of a woman who would, for no apparent reason, draw a knife across the palm of her hand. He read for the umpteenth time: *The flesh was laid open from the ball of the thumb to the root of the little finger, and the blood was oozing slowly from the wound.* And her friend's reaction was not to rush to her aid, but instead to take the knife and impale his own hand to the table. What was most striking about the scene, however, was not the bloodletting itself, but the sentence that followed it:

The waiter had seen many such incidents.

Afterwards, when the couple went to the restroom, the attendant simply bandaged their hands and sent them on their way. So what if they had mutilated themselves? Raymond longed to be in a place like the Sumatra, among the sort of people who impaled their hands to the table. Such an establishment could certainly not be found in a backwater like Saint-Louis, with its respectable cafés where you were served by middle-aged women who asked after your parents, and to whom Raymond always behaved with perfect courtesy. Raymond was not sure what to make of the scene. He had discussed it at length with Yvette and Stéphane in their booth at the Café des Vosges. Stéphane had been matter-of-fact (he had an answer for everything): 'It's an *acte gratuit*, old man,' he had said with a shrug. 'It's meaningless. That's the point.' Yvette had disagreed: it wasn't meaningless. It was an act of rebellion against the bourgeois manners represented by the woman in the fur coat at the next table. Raymond had nodded earnestly, not wishing to contradict his friends, but neither interpretation satisfied him. Neither explained the frisson he got from reading the scene, a frisson not dissimilar to that which he experienced when he passed close enough to certain girls in the school corridors to inhale their scent. Perhaps the point was not to reduce the scene to a meaning—to *explain* it—but simply to experience it as a kind of spectacle.

Raymond wore his hair to his shoulders. He had a pronounced Roman nose, inherited from his father, and his mother's long-lashed grey-blue eyes. His lips were thin and his mouth wide, so that when he smiled (which was not often) he looked quite charming. His skin was smooth, and if he had started shaving it was for form's sake only. The growth he removed was no more than an embarrassing soft down. His body was slim and lithe. His mother liked to tell him that he looked like a girl. Sometimes in the evening when he visited her room, she would have him sit on the edge of the bed and brush his hair. Raymond did not take exception to his mother's feminine view of him and even cultivated a certain girlishness in his mannerisms, if only to aggravate his father.

He had recently removed all the posters from the walls of his room and thrown away a good deal of his possessions. He had painted the walls white, so that the room now resembled a well-appointed cell. Against the wall to the right of the door was a

16

bookcase, culled of its more childish volumes, and now home to a record player with forty or fifty LPs, these carefully selected to create the right impression on anyone entering his room. He was seventeen years old.

For the last fifteen minutes or so, Raymond's mind had not been on his book. An hour ago, he had heard the tyres of a car on the gravel of the drive, before the front door opened and he heard his mother ascend the stairs. Even without the sound of her heels on the floorboards, her steps were easily distinguished from the heavy tread of his father. Since then the house had been silent. Normally by this hour, Raymond would have expected to hear his father returning home and briefly look in on his wife, before retiring to his study to read or look over some papers. Raymond's father always kept the door of his study ajar. This was less as an invitation to drop in than a way of monitoring the movements of the other members of the household. Raymond's room was next to the study and if he needed to use the bathroom or wanted to go downstairs to the kitchen to get a bite to eat, he could not do so without passing his father's door. Raymond often moved around the house in stocking-feet to avoid detection, but he always had the feeling that his father knew exactly where he was and what he was doing. Every night, when the housekeeper retired to her quarters on the second floor, Raymond would hear his father say in a stage whisper: 'Is that you, Madame Thérèse?'

The house was so quiet there was no need to shout.

'Yes, Maître,' she would reply from the landing. 'Do you need anything?'

Maître Barthelme would reply that he did not, and they would wish each other goodnight. The exchange never ceased to irritate Raymond.

The fact that Maître Barthelme had not returned home was unusual in itself. But when Raymond heard the doorbell at 23:47 (he had checked the time on the digital clock his mother had given him for his sixteenth birthday), he knew something out of the ordinary had occurred. People rarely called at the house at any time of day. The only conceivable visitor at such an hour was a policeman. And the only reason for a policeman to call was to deliver bad news. The arrival of a policeman and his father's failure to return could not, Raymond surmised, be unconnected. At the very least there must have been an accident. But would a mere accident bring a policeman to the house at this hour? Surely a telephone call would have sufficed.

When he heard Mme Thérèse make her way down the stairs and open the front door, Raymond strained to hear the conversation. He was unable to make out more than a murmur of voices. It was at the point when Thérèse climbed the stairs and knocked lightly on the door of his mother's room that Raymond got up from his chair and stood with his ear pressed to his own door. If any confirmation that the caller was a policeman was required, this was it. Thérèse was by nature suspicious and mistrustful and would never have left any other person unsupervised in the hallway. She assumed that all tradesmen were thieves who had to be watched over at all times and constantly claimed that shop-keepers had diddled her. When she returned from her marketing, she routinely weighed out the items she had bought to check that she had not been sold short.

A few inaudible words were spoken in the hallway, before two sets of footsteps ascended the stairs and made their way towards his mother's room. The door must have remained open for a short time, because Raymond was able to catch a few words of the conversation before Thérèse was dismissed and the door was closed. In the intervening minutes, Raymond reflected that he had been wrong to assume a connection between his father's non-return and the policeman's visit. Perhaps there had merely been a burglary in the vicinity and the cop had called to ask if anyone had seen or heard anything unusual. In this case, he would certainly want to speak to Raymond as well. Perhaps the cop would ask him about his own movements, and having no alibi—he had not left his room all evening—he would himself fall under suspicion.

Until this point, Raymond's day had been unremarkable. Around eight o'clock in the morning, he had drunk a cup of tea and eaten some bread and butter at the counter in the kitchen. He could feel the heat of the range at his back. The house was cold in winter—his father being generally ill disposed towards heating—but the kitchen was always oppressively warm. Mme Thérèse was preparing his mother's breakfast tray with her usual put-upon air. His father had already left.

Raymond, as he always did, called on Yvette, who lived on Rue des Trois Rois. They then ran into Stéphane at the corner of Avenue de Bâle and Avenue Général de Gaulle. As the three of them walked to school, Stéphane talked enthusiastically about a book he was reading, but Raymond had paid little attention. Little of note occurred during the day. Mlle Delarue, the French mistress, was absent, as she often was, and her place was filled by the deputy head, who had merely set the class a task and then left the room. Raymond spent the lesson staring out of the window at a pair of wood pigeons strutting stiffly around the schoolyard. At lunchtime, he ate a slice of onion tart with potato salad in the canteen. As he had no class in the final period he had walked home alone. He made himself a pot of tea, took it to his room and listened to some records. As his father dined out on Tuesdays, it was always a relief not to have to sit through the evening meal in his presence. His mother's mood was lighter and she even seemed to acquire a little colour in her cheeks. She would enquire about Raymond's day and he would amuse her with anecdotes about trivial incidents at school, sometimes impersonating his teachers or classmates. When he aped one of his teachers in a particularly cruel fashion she would chastise him, but so half-heartedly that it was clear she did not really disapprove. Even Mme Thérèse went about her business with a less sombre air and, on occasion, if there was some household business to discuss, she would join them at the table during dessert. Once, when Raymond's father returned unexpectedly, she had leapt from her chair as if she had sat on a tack and busied herself with the dishes on the sideboard. When Maître Barthelme entered, he gave no sign of having registered this breach of protocol, but to Raymond's amusement, Thérèse's cheeks had reddened like a schoolgirl's.

Five minutes passed before Raymond heard the door to his mother's room click open. He listened to the cop's footsteps approach, then pass, the head of the stairs. Raymond stepped back from the door. He grabbed his book from the floor and threw himself on the bed. This would look odd, however, as the straight-backed chair remained in the middle of the floor as if set out for an interrogation. But there was no time to rearrange things and Raymond did not want the cop to hear him scurrying around in the manner of someone concealing evidence. There was a knock on the door. Raymond did not know what to do. It would seem rude to call out *Who is it?* That would imply that admission to his room was somehow dependent on the identity of the person knocking. In any case, the question would be disingenuous: he already knew who was at the door. It was not a dilemma Raymond had ever faced. His mother never entered his room, and Thérèse only did so when he was out at school. His father refused to knock, a source of great annoyance to Raymond, as it meant that he could never fully relax in his own domain; he might at any moment be subject to inspection. He was not even sure why his father called in on him. Their conversations were brief and strained and it was difficult not to conclude that the only purpose of these paternal visits was to keep tabs on him; to remind him of the fact he was not yet old enough to warrant a degree of privacy.

In the end, Raymond got up from the bed, book in hand, and opened the door himself. The man on the landing did not look like a policeman. He was of medium height with greying hair, cut short in almost military fashion. He had a pleasant face, with mild enquiring eyes and thick black eyebrows. He was dressed in a dark brown suit with a slight sheen to the fabric. His tie was loosened and the top button of his shirt unfastened. He did not have the imposing presence Raymond would have expected of a detective.

'Good evening, Raymond,' he said, 'I am Georges Gorski of the Saint-Louis police.'

He did not offer any identification. Raymond wondered if he should have feigned surprise, but the moment passed. Instead he just nodded.

'May I?' The policeman gestured towards the room. Raymond stepped back to allow him in. The room remained almost in darkness. The cop took a few steps inside the room. He looked at the chair in the centre of the floor with a puzzled expression. He glanced around the bare walls. Raymond stood awkwardly by the bed. It was 23:53.

Gorski turned the chair around to face him, but he did not sit down, merely letting his right hand rest on it. With a matter-of-fact air he said: 'Your father has been killed in a car accident.'

Raymond did not know what to say. His first thought was: *How should I react?* He glanced at the floor to buy time. Then he sat on the bed. That was good. That was what people did in such circumstances: they sat down, as if the shock had drained all the strength from their legs. But Raymond was not shocked. As soon as he had heard the doorbell ring, he had assumed that this was what had occurred. He wondered for a moment if this had been by way of a premonition, but he dismissed the idea. What was significant was not that he had assumed his father was dead, but that—without admitting it to himself—it was what he had wanted. If he felt anything on hearing the news, it was a kind of excitement, a feeling of liberation. He glanced up at the policeman to see if he had read his thoughts. But Gorski was looking at him with disinterest.

'You mother thought it best that I break the news to you,' he said in the same business-like tone.

Raymond nodded slowly. 'Thank you.'

He felt he should say something further. What sort of person has nothing to say on hearing of the death of their father?

'A car accident?' he said.

'Yes, on the A35. He was killed instantly.'

Gorski then touched his left wrist with his right hand and Raymond understood that he was concerned about the time. He turned towards the door. 'Perhaps you should look in on your mother.'

'Yes, yes, of course,' said Raymond.

The cop nodded, satisfied that his obligations had been fulfilled. 'If you don't have any questions, then that's all for now. There will be a formal identification in the morning. You might want to accompany your mother.'

Gorski left. Raymond followed him to the door of his room and watched him make his way down the stairs. Thérèse was hovering on the landing with her hand over her mouth.

Raymond instinctively retreated. He had the feeling that when he left his room, everything would be different; that he would be required in some way to assume responsibility. He looked at himself in the mirror on the inside of the wardrobe door. He did not look any different. He pushed his hair back from his forehead with his fingertips. He adopted a solemn expression, lowering his eyebrows and tensing his mouth. The effect was quite comic and he stifled a laugh.

He entered his mother's room without knocking and closed the door behind him. Lucette was sitting up in bed. She did not appear to have been crying. It would have seemed odd to remain standing or to sit on the chaise longue, which was in any case strewn with undergarments, so he sat on the edge of the divan. Lucette held out a hand and Raymond took it. He kept his eyes fixed on the wall above the bed. His mother's nightdress was loosely fastened and the curve of her breast was clearly visible. He wondered if she had received the policeman in the same state of undress.

'Are you all right?' he asked.

She smiled listlessly. With her free hand she gathered her nightdress together. 'It's quite a shock.'

'Yes,' he said.

Raymond had not expected to find his mother weeping hysterically. He had never discerned any great affection between his parents. Since he had begun to spend time in his friends' homes he had realised that the stiff formality that characterised his parents' relationship was not usual. Yvette's parents laughed and joked with each other. When M. Arnaud arrived home, he kissed his wife on the mouth and she arched her body towards him in a manner that suggested she felt some fondness for him. When Raymond was invited to stay for dinner, the atmosphere around the table was convivial. The various members of the family—Yvette had two younger brothers—chatted to each other as if they were actually interested in the details of each other's lives. Raymond felt quite warmly towards his mother, but the atmosphere of the Barthelme household was entirely determined by his father. The only topic of conversation which animated Maître Barthelme at mealtimes was that of household expenditure. When Thérèse brought in the dishes, he would interrogate her about the cost of the various items and whether she had recently compared prices in other shops. *There's no shame in thrift*, was his favourite maxim, and one to which Mme Thérèse was a staunch devotee.

That his father was the root of the frosty atmosphere in the house was borne out by the more cheerful mood at the dinner table when he was not in attendance. Even in his absence, however, when Raymond and his mother shared a light-hearted moment, they would restrain themselves, as if their deeds might be reported to the authorities. Raymond wondered if his mother was now feeling—as he was—a certain lightness; a feeling similar to that which he experienced when the school year ended for summer, or when spring arrived and it became possible to leave the house without a winter coat.

Raymond kept these thoughts to himself. Instead he said: 'The policeman said that the body would have to be identified.'

It was odd to hear himself refer to his father as 'the body'.

'Yes,' his mother replied. 'They're going to send a car in the morning.'

It was a relief to turn to these practical matters. Raymond asked if she would like him to accompany her. She squeezed his hand and said that that would be helpful. They looked at each other for a moment and then, because there was nothing further to say, Raymond got up and left the room.

Three

FOR THE FIRST FEW DAYS after his wife's departure Gorski had taken advantage of the situation by shaving in the en suite bathroom. It was an act of defiance. As a rule he shaved in the cramped WC on the ground floor. Barely a month after they had married and moved into the house on Rue de Village-Neuf, he had been banished from the en suite. He took too long and left a ring of whiskers in the washbasin. The en suite became Céline's domain, and even in her absence Gorski felt that he was encroaching on her territory. So he reverted to using the WC downstairs. Then, after a week or so, as if to test the limits of his freedom, he had decided not to shave at all. After all, with Céline gone, he could do whatever he wanted. Over his morning coffee that same day, he had smoked a cigarette in the kitchen. He could not bring himself to leave the butt in the ashtray, however. What if this turned out to be the day that Céline chose to return? All that day, Gorski had felt self-conscious in his unshaven state, but no one at the station commented on his unkempt appearance. In the afternoon, he had called on an elderly widow in Rue Saint-Jean who claimed some tools had been stolen from her garden. When she opened the door she peered at him suspiciously. A lapdog yapped at her feet. Gorski ran his hand over the stubble on his chin. He felt slovenly and unprofessional. The tools, it turned out, were in the garden shed.

'Oh, yes,' the woman had said. 'I remember putting them in there now.'

But she had not apologised for wasting Gorski's time.

On the morning after the accident, Gorski performed his ablutions, made coffee and sat at the kitchen table. He did not smoke a cigarette. Without Céline and Clémence around, everything felt strange. Previously he would have been hard-pressed to describe the fixtures and fittings of the room in which he now sat. His attention would have been occupied by the movements and chit-chat of his wife and daughter, who had recently turned seventeen. But now there was nothing to distract him from staring at the units, tiles and work surfaces. He had imagined being called into investigate his own wife's disappearance. He would have been embarrassed to question a husband under such circumstances.

She left a note?

'Yes.'

And it said what?

'Only that she was leaving.'

He would then, for sake of thoroughness, be obliged to ask to see the note. And as it could not be produced—Gorski had thrown it in the trash—this would inevitably lead to further questions.

When did you last see her?

It would have been that morning, of course, but Gorski could remember nothing specific about the occasion. It had been a day like any other. He and Céline's actions would have been replicated on thousands of previous mornings. Certainly, there had been no clue to her intentions, or, if there had been, Gorski had not noticed it.

And have you any idea where she might have gone?

'To her parents, I suppose.'

Have you tried calling her there?

That was where the scene ended. In the two weeks since she had left, there had been no contact between them. Gorski should have called the first day. After that, the opportunity had passed. If he were to telephone now, Céline's first question would be: 'Why haven't you called?' and from there the conversation would quickly descend into a quarrel. In any case, Gorski had no ready explanation as to why he had not called. Or at least not one that he would wish to voice to Céline. The truth was that when he had read her note, he had felt little more than a mild sense of relief. But it had taken only a few days for this feeling to wear off. Now he had begun to miss her and regretted not having made contact. He could easily have stopped by her boutique, which was only a short walk from the police station, and if he had not done so, it was only stubbornness that prevented him. It pleased him that Céline must have been peeved when he had not called that first evening. Certainly she would have expected it. She would have expected him to plead for her to come home, to promise that he would change his ways. But Gorski did not want to change his ways. In truth, he did not know what he had done wrong. So he had not called. And, naturally, Céline would not be the one to end the stalemate. By not calling, Gorski felt that he had won a small victory. But it was a hollow one. He now felt her absence keenly. It had only taken a few days for the things he found most irksome about his wife—her fastidiousness, her snobbishness, her obsession with appearance—to be transformed into endearing idiosyncrasies. He missed being told over breakfast that he could not wear such and such a tie with such and such a shirt, and whereas formerly he had sometimes worn mismatched items just to needle her, he now carefully dressed in a way that he thought would meet with her approval.

But it was his daughter he missed more. The first few days he had hoped to come home to find Clémence sitting at the kitchen table, dipping a biscuit in a cup of the peppermint tea she had taken to drinking. But she had not appeared, and if he had taken to spending his evenings in Le Pot, it was partly to avoid the disappointment he felt when he returned from work to find the house empty.

It was after ten o'clock when Gorski climbed the steps to the little foyer of the police station. The desk sergeant, Schmitt, was at the counter in his habitual posture, hunched over a copy of *L'Alsace*, displaying his balding pate to anyone who entered. A cigarette burned in the ashtray by his right hand. Gorski had long since given up demanding that he present a more professional demeanour to the public. At the sound of the door, Schmitt looked up from his paper and, seeing Gorski, glanced up at the clock that hung on the wall above the row of plastic chairs that constituted the station's waiting room. He pulled an expression, clearly intended to convey that it was all right for some to swan into work whenever they chose. Gorski ignored him. He generally made a point of being at his desk by eight o'clock. He was not obliged to arrive at the station at any particular time, or even to put in an appearance at all, but he liked to set an example of good timekeeping. Nor did he want his subordinates to think that he thought himself better than them. It should not bother him what a work-shy time-server like Schmitt thought of him, but it did. Why did he feel, even now, that he was sneaking into work like a tardy schoolboy? Why did he have to suppress an urge to offer Schmitt an explanation for his lateness? In his day, Ribéry would breeze into the station at whatever hour he pleased, frequently smelling of stale wine. No one ever looked askance at *him*, even when he made lewd remarks to female members of staff. But Gorski was not Ribéry. For some reason, he did not fit in. If he tried to join in with the office banter, his contributions were invariably met with silence.

Gorski bid good morning to a few officers in the open-plan area behind the reception window. His greetings were returned, but no one paid him any special attention. He flicked through the mail on the desk in his office. It was all for show. He was due in Mulhouse at eleven o'clock for the identification of Bertrand Barthelme's body. Gorski took a coffee from the machine in the corridor and returned to his car. As he got into his Peugeot he slopped the drink on the leg of his trousers. Thankfully he had chosen a dark suit for the occasion. There was no reason that he could not have collected Mme Barthelme and her son and driven them the twenty kilometres north to Mulhouse himself. Except that he did not think it becoming for the chief of police to act as chauffeur. The journey would, moreover, be passed in awkward silence, and, having viewed the body, Gorski would then be obliged to drive the traumatised widow home. He disliked being around the bereaved. The conventional words of condolence, however sincerely intended, always sounded hollow. After his own father's funeral, he and his mother had returned to the apartment in Rue des Trois Rois. She went about making a light lunch as if nothing unusual had taken place. When Gorski glanced into the narrow kitchenette, however, she was weeping over her chopping board. Gorski had stepped back from the doorway, and by the time lunch was served Mme Gorski had dried her eyes. No mention of the funeral or his father's death had passed between them since.

So Gorski had instructed a young *gendarme* named Roland to collect Mme Barthelme. Roland was still working his probationary period and had not appeared to notice the chilly relations between Gorski and the rest of his colleagues. He was an eager-to-please type and had agreed to the mundane task with an enthusiasm suggesting he felt he had been entrusted with a mission of great importance.

The drizzle had not abated overnight and the road surface felt treacherous under the tyres of Gorski's ungainly 504. When he passed the scene of the accident, the inside lane of the carriageway remained cordoned off. A recovery truck was parked on the verge and two men were attaching a hydraulic cable to the underside of the crumpled Mercedes. Gorski congratulated himself on his decision not to collect Mme Barthelme. He arrived at the mortuary in Mulhouse a few minutes after eleven o'clock. The widow and her son were already in the waiting area. Roland was loitering awkwardly by his car. When Gorski appeared, he stood to attention in a comic fashion.

In its furnishings and decor, the mortuary's foyer was not dissimilar to that of the police station. It was distinguished, however, by the pungent smell of formaldehyde or some other chemical, and the torn posters reminding staff of the importance of good hygiene. Mme Barthelme was dressed in a light blue summer dress and a beige raincoat, belted at the waist. Her attire seemed as inappropriate to the season as to the circumstances. She seemed less pale than on the evening before, and Gorski suspected that she had applied a little rouge to her cheeks. Her dress reached to just below the knee and Gorski briefly noted her shapely calves, which were unadorned by stockings. The son stood at his mother's side. He was dressed in a flannel shirt, brown corduroy trousers and a suede jacket. Gorski had taken an instant dislike to the boy. People often acted queerly when informed of the death of a relative, but there had been something inauthentic in the young man's reactions. And now he looked at Gorski with something approaching disdain, as if it was his fault that they were gathered there.

Gorski shook hands with them both and apologised for being late. He requested that they wait a few more moments and went through the door to the cold room. A technician whose name Gorski could not remember was adjusting the blue plastic sheet that covered the body on the slab. He looked up when Gorski entered and the two men shook hands. The chemical smell was stronger here.

'Due to the damage to the left side of the cranium, I've arranged the body so that we only need to display the intact portion of the face,' he said.

He then demonstrated how he would lower the sheet and Gorski nodded his approval. He went back outside and explained the procedure to Mme Barthelme. He added that there was no need for both of them to view the body, but the son did not appear reluctant to accompany his mother. Boys were morbid at that age. He would no doubt think this fine material with which to impress his schoolmates.

They arranged themselves solemnly around the slab, Gorski standing by the head, the widow and her son to the side of the body. Gorski nodded to the technician, who then discreetly lowered the sheet. Gorski put the question to Mme Barthelme. She affirmed that it was indeed her husband. And that was it. Gorski ushered them from the room. The whole charade had taken barely thirty seconds. There might be those who would question the point of such an exercise. The possibility that the body on the slab was not Bertrand Barthelme was so slim as to be negligible. For it not to be, it would be necessary to believe that a person unknown had stolen his clothes, wallet and car and crashed while making his escape. Either that or Barthelme himself had somehow staged the accident to fake his own death. Both ideas were almost too ludicrous to merit consideration, and in such circumstances it might be thought that compelling a widow to identify her husband's remains was a pointless—even callous—exercise. But Gorski did not share this view. The procedures to administer deaths, accidental or otherwise, were not arbitrary. They had to be followed without prejudice in all circumstances. There was no place in such a system for the intrusion of personal opinion or even common sense. The state required that the causes of deaths of its citizens be properly recorded, and the correct conclusion could only be reached by establishing the firmest foundations. In any case, in Gorski's experience, no one had ever objected to taking part in a formal identification. In such situations, individuals accepted that there were certain obligations which had to be fulfilled—they perhaps even found it reassuring—and Gorski never felt guilty about putting people through the experience. He was simply following the procedure.

Gorski led Mme Barthelme back to the foyer and asked if she would like a glass of water. She gave a weak smile and shook her head, but her hands were shaking a little. The boy was gazing around the room as if he was on a school trip. Gorski went outside. Roland's car was gone and Gorski realised that he had not instructed him to wait.

'There was something I wanted to ask you, Inspector,' Mme Barthelme said when he went back inside.

Assuming that she wished to know when the body would be released, Gorski explained that a post-mortem would first have to be carried out and the accident investigation concluded.

Mme Barthelme shook her head. 'It wasn't that,' she said.

The smell of chemicals was beginning to make Gorski feel nauseous. He suggested that they talk on the journey back to Saint-Louis. Mme Barthelme waited until Gorski had pulled out of the car park before she spoke, glancing at her son before she did so.

'Something's been troubling me,' she began. 'My husband dined out in town last night.'

Gorski glanced at her in the rear-view mirror. She was leaning forward slightly in her seat, an expectant expression on her face.

'Uh-huh?' he said.

'He had dinner with some colleagues, his club he called it, every Tuesday evening. So, you see, there was no reason for him to be on the A35.'

'Where did they dine?

'They always ate at the Auberge du Rhin.' This was a restaurant on Avenue de Bâle, the least shabby Saint-Louis had to offer.

'Maybe they ate elsewhere. In Mulhouse, perhaps?' said Gorski. This would readily account for why Barthelme had been travelling south at the time of the accident.

'Why would they do that?' she said.

Gorski did not say anything. How could he possibly know the answer to such a question? It was, in any event, a matter of no consequence.

'So you can see why I'm puzzled,' Mme Barthelme persisted. 'I didn't sleep last night for thinking about it.'

'I understand,' said Gorski, 'but I'm not sure there is much I can do. If no crime has been committed, the investigation will be limited to the causes of the accident. It is a matter for the coroner rather than the police.'

Mme Barthelme slumped back in her seat and cast her eyes downwards. Gorski wondered if she was aware that he was watching her in the rear-view mirror. He had disappointed her. Her son was staring fixedly out of the window, as if he had heard nothing of the conversation, or, at least, as if it was of no interest to him. They approached the scene of the accident. The Mercedes was being lowered onto the back of the recovery truck. Gorski subtly increased the pressure on the accelerator. Mme Barthelme averted her gaze, then dabbed at her eyes with a small handkerchief. She had very delicate features. Gorski felt compelled to say something.

'I suppose that until the cause of the accident is determined, it would not be inappropriate to make some discreet enquiries about your husband's movements,' he said.

Mme Barthelme's face brightened considerably. She leaned forward and touched the shoulder of Gorski's raincoat. 'I'd be very grateful,' she said.

He creased his face into a smile. She was very pretty and he did not, in any case, have any more pressing business to attend to.

Four

Yvette and Stéphane were in the booth at the back of the Café des Vosges. Raymond had been sure he would find them there. The three of them went to the café almost every day after school. It was a humdrum place with metal tables and chairs that scraped on the grey tiled floor whenever anyone got up. The uninspiring view onto Avenue Général de Gaulle was obscured by voile curtains. Chipped gold lettering on the window announced the establishment as a *Salon de thé*. Inside, an air of gentility was cultivated by the bland watercolours adorning the walls. A large glass cabinet by the counter displayed an array of tarts and cakes. It was patronised in the main by elderly women. If the three friends frequented the place, it was for no other reason than it was on their route home from school, and perhaps also because the banality of the surroundings made them feel more unconventional than they actually were.

Stéphane broke off his conversation with Yvette when he saw Raymond approach the table.

'Well, my friends, what news?' said Raymond as he slid onto the banquette next to Yvette. 'Did I miss anything at school?'

Yvette and Stéphane exchanged a glance and Raymond was pleased with the effect his entrance had had on them. Neither of them knew what to say. The waitress with the harelip appeared at the table and took his order.

'Sorry about your old man,' said Stéphane when the waitress

had retreated to the counter. He had never referred to Maître Barthelme in this way before. The forced joviality of the phrase struck Raymond as phoney.

'So you heard?' he said.

Yvette was looking at him with a troubled expression.

'It's in the paper,' said Stéphane. 'Everyone knows about it.'

Raymond raised his eyebrows. His father would have hated that. He hated any sort of attention. He always refused to attend weddings or dinner parties and no one was ever invited to the Barthelme's home.

'What can I say?' he said with a shrug.

Yvette leaned in towards him. Raymond thought she was about to place a comforting hand on his arm, but she did not do so. The waitress arrived with Raymond's tea. The three of them sat in uncomfortable silence as she placed the smoked glass cup and saucer and the stainless steel pot of tea on the table.

'And may I have some water?' Raymond said, for no other reason than to continue his pretence that nothing out of the ordinary had happened. He poured hot water over the teabag in the glass and watched the tea infuse. Nobody said anything until the waitress had returned with his water.

'So how was old Peletière this morning?' he said. 'The usual cloud of dandruff and body odour?' Peletière was their history master.

'Raymond!' said Yvette. 'Why are you acting like this?' It was the first thing she had said since his arrival.

He looked at her and spread his hands in a gesture of innocence. 'You know I couldn't stand the old bastard,' he said. 'It'd be a bit two-faced to play the grief-stricken son, wouldn't it?'

Yvette looked away. Raymond had the impression that she had tears in her eyes, as if it were *she* he had said he couldn't stand. He felt bad.

Raymond and Yvette had met when they were eleven years old. Yvette's family moved to Saint-Louis from a village in Bas-Rhin when her father got a job as a chargehand in a concrete factory on the outskirts of the town. From the beginning, the two of them were like an elderly couple, content to sit for hours watching the pigeons peck at the dirt in the little park by the Protestant temple. Raymond always assumed they would get married. After school, he would walk her home to the end of her street, before wandering slowly back to Rue des Bois. In their early teens, however, on Saturdays when school finished at midday, they would take the long way round by the canal and sit in silence on the bank, staring silently at the motionless green water. Sometimes they kissed, or rather, they pressed their lips together. At first, this was carried out in the spirit of a game, as if they were playing mothers and fathers, but later Raymond found it arousing. It never occurred to him that it might have a similar effect on Yvette, and he kept his hand strategically positioned to conceal his erection.

Once, on a hot afternoon during the summer holidays when they were fourteen or fifteen, Yvette placed her hand on the front of Raymond's canvas shorts. She lightly clasped his penis through the coarse material, and he ejaculated immediately with a stifled groan. Yvette looked at him with a mischievous expression and gave a little giggle, but Raymond felt dreadfully ashamed, as if he had been caught committing an unsavoury act. He could not bring himself to speak. Yvette did not notice—or pretended not to notice—the dark stain that had formed on his shorts. In order to disguise it, Raymond suddenly threw off his shirt and leapt into the canal. He submerged himself in the opaque water and then bobbed up, his hair plastered to his forehead. The shock of the cold water on his body dissipated his embarrassment.

'Why don't you come in and cool off?' he called. He had a sudden desire to see Yvette pull her dress over her head and dive in. She merely smiled indulgently, the way a mother might, watching her child totter round a play park. Raymond swam to the opposite bank in a few easy strokes, dived again and came up in the rushes at Yvette's feet. He grabbed her by the ankles and playfully attempted to pull her in, but she drew up her legs and sat with her arms clasped around them. Raymond floated on his back for a while, feeling the sun dry his chest, then scrambled out.

After that, their amorous activities ceased for a while. When they did kiss, it was Raymond who broke it off. He did not want Yvette to think that her previous act was now expected of her. More worryingly she might expect him to reciprocate in some way. It was not that he was not curious about what lay between Yvette's legs, but it would have seemed indecent to touch her there. More recently, however, things had moved on. Yvette's body had matured and one evening in her bedroom, she had detached herself from their embrace and wordlessly unfastened the second and third buttons of her blouse. It was hardly the most wanton act, but Raymond could not fail to interpret it as anything other than an invitation to slip his hand under the fabric. This he duly did. He was not rebuffed, but he did not dare go so far as to push aside the material of her brassiere. Nevertheless, the presence of his hand elicited a moan of pleasure from Yvette. This sound was enough to cause Raymond to spend himself. He then said in a childish voice: 'I think I've had an accident,' and Yvette replied in a maternal tone that he was a very naughty boy. It became a regular occurrence for Raymond to fondle Yvette's breasts while she pushed the heel of her hand in to his crotch. He began to feel guilty that their lovemaking—as he thought of it—was not reciprocal, but he had only the vaguest idea of the mechanics of pleasuring a woman. Yvette, for her part, betrayed no dissatisfaction with the arrangement, and afterwards would silently hand Raymond a handkerchief to mop up his emission.

Raymond had contemplated asking Stéphane for some advice. On account of the fact that his friend was nine months older and had lived elsewhere, Raymond assumed that he was a great deal more worldly. But no mention was ever made of he and Yvette's activities. When they were in Stéphane's company, they kept their hands to themselves. Similarly, at school, they behaved as if they were no more than friends. Raymond occasionally wondered if Yvette might share similar intimacies with Stéphane. He even found it arousing to think of his two friends together, but he was sure that nothing of that sort had ever occurred. In any case, the two of them were never alone together. As it was, the clandestine nature of Raymond's activities with Yvette only gave them a greater frisson.

One afternoon, towards the end of the summer, the threesome cycled to the Petite Camargue for a picnic. They laid out a rug by the edge of the lake and sat eating the pâté and cheese they had brought with them. Stéphane was discoursing volubly on the absurdity of choosing to continue to exist in a Godless universe, but Raymond was not listening. He could not imagine anyone less likely to commit suicide than Stéphane. The trees around the edge of the water were already changing colour and he had a melancholic sense that something was coming to an end. Somewhere, a wood pigeon cooed in the trees. They would soon enter their final year at school and after that the threesome would be broken up. Yvette and Stéphane's most frequent topic of conversation had become the relative virtues of the colleges they were considering. Yvette favoured Strasbourg, while Stéphane had set his sights on Paris. 'Why would you choose to go anywhere else?' he declared frequently. It was a conversation in which Raymond felt unable to participate, and he would continually disrupt his friends' discussion with irrelevant remarks. He was a mediocre student. The recurrent allegation of his school reports was of an intelligent pupil who refused to push himself. Once a year Raymond's father would invite him into his study for a discussion of his progress.

'I am baffled by these reports,' he told his son when he was eleven or twelve years old. 'I myself see no evidence of this intelligence your teachers speak of. Certainly your grades do not support this assertion. Perhaps you could enlighten me?'

When Raymond failed to respond, Maître Barthelme shook his head and said: 'I suppose it is a lesser crime to be stupid than to fail to make use of one's talents.'

It was true that Raymond had made little effort with his schoolwork. It was a kind of listless defiance of his father. As he passed through his teenage years, the assumption that the firm of Barthelme & Corbeil would one day become Barthelme, Corbeil & Sons had receded. If Raymond buckled down enough to improve his grades, his father would insist on him studying law. Nevertheless, by indulging in this self-sabotaging behaviour, Raymond was wrecking his prospects of ever escaping Saint-Louis. He had no desire to end up working in a bank on Rue de Mulhouse and throwing himself under a train before he was forty. He had thus resolved to improve his performance. The process was not, however, as straightforward as he imagined. He had long since accepted the comfortable designation of underperforming student. But what if it transpired that he was not as intelligent as his teachers—and he—believed? What if his grades were an accurate reflection of his abilities? It was more humiliating to fail when one had made an effort. If one did not lift a finger, it was possible to preserve the illusion that one was lazy rather than dim-witted. Nevertheless, the prospect of being trapped in the stagnant backwater of Saint-Louis spurred him on. At first, he struggled. He had not acquired the habits of concentration and self-discipline expected of students his age. But his grades slowly began to pick up. He was careful to maintain his outwardly diffident attitude, but his teachers took notice of his improvement and encouraged him. Still, his prospects of passing the baccalaureate remained in the balance.

After they had eaten their picnic, Stéphane declared that he was going to take a turn around the lake. He had a surfeit of energy and was incapable of remaining inactive for any length of time. Raymond took off his shirt and lay back on the rug with his hands behind his head. He was happy where he was. Yvette, as Raymond knew she would, said that she would stay too. She tried to persuade Stéphane to remain, but her protests were half-hearted. Stéphane shook his head at their lethargy and set off at a brisk pace through the trees.

Raymond took out his copy of Zola's *La Curée,* which they would be studying the following term. He had resolved to get ahead with his reading, but he had been unable to get past the first chapter. He complained to Yvette, who had finished the book in a few days, that the opening description of the carriages circling the Bois de Boulogne was interminable.

'It's five pages,' she replied earnestly. 'He's introducing us to the milieu of the novel.'

'It's so tedious,' Raymond groaned.

He started to read to her in an exaggeratedly monotonous tone:

'The lake, seen from the front, in the pale light that still hovered over the water, became rounder, like a huge tin fish; on either side, the plantations of evergreens, whose slim, straight stems seemed to rise up from its still surface, looked at this hour like purple colonnades—'

Yvette lay next to him and placed her hand on his chest. She brushed her lips against his ear. Raymond continued to read aloud:

'—delineating with their even shapes the studied curves of the shore; and shrubs rose in the background, confused masses of foliage forming large black masses that closed off the horizon.'

Yvette kissed his neck and traced circles on his chest with her fingers. Raymond laid aside the book and turned to kiss her. There was a new seriousness in the way they went about their business. Raymond placed his palm on the bare skin of Yvette's stomach and pushed his hand inside the waistband of her denim shorts. Yvette made no objection and even undid the metal button to facilitate his progress. The tips of Raymond's fingers reached her pubic hair, which until then he had not even seen. His middle finger came to rest on a slick nub of gristle. Yvette inhaled sharply. Raymond did not know what to do, so he merely left his hand where it was. Yvette gripped his wrist and pressed his hand against her sex. She slowly rotated her hips. Her breathing quickened. Her face was buried in the crook of Raymond's neck.

Sunlight flickered through the yellowing leaves on the branches above them. Raymond's wrist was at an awkward angle and was becoming quite painful. Yvette gripped it more tightly and pushed it further between her legs. Her breath arrived in short gasps that reminded Raymond of a steam train picking up speed. Just then, they were distracted by a couple on the opposite side of the lake. It was not possible to hear what they were saying, but it was clear that they were arguing. Raymond raised himself onto one elbow to watch the scene through the trees. The woman slapped her companion across the face and stormed off into the woods. The man was left holding his face and looking around to see if anyone had witnessed the incident. Raymond removed his hand from Yvette's shorts and massaged his numb wrist. He made a silly comment about what the man must have said to deserve such a slap. Yvette turned her back to him. When Raymond put his hand on her shoulder, she shrugged it away. He put his fingers to his mouth and tasted the salty residue that had been left there. Then he picked up his book and pretended to read. They did not speak until Stéphane returned, excited by the incident with the couple, which he had witnessed close at hand. Neither Raymond nor Yvette were interested, however, and they quietly packed up their things and returned to where they had left their bicycles.

Raymond took a sip of his tea. The harelipped waitress was watching him from behind the counter. Perhaps she also knew about the accident and was curious about his behaviour. There might even have been a photograph of his father in *L'Alsace*. Such articles often ended with a line such as: *The deceased is survived by his wife and son.*

Yvette started packing her things into her satchel. She stood up to go.

'I don't know why you have to act like that all the time,' she said.

Raymond adopted an innocent expression. 'Like what?' he said.

'Like you don't care about anything. Or anyone.' She put her bag over her shoulder.

If Stéphane had not been there, Raymond might have said something conciliatory. Indeed, if he had been alone with Yvette, he would not have acted as he had in the first place. His display of indifference had been entirely for Stéphane's benefit. But he could hardly change course now, so he shrugged and said: 'Maybe I don't care about anything.'

Yvette shook her head dismissively.

Stéphane intervened: 'He's just upset.'

Raymond had no wish for Stéphane to speak up for him, but he regretted his behaviour. He did not want Yvette to leave.

'I'm sorry,' he said quietly. 'Maman and I had to identify the body this morning.'

He had played his trump card. Yvette could hardly walk out after such a revelation.

'Oh,' she said. She sat down and placed her satchel on the floor.

'That can't have been much fun,' said Stéphane.

Raymond described how he and his mother had passed his father's car on the road to Mulhouse. There was, in truth, little to say about the process itself. He did not tell them how, as they had entered the mortuary, an image from *Frankenstein* had flashed through his mind and he had half-expected the body under the sheets to slowly rise from the slab.

'It was all over in a few seconds. They tried to hide it but I could tell he was pretty smashed up. Maman didn't faint or anything. The whole thing was pretty weird.'

Yvette nodded earnestly. 'It must have been horrible.'

Raymond shrugged, but not maliciously. He gave her a little smile. He was glad Stéphane was there. He had no wish to go into more detail, to explain how, despite everything, he had had to choke back a sob when the sheet had been drawn back from his father's face.

'The funniest thing was the cop. I think he's got his eye on Maman already.' He patted Yvette's arm in imitation of Gorski. 'There, there, Madame Barthelme. I must apologise for putting you through this, Madame Barthelme.' Then he wrung his hands in an obsequious manner and made a smacking noise with his lips.

Yvette and Stéphane laughed drily, but it was clear that neither of them found his comments amusing. Raymond noticed the glance that passed between his two friends. A silence fell over the table. Stéphane looked at his watch and said that he had to pick up a book from the library. Raymond expected Yvette to say that she would stay for a while, but she too said she had to leave. They calculated their share of the bill, as they always did, and placed the coins on the pewter salver.

They parted with Stéphane on the pavement outside. His statement was clearly untrue. If he had needed to visit the library, he would have done so before leaving school. Nevertheless, Raymond was pleased to be alone with Yvette. He was sorry he had acted as he had. He was about to say as much, but something prevented him. He felt a sudden resentment towards Stéphane, as though it was his friend who was responsible for his behaviour.

Raymond and Yvette walked slowly along Rue de Mulhouse. The longer they remained in silence, the more intractable it became. Now that he had missed his chance to apologise, he could only think of silly, flippant remarks to make, and that would only compound the callous impression he had made in the café. He thought of asking Yvette what she was thinking about, but it always annoyed him when she asked him that, usually in the moments after they had engaged in some sort of sexual activity.

A fat man with a rolling gait approached. He was wearing a Tyrolean hat with a little feather in the band. His face was florid and they had to step aside to allow him to pass. Normally Raymond would have passed some comment about his cauliflower nose. But things had changed. It was no longer appropriate to make fun of passers-by. Raymond wondered how much time would have to pass before it would once more be acceptable to do so. Or if, perhaps, they had entered a new phase of their lives in which they would have to behave at all times in a solemn adult manner.

Ah, yes, Raymond imagined people commenting of him, *he never smiles. He's never been the same since his father passed away.*

He stole a glance at Yvette. He liked her profile. She had a small nose and long eyelashes. He mouth was naturally down-turned, but her general expression was calm, rather than sad, as if she found the world around her vaguely amusing. He felt a surge of emotion towards her.

They reached the corner of Rue des Trois Rois, where they usually parted. Yvette offered him a sympathetic smile. She held out her hand and lightly touched his wrist. Raymond grasped the opportunity afforded by her gesture. 'I'm sorry about before,' he said. 'I was an ass.'

Yvette shrugged in a resigned fashion. She expected little else.

Five

THE OFFICES OF BARTHELME & CORBEIL did not re-open until
two o'clock. Gorski decided to lunch at the Restaurant de la
Cloche. He was not hungry, but he had no wish to pass the
intervening time at the police station. Even alone in his office
he felt ill at ease there. It was possible to enter the station from
the car park behind the building—avoiding any interaction with
Schmitt or whoever else happened to be manning the desk—but
this always made Gorski feel furtive. Furthermore, if he used the
rear entrance, no one knew he was in his office and any calls
would not be put through. In order to avoid this, it was necessary
for Gorski to proceed along the corridor and put his head around
the door of the communal area. No matter how breezily Gorski
greeted his colleagues, he always suspected that they thought
he was trying to eavesdrop on their conversations or catch them
slacking. In order to dispel this notion he was obliged to stand
in the doorway and engage in some strained small talk, before
announcing: 'Well, I'll be in my office if anyone needs me.'

So even when he parked behind the station, he entered from
the front, the curt nod to Schmitt being a small price to pay
to avoid these other difficulties. Once in his office, he kept his
door ajar so as not to appear aloof from his staff. He would have
liked to discontinue this practice—it added to his feeling of
self-consciousness—but were he to start closing his door after so
many years, his colleagues would surely wonder what clandestine

activities had prompted this alteration in his habits. Whenever possible, Gorski avoided the station altogether.

It was 12:45 when he entered the Restaurant de la Cloche. The lunchtime service was in full swing. Despite having an armful of dishes, Marie bustled over to him and showed him to a table by the window overlooking the car park in Place de l'Europe. Since Céline's departure, Gorski had promised that he would not visit la Cloche more than two or three times a week. Even after he retired, Ribéry had lunched there every day. His old mentor had been dead fifteen years, but Gorski still resisted Marie's attempts to sit him at his regular corner table. In a similar way, he even avoided sitting at the same table on consecutive visits. Naturally, Gorski was not unaware that this petty assertion of freedom did in itself constitute a routine of a kind. Today, however, he was happy with his place. He had his back to the corpulent hairdresser who occupied the table by the door. Lemerre was as objectionable in character as he was in appearance, and he never failed to try to draw Gorski into tittle-tattle about the goings-on of Saint-Louis. The sullen waitress, who had recently been the focus of the town's attention, was working the tables on the opposite side of the restaurant. Gorski was relieved. Despite the fact that she never so much as acknowledged him, her presence made him uncomfortable. He had to consciously prevent himself from following her movements around the room.

Marie arrived to take his order. Just as he refused to sit at the same table, Gorski never repeated his order. Ribéry had eaten the same lunch of *salade de viande*, *pot-au-feu* and *tarte aux pommes* every day for thirty years, the only exception being made on Thursdays—market day—when he had the *baeckeoffe*. It must have seemed odd that Gorski could not settle on a regular order. So now when Marie asked: 'What'll it be today?' it was with a particular emphasis on the final word, as if she was addressing a capricious child. Did he not know what he liked? So it was with studied consideration—he tapped his forefinger against his lips—that he scanned the blackboards on which the menu was displayed. What he ate was, in any case, of little importance. Gorski could not deceive himself about his real motive for visiting la Cloche. Just as Marie was moving away from his table, he said, as if as an afterthought: 'Oh, and I'll have a *pichet* of wine.'

'Of course, Inspector.' If she disapproved, she did not show it. His wine secured, Gorski relaxed a little. He would, in truth, have been more comfortable in Le Pot, where he could order as many beers as he liked without Yves raising an eyebrow, and where he was not obliged to sit at the window in plain sight of passers-by. He preferred to drink beer. White wine did not agree with his stomach, and he had taken to carrying a tube of antacids in the pocket of his raincoat.

Gorski's first course arrived without his wine. He ate his soup dutifully, like a child that has been promised a reward for eating its greens, but with growing anxiety. He hoped that he would not have to demean himself by prompting Marie. But she was merely waiting for her husband, Pasteur, to decant his wine into the little jug. When it was placed on the table, Gorski started slightly, as if he had forgotten he had ordered it, then smiled his thanks to the *patronne*.

Behind him, Lemerre was turning the pages of *L'Alsace* and providing a commentary on the day's news to a local pharmacist, Cloutier, who had joined him at his table. Cloutier liked to talk behind his hand about the medications he supplied to his customers, these nuggets of gossip routinely followed by a remark such as: 'I wouldn't rule out a dose of the clap,' accompanied by a complicit wink. Gorski stared fixedly out of the window. Marie brought his schnitzel. He cut the breaded meat into thin slices and chewed them slowly. After each mouthful, he allowed himself a sip of wine. He was thinking about Lucette Barthelme and the grateful expression that had flashed across her eyes when he had agreed to make enquiries on her behalf. He had no legitimate reason for doing so. Still, there could be no harm in it, and he had, in any case, little else to do.

His thoughts were interrupted by Lemerre. Gorski reluctantly turned round, leaning his elbow on the back of the chair. The hairdresser was pointing to a headline in the inner pages of his newspaper.

'A juicy case here,' he said with relish.

A woman had been strangled in her Strasbourg apartment.

'Seems she was quite a girl,' Lemerre continued. '*Was known to entertain frequent gentleman visitors*,' he read, before repeating the final phrase with relish. 'A real *crime passionnel*, it seems.'

Gorski nodded curtly. The crime of passion was a myth—an idea cherished more by novelists and spinsters than investigators—but he knew from long experience that it was a mistake to be drawn into debate with Lemerre. 'No doubt,' he replied. He began to turn back to his lunch, but Lemerre had not finished.

'Not many of those round here.' He gestured in the general direction of the town.

'I'm sorry?' said Gorski.

'Crimes of passion,' he said. 'Not much of that sort of thing in Saint-Louis.'

'No,' said Gorski.

'Makes me wonder what a chief of police has to do with himself all day.'

Gorski smiled thinly at him. Lemerre then apologised for interrupting his lunch. 'I can see how busy you are, Inspector.' Cloutier joined in his laughter. Gorski drained his glass then filled it to the brim with no regard for who was watching. He forced himself to finish his veal, but did not eat the mound of potato salad that accompanied it.

The offices of Barthelme & Corbeil were unremarkable. The solicitors' names were inscribed on a discreet brass plaque at the entrance of what otherwise appeared to be a residential building. The plaque spoke of a firm that did not have to flaunt its presence or tout for business. Gorski pressed the buzzer and was granted access. The offices were on the first floor. It was only on the frosted glass of the door that the nature of Barthelme & Corbeil's business was indicated: *Solicitors and Notaries*.

Gorski entered without knocking and was greeted by a secretary seated behind an impressive oak desk. She was a petite woman of around forty. Her hair was loosely arranged around her face. She was dressed in a green, paisley-patterned blouse and wore a pendant with an Eastern symbol around her neck. Her eyes were red-rimmed and the tip of her nose was a little florid. She must have been informed of Barthelme's death only on her arrival at work. It was revealing that she had not been sent home and, indeed, that the business had remained open at all. The outer office was unprepossessing. Aside from the oak desk, the furnishings were tatty. The carpet was threadbare in the areas that saw most traffic. Yet the impression was not of a firm that was down at heel, rather of one that was sheltered from the external world. It was a place where delicate conversations could be held in hushed tones. Barthelme & Corbeil was the intermediary between the families who shielded themselves behind the rows of sycamores on Rue des Bois and the grubby world beyond.

Gorski smiled sympathetically and expressed his condolences to the secretary.

The woman forced a smile. 'It's been quite a shock,' she replied. Despite her tears, there was a liveliness in her eyes at odds with her surroundings.

Gorski asked if he might have a word with Maître Corbeil. The woman took his card and with a gentle knock entered the room to the left of the desk.

Corbeil was at his desk perusing some papers, and continued to do so, even after Gorski's presence had been announced. Without looking up he pointed towards a pair of green leather armchairs. Not wishing to acquiesce to Corbeil's ill-mannered gesture, Gorski remained standing in the middle of the floor. Ribéry would never have tolerated such treatment. He would have marched over to the desk and torn the papers from under the solicitor's nose. Not that the situation would have arisen in the first place. For all his failings, Ribéry had been one thing

Gorski would never be: he was clubbable. He knew everyone in town, from mayor to bartender, and neither Corbeil nor anyone else would have treated him with such disrespect. As if to demonstrate that he was unperturbed by Corbeil's discourtesy, Gorski wandered over to the window and looked out onto the street. Lemerre was ambling back to his premises on the opposite pavement, breathing heavily through his mouth. Gorski lit a cigarette. The sound of his lighter caused Corbeil to glance up, as if he had forgotten he was there. He unscrewed the lid of a heavy fountain pen and added his signature to the foot of the document he had been reading. Then he stood up and walked across to where Gorski was standing. He held out his hand.

'So you are our famous Inspector Gorski, eh?'

Gorski returned his gaze. The remark irked him, as it had no doubt been intended to. It was not so much the clearly ironic 'famous', as the use of the word 'our', implying as it did that Gorski was somehow the property of the worthies of the town. The solicitor showed no sign of being upset about the death of his partner. He was of medium height with unblemished pink skin. He was completely bald save for a few neatly trimmed tufts growing above his ears. He was dressed in an English tweed suit and brown brogues. His movements were precise and somewhat effeminate. Gorski had the impression that the two colleagues would never have called each other by their first names and would certainly never have addressed each other as *tu*. Indeed, when Gorski explained the reason for his visit, it was as if Corbeil had already forgotten the circumstances of his colleague's death.

'From what I understand, it was nothing more than an accident,' said the solicitor. 'So I fail to see what reason you have for'—he paused, as though searching for the most offensive phrase—'for sniffing around here.'

Before Gorski had the chance to answer, Corbeil guided him across the room to the armchairs he had indicated earlier. Between them was a low table with a large cut-glass ashtray and a decanter of sherry. He took a seat and invited Gorski to do the same. He crossed his legs, then immediately leapt up. He fetched two glasses from a cabinet behind his desk.

'I'm forgetting my manners,' he said. He resumed his seat and poured out two large measures of sherry. 'If memory serves, your predecessor always appreciated a little lubrication. I don't expect you're any different.'

Gorski took a sip of his sherry, resisting the desire to knock it back in a single draught. The wine he had drunk at the Restaurant de la Cloche had only sharpened his thirst.

'You were explaining the nature of your visit,' said the lawyer.

The sherry left a sticky coating on Gorski's tongue. 'I am merely trying to establish Maître Barthelme's movements prior to the accident.'

Corbeil's expression did not change. His face was so bland it was hard to imagine it expressing anything at all. 'Is there some indication of foul play?'

Foul play. It was a phrase people only ever used when addressing a cop, a way of avoiding the more brutal phrases.

'The Accident Investigation Unit has not yet submitted its report,' said Gorski.

'Nevertheless,' replied Corbeil, 'the assumption seems to be that it was nothing more sinister than an accident. You used the word yourself only a moment ago. If that is the case, I fail to see the need to delve into my colleague's "movements", as you call them.'

The solicitor's attitude irritated Gorski. He would never have spoken to Ribéry this way. It was curious too that he spoke of an 'assumption'. The report in *L'Alsace* had carried only a rudimentary description of the scene and a few lines about the victim. There had been no speculation as to the cause. Perhaps Corbeil had already made a few phone calls of his own.

'I try not to proceed on the basis of assumptions,' said Gorski. 'Regardless of the findings of the Road Accident Investigator, certain questions have to be addressed.'

51

'I'm not sure I agree, Inspector. Just because an individual has the misfortune to be involved in an accident, I fail to see why that gives you the right to pry into his affairs.'

Gorski could no longer hide his impatience. 'Maître Corbeil, I am not "prying". I am carrying out an investigation into a fatal'—he pulled himself up before using the word *accident* again—'into an individual's death, and I see no reason for you to adopt such an obstructive attitude.'

He took out a second cigarette. Corbeil stood up and took a cigar from a box on his desk and lit it with a weighty onyx lighter. He puffed on it for a few moments, appearing to be lost in appreciation of the fine tobacco. Then he gave a little shake of his head, as if suddenly recalling that Gorski was there.

'You're quite right, my dear Inspector. I have no wish to be uncooperative, quite the contrary. You must forgive my legalistic propensity to parse everything.'

He resumed his seat. Gorski forced a smile.

'My enquiries, at this point, relate only to why your colleague was travelling south on the A35 when the incident occurred. I cannot imagine that the same question has not crossed your mind.'

Corbeil shook his head slowly. 'I don't see why it should have, but nevertheless—' He gestured with his cigar for Gorski to continue.

'Maître Barthelme's car left the road sometime after 9pm. My question merely regards what time you parted company and whether he gave any indication of where he was going?'

Corbeil's eyes betrayed a flicker of confusion. 'I'm not sure I follow,' he said.

'It's a straightforward question,' said Gorski.

'But it seems to be based on a misapprehension on your part,' said Corbeil. 'I did not see Maître Barthelme after I left these premises.'

Gorski suppressed a smile. He felt vaguely that he had won a small victory. He confined his reaction to a slight nod, intended to give the impression that he had somehow tricked the lawyer into making this admission.

'So you did not have dinner with Maître Barthelme at the Auberge du Rhin?'

Corbeil gave a bemused laugh. 'I did not.'

'It is my understanding that you and your partner dined together every Tuesday evening.'

The lawyer looked askance at Gorski and replied that he was mistaken. He had never so much as set foot in the restaurant. 'I cannot imagine what gave you such an idea,' he said.

'In that case, can you tell me what time you last saw him?'

'Sometime in the afternoon, here at the office.'

'And when was that?'

Corbeil puffed out his cheeks to indicate that he could not possibly be expected to remember something so trivial.

Gorski pointed out that it was only the previous day. 'Perhaps your secretary has a better memory,' he suggested.

Corbeil looked at him grudgingly, before getting up and stepping over to his desk. He consulted a large diary and stated that he had been out of the office. He then pressed a button on an intercom system and asked the secretary to join them. He could just as easily have gone to the door, but no doubt thought the silly device bestowed some gravitas on him.

The woman entered a few moments later and loitered uneasily in the doorway. Corbeil invited her to come further into the room, but he did not offer her a seat.

'Irene, the inspector here would like to ask you one or two questions about Maître Barthelme.'

The woman's eyes darted between the two men. Gorski smiled to put her at ease.

'It's nothing to be concerned about,' he said. 'I simply want to know when Maître Barthelme left the office yesterday afternoon.'

'It was four o'clock, or a little after.'

'Did he have an appointment?'

'There was nothing in the diary.'

'He didn't tell you where he was going?'

Irene stifled a sob. She looked at Corbeil in the hope that he might intervene.

'But it was around four o'clock?' said Gorski.

'Yes.'

'And did he return to the office?'

She shook her head.

'And what time did you leave?'

'Shortly afterwards.' She glanced again towards Corbeil, who was regarding her with some distaste. 'Maître Barthelme told me that if I was finished for the day, I could leave.'

'So it's possible he might have returned to the office after you left.'

She dabbed her eyes with a handkerchief she had balled up in her hand.

'I fail to see the relevance of this,' said Corbeil.

Gorski resisted the temptation to tell the solicitor that what he thought was of no importance, but he did not pursue the point. The secretary appeared to be the only person in the least upset about Barthelme's death and he saw no need to add to her distress.

Six

THE SHORTEST WAY BACK TO the police station would take
Gorski past Le Pot. It was perfectly possible to take an alternative
route, but were he to take a detour, would that not constitute
an admission that he had some kind of problem: that he was
incapable of walking past a bar without entering it? On the other
hand, what would be more natural than to stop off for a quick
beer to mull over his conversation with Corbeil? It was not that
he had a craving for a drink. It was simply that it would be more
agreeable than returning to his office. Even so, had he not, only
that morning, resolved to spend no more time in Le Pot? He
did not enjoy sitting alone drinking, and he was well aware of
the effect that the presence of a cop had on the atmosphere of
the bar. It had simply become a way of avoiding spending his
evenings in the house on Rue de Village-Neuf.

He turned into the street in which Le Pot was located. The
act of resisting the temptation to enter the bar would have little
value unless he actually passed it. He even crossed to the opposite
pavement so that he would have to walk right past the door. A
few metres from the entrance, Gorski glanced at his watch and
adopted an expression intended to suggest to anyone who might
be observing him that he was suddenly surprised to find that he
had more time on his hands than he thought.

Three men in work clothes were standing by the counter,
a newspaper open between them. Gorski slid onto the ripped

vinyl banquette and mimed the motion of pulling a beer. Only when Yves had wordlessly placed his drink on the table did he stand up and remove his raincoat. He let the beer sit for a few moments. Now that it was here, he was in no hurry. He watched the bubbles rise and settle on the underside of the foam, which the bartender had adeptly skimmed with a palette knife he kept by the tap for this purpose. The men at the bar exchanged some lewd remarks about the victim of the Strasbourg murder. At this point, Yves gave an almost imperceptible nod to alert them to Gorski's presence and the conversation fizzled out.

Gorski was intrigued by his exchange with Corbeil. The greater part of his work as a cop was entirely mundane. It is a misconception that detectives spend their time unravelling dark mysteries. They do not. In the vast majority of cases, the perpetrator of a crime is either known from the outset, or, in the cases of petty theft or burglary, unlikely ever to be apprehended. The police go through the motions of investigating crimes not primarily in the hope of finding the culprit, but simply to assure the citizens whose taxes pay their salaries that they are protected from the villains the press encourages them to believe are ready to rob, rape or murder them. In the rare event of an investigation resulting in an arrest, it is more likely the result of days of tedious legwork than some moment of intuition. So it is, at least in a town like Saint-Louis, which—a few habitual thieves aside—is blessed neither with a proper criminal class nor with any great tendency towards violence. It is a peaceful place, mostly untroubled by drama. At social gatherings, Gorski was invariably expected to entertain the company with anecdotes about the baffling cases he had solved, but when, instead, he tried to explain the real nature of police work, the conversation would swiftly move on to another topic.

So Gorski was intrigued simply because he had found something out that he didn't know before; something that ran contrary to the previously accepted version of events. Truth be told, it was not much. A man had lied to his wife. On the night he died, Barthelme had not been where he said he would be. But more than that, he had not been where he said he was every Tuesday evening for the duration of his married life. The most likely explanation was perfectly obvious, but it was curious nevertheless. Bertrand Barthelme did not seem the type to keep a mistress. Moreover, Corbeil's obstructive attitude suggested that he knew his colleague had something to hide. The solicitor's unhelpfulness could be plausibly explained by a desire to protect the dead man's reputation—and, by extension, that of the firm—but it also suggested that there might be something lurking behind the stuffy bourgeois image Barthelme had projected to the world.

Gorski sipped his beer. He reminded himself that the unaccounted hours in Barthelme's life were of no feasible interest to the police. No crime had been committed. He had made his enquiries only out of a silly desire to please Lucette Barthelme. It was quite improper, as Corbeil had been all too aware. He should report his findings, such as they were, to the widow and leave it at that. But, if only to spite Corbeil, he did not want to leave it at that. He had been drawn in. He imagined Ribéry sitting next to him with his lunchtime *pichet*. As a cop he was Gorski's opposite: all instinct and hunches. If his gut did not offer up an instant solution to a case, he would most likely shrug and blame the gypsies (a group he regarded as outside his jurisdiction). Not for him the wearing out of shoe leather, knocking on doors, or poring over cuttings and criminal records.

Gorski got up and asked Yves for a *jeton* for the telephone booth in the corner of the bar. He called Lucette Barthelme. Perhaps she had simply been mistaken about whom her husband dined with. There was probably a perfectly innocent explanation. When the housekeeper put the widow on the line, she sounded disoriented, as if she had just woken up. Gorski apologised for disturbing her and explained that he had been unable to see Maître Corbeil. He asked if she could think of anyone else her husband might have spent the evening with.

'Oh, I'm not sure,' she said.

'You referred to a club of some sort,' he said.

'Yes,' she said, 'that's right. What a good memory you have, Inspector.'

Gorski gently pressed her for some names.

After some thought, she provided two: one an *agent immobilier*, the second the owner of a factory on the outskirts of the town. Gorski thanked her and said that he would keep her informed of any developments.

Henri Martin's offices were set back from the main thoroughfares of Saint-Louis, on the ground floor of a residential property on Rue des Vosges. There was no window displaying properties for sale or rent. Next to the bell was a sign: *Consultation by appointment only.*

One of the first lessons Gorski had learned from Ribéry was never to call ahead. Don't give a witness the chance to get their story straight in advance. Still, Henri Martin did not seem at all surprised by Gorski's visit. He was a small man, neatly dressed in a dark three-piece suit. Without asking whether he wanted it, he poured Gorski a whisky from a decanter, before inviting him to take the seat opposite his desk.

'I don't imagine you've come to enquire about a piece of real estate,' he said, as Gorski settled himself.

'No? Why not?' said Gorski. 'As a matter of fact, I am thinking of moving.'

Martin looked embarrassed. He smiled apologetically.

'The service we offer is quite exclusive,' he said by way of explanation. 'We are brokers rather than dealers. Our clientele is rather'—he searched for the correct word—'rather well heeled. I would be happy to recommend the services of one of the other firms in town.'

Gorski creased his mouth into a smile to indicate that he was not offended, but he postponed explaining the purpose of his visit. Martin had put himself on the back foot, and when people were on the back foot, they found silence uncomfortable. Martin sat down behind the desk and placed his own drink carefully on a coaster. He was playing for time. Gorski was convinced that Corbeil had already called him. He sipped his drink. He knew little about whisky, but he could tell that it was not the workaday stuff one drowns in soda.

'So,' Martin began, 'if you are not here for a consultation, can I assume your visit is in connection with the death of Maître Barthelme?'

'Why would you assume that?' said Gorski.

Martin made a gesture with his hand. 'What else would it be about?'

The purpose of Gorski's visit was quite mundane: to confirm that Martin had not had dinner with Barthelme on the night of his death. It could be accomplished with one simple question, but Gorski determined to make the most of his visit. 'Go fishing,' Ribéry would have told him.

'I wanted to ask about this club of yours.' He kept his statement deliberately vague.

'What club would that be?' said Martin with a little shake of his head.

'The club which yourself, Maîtres Corbeil, Barthelme and'—Gorski took his notebook from the inside pocket of his jacket to remind himself of the name—'Monsieur Tarrou are members.'

He was pleased with the effect of his question. Martin became suddenly concerned that the cuffs of his shirt were not properly shot. He wore gold cufflinks inscribed with his initials. The pupils of his eyes darted upwards as though he was trying to access a forgotten recess of his memory, an involuntary reaction Gorski had observed numerous times. He swirled his whisky beneath his nose then took a sip.

'I'm afraid, Inspector,' he said eventually, 'you have me at a disadvantage.'

'How so?'

'I know of no such club.'

'But you know these gentlemen?'

'Well, yes, but there is no "club", as you call it.'

'The word is Maître Barthelme's, not mine,' said Gorski.

'Nevertheless.'

Gorski knew the answer to his next question before he asked it. 'So may I ask when you last saw him?'

Martin shook his head in response. 'If I didn't see him last night, I hardly see why it matters.'

'Perhaps you could indulge me.'

Martin blew out his cheeks. He was becoming exasperated, just as Gorski intended.

'I couldn't say exactly, two or three weeks ago.'

'And the nature of your relationship? How would you characterise it?'

M. Martin drew his shoulders back and tucked his chin towards his narrow chest, but he kept his tone affable.

'Do you mind if I ask what necessitates such an enquiry? As I understand it, Maître Barthelme's death was nothing more than an accident.' It was precisely the phrase Corbeil had used.

'Have I suggested otherwise?' said Gorski innocently.

'That being the case, I don't see what the nature of our relationship has got to do with anything.'

Gorski decided on a different tack. He leant forward in his chair. 'If I can count on your discretion, Monsieur Martin, there are certain circumstances surrounding Maître Barthelme's death that oblige me to look into his affairs.'

Martin looked at him sceptically. 'May I ask what you are referring to?'

Gorski smiled apologetically. He made a gesture with his hand intended to suggest that he was not at liberty to share such information.

'Now, as to your relationship?'

Martin looked uncomfortable. 'I suppose you could say we were associates,' he said. 'Business associates.'

'Business associates,' Gorski repeated gravely, as if committing the phrase to memory. He drained the remains of the whisky then abruptly stood up. 'I won't take up any more of your time.' He held out his hand. 'I hope I can rely on your discretion. You know how people like to talk.'

'Of course,' said Martin solemnly.

Outside, Gorski strode off down the street. Then after a safe distance, he doubled back and peered through the window of Martin's office. He was already making a telephone call.

Seven

MARC TARROU WAS ON THE telephone when Gorski entered the prefabricated hut which served as his office. The cabin was set on breeze blocks in the potholed car park of his concrete factory. He gestured in a friendly manner for Gorski to take a seat on a plastic chair. The walls were lined with plywood veneer and covered with miscellaneous year planners and advertisements for building supplies. Most of the floor space was taken up with piles of paper and bulging ring-binders. It could hardly be more different from the offices of Barthelme & Corbeil. Gorski remained standing. His eyes were drawn to a calendar, five years out of date, displaying a photograph of a girl in a bikini kneeling in the shallows of the sea on a Caribbean beach. Her legs were parted and her head thrown back as a wave broke over her.

Tarrou continued his conversation, which concerned a delay in an order, for some minutes, occasionally breaking into a language Gorski guessed to be Arabic, while theatrically rolling his eyes and shaking his head at his visitor. He was a handsome man with an olive complexion and thick dark hair, swept back from his forehead. Despite the fact that there was no heating in the cabin, he was in his shirt-sleeves. A blue blazer with gold buttons hung over the back of chair. Beneath the desk, the cuffs of his trousers were spattered with pale clay mud from the car park. Tarrou ended his conversation with a series of gaudy oaths and settled the receiver gently back in its trestle with a wink.

'Fucking Arabs,' he said. 'That's the only language they under-stand.' Then, as if to legitimise his sentiments, added: 'I'm half-Arab myself, on my mother's side. A Marseillaise mongrel, ha ha.'

Gorski wondered how often he had trotted out that line. It was hard to believe that Bertrand Barthelme and his cronies would associate with such a man.

Tarrou emerged from behind his desk, his hand outstretched. 'So the cops, eh? What have I done this time? Inspector Gorski, isn't it?'

Gorski grimaced at the joke. The manufacturer cleared the papers from two plastic chairs and they sat down. Then Tarrou leapt to his feet. He produced a bottle of wine from the top drawer of a filing cabinet.

'A snifter to oil the wheels, eh?'

There were two unwashed glasses on the table between them. One was stained with lipstick. Tarrou found a paper towel and gave them a cursory wipe. He poured out some wine and handed one to Gorski. He kept the lipstick-stained glass for himself.

'Chin-chin,' he said.

He sat down opposite Gorski, leaning forward with his elbows resting on his splayed knees. 'I expect you're wondering how I know who you are,' he said. 'Well, I'll tell you. That snake Corbeil rang and told me you were sniffing about. Told me I could expect a visit from you.'

'I see,' said Gorski. 'And why do you think he felt the need to do that?'

Tarrou puffed out his lips. 'You'd have to ask *him* that, wouldn't you, Inspector?'

Gorski did not know what to make of this apparent openness. In his experience, such tactics were usually a smokescreen. He had encountered plenty of these hail-fellow-well-met types, whose eagerness to parade their candour only raised the suspicion that they had something to hide. Nonetheless, there was something likeable about Tarrou. Bogus or not, his genial manner was preferable to the veiled hostility of Corbeil and Martin.

'So,' he continued, 'if you've got some sniffing around to do, sniff away!'

Gorski placed his glass on the table between them. 'How would you describe your relationship with the deceased?'

'The deceased? Is that what we're calling him?' He gave a great shrug.

'Would you describe him as a friend?'

'A friend?' He seemed to find the suggestion amusing. 'I don't think Barthelme had any friends.'

'What then?'

'We did a bit of business together. You don't need me to tell you that there's not much gets done in Saint-Louis without old Barthelme getting his nose in the trough.'

Gorski nodded as if he knew exactly what he was referring to. Perhaps Tarrou was actually as ingenuous as he appeared.

'And when did you last see him?'

Tarrou ran through a whole repertoire of gestures: pulled a face, shook his head, puffed out his cheeks, exhaled noisily. 'Not sure I could say… couple of weeks ago. Three maybe.'

'Not yesterday, in any case?'

'No.'

'Tell me about this club of yours.'

'What club would that be?'

'The club you belonged to with Barthelme, Corbeil and Martin.'

Tarrou looked genuinely puzzled. He shook his head. Then he knocked back his wine and topped up their glasses.

'You never met these gentlemen for dinner?'

'I did. On occasion,' said Tarrou. 'But I wouldn't call it a club. Is that what Barthelme called it? Ha ha. The pompous asshole!'

'But, regardless of whether you called it a club, you were in the habit of dining with these gentlemen?'

'In the habit? No. We met now and again to discuss… to discuss our mutual interests. There was nothing more to it than that. If there was some sort of club, I wasn't part of it.'

He put down his wine, as though afraid that he might become loose-tongued.

Gorski nodded. It was of course perfectly possible that this club was nothing more than a fiction Barthelme had invented to deceive his wife. But there was clearly some kind of association between the men, and it intrigued him that it was one from which they were all so keen to distance themselves. Nevertheless, he sensed an ally in Tarrou and did not wish to push his luck.

'In any case, you did not have dinner with Maître Barthelme yesterday evening?' he asked.

'No.'

'And you didn't see him between 4pm and the time of his death?'

'Well, I don't know what the time of his death was, but no.'

Gorski drained his glass and stood up.

'I was under the impression that this was nothing more than an accident,' said Tarrou.

'All I can say is that an investigation is underway,' replied Gorski. Then he added, knowing that Tarrou would be the last person to keep any titbits of information to himself: 'There are a couple of loose ends.' He made a throwaway gesture with his hand, as if it was a matter of no consequence, but he noted the inquisitive expression that passed across the factory owner's face.

Tarrou walked him to the door.

'Give my regards to Madame Barthelme,' he said as they shook hands.

Gorski looked at him. He felt the colour rise to his cheeks. Tarrou nudged him on the upper arm: 'Wouldn't want a nice bit of stuff like that to go to waste, would we?' He laughed heartily at his own joke.

Gorski stepped down the breeze-block steps of the hut into a pothole. Muddy water seeped into his shoe. He got into his car and lit a cigarette. He was not thinking straight. Barthelme's death was in all likelihood an accident, yet here he was running round making baseless insinuations. He had allowed himself to get carried away. So what if a group of businessmen got together for dinner once in a while. And so what if the victim of a road accident had lied to his wife about his whereabouts. There was no reason to believe the two things were connected. And Tarrou's lewd remark suggested he had seen right through him. He was less interested in the affairs of Bertrand Barthelme than in the agreeable Lucette.

GORSKI HAD ALWAYS HATED the house on Rue de Village-Neuf. The development on the northern edge of Saint-Louis had been built twenty years before. The houses were ersatz rustic. Fake beams mimicked the style of the traditional Alsatian farmhouse. The shutters on the windows were PVC rather than wood. Before they married, Gorski had imagined taking an apartment like that of his parents, but Céline would not hear of such a thing and before he knew it the matter had been taken out of his hands. Céline's father, already by that time deputy mayor of the town, had purchased the house and presented it to the couple as a wedding gift. Céline was delighted and swept from room to room, pronouncing about colour schemes and furnishings, while Gorski and M. Keller stood awkwardly in the hall.

The size of the couple's new home did not go unnoticed at the station, and Schmitt and his cronies missed no opportunity to make insinuations about how he could afford such a house on a detective's salary. 'Perhaps he's taking kickbacks,' was the usual refrain. 'Do you have to apply for planning permission to fuck your wife?' was Schmitt's favourite line. It had been Gorski's mistake not to put an end to this from the outset. If he had not done so, it was out of a misplaced desire to be one of the boys—to show that even though he was the boss, he could take a joke as well as anyone. He had only succeeded in making himself a figure of derision.

If Gorski avoided returning to the house on Rue de Village-Neuf, it was because, even after twenty years, he felt like a caretaker wandering onto a stage set after the theatre had emptied.

There was nowhere he could sprawl out with his newspaper or put down a bottle of beer without worrying about making a ring on the table. Tonight he had at least forced himself to leave Le Pot before Yves wearily turned around the little sign on the door. But as he pulled up outside the house, he regretted having gone to the bar at all. He could see the glow of the hall lamp through the glass panel at the side of the door.

The front door was locked. When he stepped into the hall, he called out a tentative greeting. There were no other lights on in the house and no one replied. He turned on the light in the kitchen and then went upstairs. The door to his daughter's room was ajar. Clémence must have come to collect some of her things. Gorski cursed himself for missing her. He went back downstairs and uncorked a half-empty bottle of wine. As he poured himself a glass he spotted the little note propped against the cruet set on the kitchen table.

Hi Pops. Swung by to pick up some bits and pieces. Expect you're busy busting some international criminal gang. Maman's driving me crazy by the way! C x

PS You're not thinking of wearing that tie with that shirt are you!?

Gorski smiled. The last line was a private joke between them. But at the same time he felt a smarting at the back of his eyes. He had to swallow hard to suppress a sob. How wretched to have been sitting in Le Pot like a pitiful drunk when Clémence had been here. He knocked back the glass of wine he had poured and transferred the remains of the bottle into his glass.

At that moment, the telephone rang. Gorski snatched up the receiver. The set was attached to the wall next to the kitchen door.

'Clémence?' he said.

'Georges! I'm so glad I've caught you.' It was his mother-in-law. She addressed him in her usual sing-song voice, as if nothing was amiss.

Gorski felt a sinking in his chest. 'Evening, Madame Keller,' he said. Despite her many rebukes, he could never bring himself to call her by her first name. He would have felt somehow that he was flirting with her.

'Now, Georges,' she began in a mock-reproachful tone, 'what *is* going on with you and Céline? She's moping around here like a lost child. You need to give her a little ring. I'm sure you can sort all this out. It's so silly.'

Gorski liked his mother-in-law and did not resent her interference. He was even rather heartened to hear what she had to say. Nevertheless, he felt obliged to put up a bit of resistance. 'Don't you think it's she that should be calling me?' he said.

He prised his shoes from his feet. They were caked with the pale mud from Tarrou's car park. He had left a trail of footprints across the parquet. He drained the dregs of the wine from his glass.

'Georges, you know how stubborn she is. You're the sensible one. One little phone call is all it will take.'

He stretched the telephone cable to its limit and opened the fridge. He took a bottle of beer from the door and held the receiver in the crook of his neck while he opened it. 'I'll think about it,' he said. 'Perhaps I could have a word with Clémence though?'

'Céline's here now if you want to speak to her,' she said.

'I don't think that's a good idea.' But he could already hear Mme Keller calling her daughter.

She must have put her hand over the mouthpiece, because some moments of muffled conversation ensued. Gorski took a good swallow of beer and rolled his head on his shoulders. He did not want to hang up out of courtesy to Mme Keller. She came back on the line.

'Here she is now,' she said. 'She was just powdering her nose. Ta ta!'

Gorski could imagine Céline holding the receiver warily with the tips of her fingers, as if it carried the danger of infection.

'Georges,' she said. Her tone was as it always was: flat, a little curt.

'How are you?' he said.

'I'm fine. Is that what you called to ask me?'

Gorski was about to tell her that it was not he who had called at all, but thought better of it.

'And Clémence?'

'Clémence? Fine, I suppose. Why shouldn't she be?'

Gorski could not think of an appropriate response.

'Was there anything else?'

'Perhaps we should meet?' he suggested, without conviction. Part of him wanted Céline back, but, as yet, the novelty of not having to answer to her had not entirely worn off. 'I miss you,' he added, because he felt that he should.

'Oh, come on, Georges,' said Céline. 'Let's not get sentimental. Have you been drinking?'

'I just got in,' he said. It was not—technically—a lie.

There was a silence. Then Céline said: 'Was there anything else?'

Gorski pressed on. 'Perhaps we should have dinner or something. I suppose there are certain things we need to discuss.' Even if she refused, he would be able to tell Mme Keller he had tried.

Céline gave a great sigh before, to Gorski's surprise, agreeing.

'Is Clémence around?' he asked.

'Sulking in her room, as usual,' said Céline.

'Perhaps you could—' But Céline had hung up. Gorski took his beer to the living room. He turned the television to a current affairs discussion. He took off his jacket and loosened his tie. He sat down on the sofa and was asleep within minutes. The bottle of beer slipped from his hand and emptied its contents onto the carpet.

Eight

RAYMOND WAS ON THE TRAIN to Mulhouse. It was early afternoon and the carriage was almost empty. He took his book from his satchel and retrieved the scrap of paper he had secreted inside its pages. He examined it for the third or fourth time. After dinner the previous evening, he had gone into his father's study. He had rarely been there alone, and then only to fetch something for his father or to check that the shutters were properly fastened. It was not a room in which one set foot without the proper authorisation. So when Raymond entered, it had not been with any particular purpose in mind, but simply because he could. At first he had paced slowly around the bookcases that lined the walls, warily circling the desk that formed the room's centrepiece. He ran his fingers over the spines of the volumes on the shelves. Then he sat down in the armchair at the window. The green leather of the chair was cracked and worn to a patina. The base bore the indentation of his father's buttocks. The antimacassar upon which Raymond rested his head was infused with the aroma of pipe tobacco.

Raymond's earliest recollection of his father was this smell. He associated it primarily with the coarse fabric of his suits and wiry whiskers of his beard, but it permeated everything. It seemed strange that this aroma persisted, as if his father was still present in the room. Raymond recalled sitting at his father's feet while he sat reading in this very chair. He was perhaps three or four years old. He brushed his fingertips along the cuffs of his father's trousers, enjoying the ticklish texture of the tweed. But it was the smell he remembered most, the nutty, complex smell of a world to which he did not belong. Even then, Raymond knew that his father was not to be disturbed, but he craved some sign of affection from him, for him to lower his hand from the arm of the chair and tousle his hair. Instead, however, Maître Barthelme had flicked out his foot as if a fly had alighted on his ankle. Raymond scuttled from the room.

Raymond got up and walked over to the desk. He sat down in the chair from which his father had delivered his annual lecture on Raymond's educational failings. There were no papers on the surface of the desk. The only items were the green-shaded reading light with its old-fashioned fabric cable, a telephone, a pipe rack, a jar of ink and a fountain pen. Raymond picked one of the pipes from the rack and put it in his mouth. The stem tasted bitter and he put it back, rubbing his lips with the back of his hand to get rid of the flavour. He opened each of the six drawers in turn. To his surprise, five of them were entirely empty. Only the drawer on the top left contained a few miscellaneous items: a box of pipe cleaners, some matches, paperclips and such like. It was in this drawer that Raymond had found the scrap of paper he was now inspecting. It was approximately four centimetres by two and had been torn from the page of a notebook or diary. The paper was of good quality and yellowed with age. There was a faint tide-mark on the bottom corner and the ink of the final few letters had bled into the fibre of the paper. Perhaps it had once been passed across a café table where there was some moisture from a drink. Written on it was an address: *13 Rue Saint-Fiacre, Mulhouse*. The handwriting was rounded and feminine. The capital 'S' and 'F' of Saint-Fiacre were written with a flourish, suggesting a flamboyant, outgoing nature. The 'e' of Mulhouse ended in a little curlicue. The address was not accompanied by a name and the fact that there was no area code suggested that it had been written down so that the recipient might pay a visit rather than post something there.

The train stopped at Bartenheim and a woman with a small child got on. Although the carriage was almost empty, they took the seats opposite Raymond. He slipped the address back between the pages of his book and returned it to his satchel. He stared fixedly out of the window. He did not want to fall into conversation and be questioned about his destination or the nature of his business there. The woman occupied herself talking in a childish voice to her toddler, an ugly child with red hair and a lazy eye.

When the train pulled into the stop before Mulhouse, Raymond got up and walked to the opposite end of the carriage. He stepped off the train and then got into the adjacent carriage. He was quite proud of his little charade until he realised that the woman was most likely also travelling to Mulhouse and would spot him on the platform there. When the train pulled into the town a few minutes later, Raymond disembarked as soon as the train came to a halt and headed for the stairs that led to the underpass. He allowed himself a glance over his shoulder. The woman was coaxing her offspring onto the platform.

Despite its proximity, Raymond had rarely set foot in Mulhouse. If he and his mother required something that could not be obtained in Saint-Louis, they generally went to Strasbourg. In Raymond's mind, Mulhouse was little more than a larger version of his home town, equally dreary and no less provincial. What he did not realise is that in a town of one hundred thousand people, rather than twenty thousand, there is room enough for a few individuals who do not conform to the conventional way of life. Bars and restaurants can offer something more exotic than the staples of the regional cuisine. While a town the size of Mulhouse is unlikely to be a hotbed of anarchism, it is large enough for those with unorthodox views to meet like-minded souls and find a conducive place to exchange them. It is similarly possible in a town like Mulhouse to lead, if one wishes, a life of relative anonymity. The population is more fluid and the inhabitants are less concerned with the petty affairs of their neighbours.

The smaller the town, the more inward-looking its residents. Fewer people arrive and settle in our smallest towns. Change, if it occurs at all, takes place over generations. The citizenry become set in their ways, and anyone deviating from these norms is made to understand—one way or another—that they are not welcome. Our larger towns and cities thus exert a pull on those individuals who, for whatever reason, do not fit in elsewhere.

None of which is to say that Mulhouse is a metropolis like Paris, Lyons or Marseilles. It is not. It is a provincial town where the vast majority of citizens would baulk at the idea of living in a larger place. Mulhouse is just right. It is served by a well-regarded theatre and several cinemas. There is an art gallery and a reputable university. The centre boasts a picturesque town square, surrounded by winding streets lined with cafés and artisanal shops. The larger chains are also represented. What need, the denizens of Mulhouse ask, could one have for anything more? The larger cities are awash with crime. They are filthy and dilapidated. Vagrants and blacks grasp your wrist as you pass, begging for a few centimes. Drug dealers and whores peddle their trade in unlit alleyways, eager to lure your children into a life of ruination.

Nor do the citizens of Mulhouse crave the rural life. Who would want to live in a village where there is nothing to do in the evening, and where the locals have nothing better to do than stand at shop counters gossiping in coarse dialects? No, Mulhouse is just right. No one in Mulhouse would ever want to live anywhere else.

Outside the station, Raymond was confronted by a sizeable bus concourse. Busses stopped outside the station in Saint-Louis too, but there was never any need to take one. Raymond spotted a plan of the town behind the scratched perspex of an information board, but it was torn and faded and bore only the names of the main thoroughfares. There was no sign of a Rue Saint-Fiacre. The woman from the train emerged from the entrance of the station and looked at Raymond with a puzzled expression. He turned away and followed a sign to the town centre. He found himself in a maze of winding streets and quickly lost his bearings. He was surprised by the variety of shops and restaurants Mulhouse had to offer. He passed an alley in which a group of shifty men dressed in tracksuits were loitering. One of them caught Raymond's eye. 'Hashish?' he whispered. Raymond hurried on. After half an hour or so, it became clear that he was unlikely to find Rue Saint-Fiacre by wandering around in an arbitrary fashion. He felt discouraged, but he told himself he had embarked on an adventure. It was liberating to be in a place where he was not recognised at every corner.

At the junction of two thoroughfares, he looked around for a suitable person to ask directions. It was around three o'clock and the streets were quiet. A few women shopped for the evening meal. Waiters dallied in the doorways of cafés, waiting for trade. Raymond fished out the slip of paper and scrutinised the address, as if it would miraculously reveal its location. A man in a suit passed, walking rapidly. Two youths, a little older than Raymond, stood on the opposite pavement, smoking. They eyed Raymond impassively, as if they sensed an interloper on their territory. Raymond walked quickly away. An attractive woman in her mid-twenties approached. She was wearing a short blue coat and a skirt reaching midway down her thighs. Her heels clacked on the pavement. She did not seem to be in a hurry. She caught Raymond's eye and looked at him questioningly, as though she was expecting him to proposition her. Raymond blushed and strode past her. He turned into a side street and collided with a young woman bending over a pushchair. He apologised and then, because the ice had been broken between them, said: 'Perhaps you can help me. I'm looking for Rue Saint-Fiacre.'

He held out the paper, as if to corroborate his story. The woman took it from him. She repeated the name of the street and then slowly shook her head. 'Sorry,' she said, 'I don't know it.' She had dark rings under her eyes.

A man in his thirties stepped off the pavement to pass them. The woman held out her hand to attract his attention. 'Monsieur, this young man is lost,' she said, as if Raymond was a foreigner, unable to speak the language.

She handed the address to the man. A cigarette dangled from the corner of his mouth. Raymond did not like the fact that his note was now being passed around willy-nilly. Half of Mulhouse would soon know the nature of his business.

'Rue Saint-Fiacre?' said the man. He pushed his hat towards the back of his head, and took the cigarette from his lips. 'Yes, I know it.' He was about thirty-five and had pockmarked skin.

He turned and gestured down the street with an outstretched arm, his cigarette pinched between two fingers. He began to provide the woman with elaborate directions, as if it was her that wanted to go there. Raymond nodded along, but he was barely listening. The man's instructions petered out. He rubbed his mouth as though he too had lost his bearings.

'Well, it's somewhere down that way.'

The woman's child started to cry. Raymond thanked the man and started to move off in the direction he had indicated.

'Wait,' he said. 'It's on my way. I can show you.'

'That's not necessary,' said Raymond.

But the man had already fallen into step with him. Raymond had no choice but to comply. The woman was murmuring softly to her child. Raymond thanked her for her help, but she did not look up from the pushchair. As they moved away, the man cast a lingering glance at the woman's behind.

'Single mother,' he said meaningfully.

Raymond nodded in vague agreement. The pavement was too narrow for them to walk comfortably abreast and Raymond stepped into the gutter. The man still had the address in his hand. Raymond asked if he could have it back. He had a sudden fear that it would later be used in evidence against him; that it had been a mistake to show it to anyone, or even to ask directions. He had drawn attention to his presence in Mulhouse. The man handed him the paper and he pushed it into his back pocket. When he got home, he would return it to his father's desk before its absence was noticed.

They walked in silence for a few minutes. Then the man asked what was happening in Rue Saint-Fiacre. Raymond had been dreading the question. He could certainly not tell the man the truth. He had assumed that 13 Rue Saint-Fiacre was a residential address and had even formed a mental image of the street. But for all he knew, it might be a bar, a shop, or the premises of some other business. Perhaps it was the office of a legal colleague of his father's. But he could hardly admit to this stranger that he did not know what was there or why he was going there.

When he didn't reply immediately, the man turned and looked questioningly at him. Raymond said: 'I'm meeting a friend.'

It was as good an answer as any. Even if the man accompanied him all the way there, he could simply wait outside the address for his imaginary friend. Of course, it did not really make sense that he would arrange to meet someone at a location he did not know, but the man merely gave a cursory nod and Raymond realised he had only asked to break the silence between them. They emerged into a busier thoroughfare, turned right and continued for some minutes. The man paused and shook hands with an acquaintance outside a bar. They exchanged a few words while Raymond stood awkwardly at the kerb.

At the end of the street, the man indicated that he was going in the opposite direction. Raymond looked over the man's shoulder and noted the name of the street: Rue de la Sinne. He instructed Raymond to carry straight on, then to take the third or fourth street on the left. He shrugged. 'I'm sure you'll find it,' he said.

The man shook his hand and wished him good luck. It struck Raymond as a strange thing to say, as if he suspected there was more to Raymond's mission than he had let on. In any case, his directions proved accurate.

Rue Saint-Fiacre was exactly as Raymond had pictured it, so much so that he wondered if he had been there before. It was a narrow street with four-storey apartment buildings on either side. Cars were parked along the right-hand side only. Halfway along was a shabby philatelist's shop. In chipped gold lettering on the window were painted the words:

TIMBRES POSTE
ACHAT – VENTE

At the far corner of the street was a small café with two folding metal tables set on the pavement outside. No.13 was opposite the philatelist's. It was an ordinary turn-of-the-century apartment building with a heavy wooden door, painted brown. Raymond glanced around, then stepped inside. His heart was beating quickly. Of course, he was not, in essence, doing anything wrong. Yet he felt that he was engaged in something illicit. If challenged, would he tell the truth about why he was there? *Ah, yes*, he imagined saying, *I found this address written on a scrap of paper in my father's desk and I thought he might have been here the night he died.* It sounded ridiculous. It *was* ridiculous. And yet he was here.

The only light in the hallway came from a window on the first-floor landing of the stairwell. The switch of a light glowed orange, but Raymond did not dare turn it on. He allowed his eyes to adjust to the semi-darkness. He tried to breathe evenly. Along the wall on the right of the passage was a series of metal mailboxes. The dark green paint was bubbled and chipped. Raymond bent to read the nameplates on each box. None of them meant anything to him. The final box, which was overflowing with advertising brochures, had no name on it. From this, Raymond concluded that one of the apartments in the building was empty. There was nothing to indicate which mailbox belonged to which apartment. Above him, Raymond heard the sound of a door opening. He did not wait to find out if someone was coming. He exited the building and hurried off, without looking back to see if anyone emerged from the building. He recited the names he could remember from the mailboxes under his breath: Abbas, Lenoir, Comte, Ziegler or something similar. Had he thought things through, he would have brought a notebook and pen. He continued to the far end of the street and leant against a lamp post in a studiously casual fashion. Some children were playing in a small square, but they paid no attention to him. No one emerged from the building. The whole excursion now seemed quite ill-conceived. He had thought no further ahead than locating the address on the piece of paper. What had he expected to find? Short of knocking on the door of each apartment and explaining who he was—a course of action that was out of the question—it was hard to see how he could learn anything meaningful.

Nevertheless, he was here now and he did not have to be home for two or three hours. Next to the philatelist's was an archway leading to a cobbled courtyard. It provided an ideal vantage point. Having first gone into the café to purchase a packet of cigarettes, Raymond took up position. He did not particularly enjoy smoking. Sometimes he and Stéphane shared a cigarette or two in the Café des Vosges, but it was more for effect than for any pleasure in the taste of tobacco. At first, Yvette had chided them for ruining their health—the boys liked it when she told them off—but after a while she had joined in, holding the cigarette ostentatiously between the tips of her thumb and index finger, but rarely inhaling.

The apartments on the upper two floors of the building each had a small balcony with a wrought iron balustrade, large enough only for a pair of small chairs, and accessed by a louvred door. On the right-hand balcony of the second floor was a rusting child's bicycle and a turret of unused plant pots. On the adjacent balcony, a pair of unloved geraniums clung to life. The paint on the ironwork was peeling. Weeds grew from the guttering and the plasterwork of the walls was crumbling and stained with watermarks. The general impression was one of decay. Raymond pictured his father emerging from this rundown building, glancing furtively around before getting into his Mercedes.

He felt conspicuous in the archway. Any passers-by or residents looking out of their windows could hardly fail to spot him and would surely wonder what he was doing there. After twenty minutes or so, an old woman with a pug emerged from the building. She was dressed in a thick mauve overcoat with a matching felt hat. The pair crossed the road and approached the archway. The dog commenced a wheezing inspection of the weeds sprouting from the base of a drainpipe. The woman looked at Raymond, but she did not greet him and her expression showed no curiosity. Her dog cocked its leg against the wall before they moved off in the direction of the town centre. A trickle of urine made its way across the narrow pavement.

Half an hour passed. No one else entered or left the building. Few people passed along the street, and those who did paid no heed to Raymond. He smoked another cigarette. He began to forget the original purpose of his mission. He was not bored. On the contrary, each tiny event on the street held some interest. He found himself speculating about the lives of the people he saw: the middle-aged woman who entered the philatelist's shop with a cardboard box of goods and left empty-handed a few minutes later; the old man with a terrier who, despite the drizzle that had started to fall, sat outside the café for ten minutes without ordering anything, before getting up and returning in the direction from which he had come. From one of the apartments above, Raymond heard the sound of a badly played piano. A few minutes after the music ceased, a girl of thirteen or fourteen emerged from the building and walked slowly along the street, the fingers of her right hand playing an arpeggio by her side.

The apartment building began to reveal more details to him. To the left of the door was a patch of fresh paint where someone had clumsily covered over some graffiti. Above the door was a small gargoyle, with a horned head, bulging eyes and a tongue protruding lewdly from its mouth. The pavement to the left of the door was strewn with cigarette ends, presumably dropped from one of the balconies above. The windows of the apartment on the ground floor to the right of the door were hung with yellowing curtains. The glass did not appear to have been cleaned for years. It seemed remarkable that Raymond should not have noticed these things immediately. Similarly, it was only after he had been there for an hour that he noticed the stale smell in the archway. And if he took a step out onto the pavement, a breeze from the far end of the street carried a faintly industrial smell, perhaps from a tannery.

The old woman with the pug returned. She was carrying a canvas bag of vegetables and moving even more slowly than before. Raymond did not want her to see him again. It would seem odd that he had been loitering there since she had left the building. He emerged from the archway and ducked into the philatelist's. A little bell rang above the door. The shop smelled of old books. It was more of a bric-a-brac shop than a philatelist's. Aside from a glass counter displaying pages of stamps, behind which sat the proprietor, there seemed little to justify the sign above the door. A cabinet to the left of the counter was filled with items of costume jewellery. The walls were hung with old-fashioned ski shoes, musical instruments and tatty hunting trophies. The sound of the bell caused the proprietor to look up from the catalogue he was reading. He looked at Raymond without interest. The window was piled high with goods, so that it was difficult to see out into the street. Raymond positioned himself where he could see through the glass panel of the door and occupied himself by flicking through a leather-bound edition of the complete works of Balzac. The old woman must have been walking exceptionally slowly, for it seemed an age before she passed the door. Raymond felt the eyes of the proprietor on his back.

'You can have the set for fifty francs,' he said.

Raymond glanced over his shoulder. The shopkeeper was looking at him over the rims of his spectacles. Raymond nodded and moved away from the books. It was then that his eyes alighted on the knife. It was set atop a stack of battered leather suitcases. The blade was ten or twelve centimetres long, curving elegantly to a point. The handle had been carved from horn or antler. It came with a dark leather sheath, stitched with yellow thread and worn to a smooth sheen. Raymond picked up the knife and weighed it in his hand. He was aware that the shopkeeper was observing him.

'How much is this?' he asked, trying to make his enquiry sound as casual as possible.

The proprietor told him the price, then added by way of explanation: 'It's antique. A nice piece.'

Raymond nodded and put it down. He did not have the amount in question or anything like it. He had not seen the old woman pass by, but he had been distracted by the knife. He bid the shopkeeper good day and left. The street was deserted. It was now five o'clock. Raymond was not dissatisfied with his afternoon's work. There was no evidence to suggest that his father had ever visited this place, yet the scrap of paper had clearly lain in the drawer for years. At some point it had been of sufficient importance for his father not to have discarded it. Raymond was not accustomed to thinking of his father as someone with secrets. Until this point he had accepted, as all children do, the image that his father presented to the world. But this scrap of paper written in feminine hand represented a crack in that façade. Raymond could happily have spent the evening maintaining his vigil on the apartment building, but he was due at home for dinner at half past six and he had no desire to elicit any questions about where he had been. As he walked back to the railway station, he was already planning to return the following day.

Nine

THE ACCIDENT INVESTIGATION AND post-mortem reports were on Gorski's desk. The former began with a banal description of the stretch of the A35 on which the incident occurred, this accompanied by a map with arrows showing the direction of travel and final resting point of the vehicle. The climatic conditions were described, supported by data from a local weather station. The report then moved to the vehicle itself. The specification and general condition of the vehicle were painstakingly detailed. A full service history had been recovered from the glove compartment and there was nothing to suggest that the vehicle was not in perfect running order. This more or less eliminated the possibility that the crash had been caused by mechanical failure. There then followed a list of twenty-nine separate items of damage to the vehicle, each with a description and probable cause. The cause of almost every item of damage was listed as 'Impact of collision with tree'. It was tedious stuff, but Gorski read every word. The report ended with a series of calculations and the conclusion that the vehicle had left the carriageway at the point indicated on the map while travelling at between 104 and 110 kilometres per hour.

The post-mortem was similarly meticulous. Following an account of the height, weight, age and general condition of the body, each injury was described and ascribed a probable cause. The style of language and even some of the vocabulary—

'abrasion', 'fracture', 'rupture'—was indistinguishable to that of the vehicle report. There was no reason it should be any different. Barthelme's body, like his car, was no more than a piece of evidence. The fact that one was composed of tissue, skin and bone and the other of metal, glass and plastic, was immaterial. Gorski read the two reports with the same detachment. Aside from the injuries to the cranium, which would have proved instantly fatal, the ribcage had collapsed on impact with the steering wheel and the damage to the organs in the chest cavity would also have resulted in death. None of this added much to the observations that Gorski had made at the scene. Yet this thoroughness reassured him. The state was not satisfied with vague impressions or probabilities. The state—like Gorski—required certainty. And if certainty could not be achieved, then any conclusions about probable cause must at least be based on quantifiable, verifiable evidence. No matter how clear the cause of a citizen's death appeared, due process must be adhered to. Ribéry always derided these niceties as a waste of money and refused to even open the manila covers of such reports. 'If you learn something from a post-mortem that you didn't see with your own eyes, then you're not doing your job, my boy,' he liked to say. 'God put two eyes in your head, not a pen in your hand.' Gorski always nodded along with this chapter from the Ribéry gospel, but in truth he found it simple-minded. While there was no substitute for keen observation of a crime scene, there was much the eye could not see. In this case, the post-mortem report contained two pieces of information that could not be discerned from a visual examination of the evidence. The first of these placed the time of death, based on the ambient temperature recorded at a nearby weather station, at between 22:25 and 22:40. This meant that the accident had occurred between five and twenty minutes before the call reporting the incident had been placed. There was nothing untoward in that. The road had been quiet and the vehicle had not been immediately visible from the carriageway.

The second noteworthy piece of information was that a considerable amount of alcohol—the equivalent of more than one bottle of wine—was present in the victim's bloodstream. Such a quantity of alcohol, the report concluded, greatly increased the possibility that the driver had fallen asleep at the wheel and would have significantly impaired the subject's ability to bring the vehicle under control.

It was all very neat and tidy. But, ironically, it was Ribéry's advice that caused Gorski to turn back to the accident report. Everything contained there led to a single conclusion, but there was an omission. Gorski lit a cigarette and ran his finger down the twenty-nine enumerated points of damage to the Mercedes. He then turned to the signature at the end of the report. He consulted the directory he kept on the window sill behind his desk and dialled the number of the investigating officer. His name was Walter Lutz. He had attended the scene on the night of the accident, and Gorski and he had exchanged a few words while they stood on the verge smoking. He was a stocky man, with a brusque, down-to-earth manner.

He picked up on the third or fourth ring. 'Lutz,' he said.

Gorski explained why he was calling.

'Everything's in the report,' said the investigator.

'Yes, of course,' said Gorski. 'I just wanted to clarify a couple of details.'

'It's all pretty clear, isn't it?'

'Very clear.'

'So?' Lutz was trying hard not to sound impatient.

Gorski had no desire to aggravate his colleague by suggesting that his report was shoddy. 'I just had one question, a very small point. I'm sure you can put my mind at rest.'

Lutz made a grunting to noise to indicate that Gorski should continue.

'It's about the scratches on the offside of the vehicle.'

'What about them?'

'There's no mention of them in your report.'

'And?'

'Any reason why not?' said Gorski. He kept his voice casual.

'I didn't consider them to be evidence.'

It was impossible for Gorski to proceed without implying some criticism of his colleague. 'Surely all damage to the vehicle should be accounted for in your report,' he said.

'All damage relevant to the incident,' said Lutz.

Gorski resisted the temptation to disagree on this point. 'So you didn't consider the scratches relevant?'

Lutz exhaled loudly. 'They weren't caused by the impact on the vehicle, so, no, I don't consider them relevant. They could have been there for months, for all I know.'

Bertrand Barthelme did not, Gorski thought, seem like the kind of man who would drive around in a less than pristine vehicle. 'So because the scratches did not fit with your conclusion about the cause of the accident, you do not consider them evidence.'

'Correct,' said Lutz.

Gorski was silent for a moment. With his free hand he tapped a cigarette out of the packet on the desk. 'I'm sorry,' he went on, 'but if your conclusion cannot account for how the scratches came to be on the vehicle, shouldn't you then revise it?'

'I don't see why,' said Lutz. 'All the evidence points to the conclusion I reached.'

Gorski did not see anything to be gained in pointing out that that was inevitable if one discounted any evidence which contradicted the said conclusion. Instead, he adopted a conciliatory tone.

'Just to satisfy my curiosity, what in your professional opinion might have caused the scratches?'

He could almost hear Lutz shrug.

'Is it possible,' Gorski suggested, 'that the car turned on its side as it made its way down the slope and righted itself before it collided with the tree?'

'It's possible,' said Lutz. Clearly he would accept anything

Gorski suggested, if only to bring the conversation to a close.

'But if that was the case, would you then not have to revise your estimate of how fast the vehicle was travelling prior to the accident?'

'I suppose so,' said Lutz, 'but it wouldn't have any bearing on the general conclusion.'

'No, it wouldn't,' Gorski agreed. 'What about this: could the scratches have been caused by a collision with another vehicle?'

'How do you mean?'

Gorski was already resigned to making an enemy of Lutz. 'For example, if another vehicle came alongside and forced the Mercedes off the road.'

Lutz was silent for a few moments. 'I think that's highly unlikely.'

'No, not likely, of course.' Gorski gave a little laugh as if he was dismissing his own suggestion. 'But it would account for how the scratches came to be there.'

Lutz seemed to cheer up a little, as if he accepted that they were merely engaged in a hypothetical discussion which did not imply any criticism of his work. 'If that had been the case, the driver would have applied the brakes or taken some other avoiding action. There would have been tyre tracks on the road.'

'But it had been raining,' said Gorski. 'The road surface was greasy. Wouldn't that mean that no skid marks would be left?' He also recalled that the amount of alcohol in Barthelme's bloodstream would have impaired his ability to take avoiding action.

Lutz grudgingly conceded the point.

'So, given the evidence of the scratches to the side of the car,' Gorski went on, 'the idea that the car was run off the road by another vehicle cannot be entirely discounted.'

'Look, Inspector,' said Lutz, 'you've got my report. The evidence supports my conclusion. If you want to pursue fantasies, go ahead. I've got better things to do.'

Gorski apologised for taking up his time and hung up. In all likelihood, Lutz was right: he was a fantasist. That was what Ribéry would have called him. He would have laughingly told him to stop overthinking things. Gorski stubbed out his cigarette and went to Le Pot.

It had reached the point that Yves poured him a beer before he had even taken his seat. When the bartender brought it to his table, Gorski asked for a hotdog. He did feel not hungry, but he was conscious of the need to eat something. Yves' hotdogs were, in any case, insubstantial. The meat dissolved on one's tongue and the bread which enclosed it was of a spongy, sugary texture that required no mastication. The only real flavour came from the thick yellow worm of mustard. Gorski reached for a copy of *L'Alsace* that had been discarded on the banquette. The Strasbourg murder had been relegated to the inside pages: POLICE BAFFLED BY STRANGLING. He was already familiar with the bare facts of the case. A woman, Veronique Marchal, had been found strangled in her apartment. There was no sign of forced entry nor had anything been stolen. The police had so far been guarded about the circumstances in which Mlle Marchal was found, but it was assumed—and the article made reference to sources close to the investigation—that the motive was sexual. Neighbours had testified that men often visited the woman's apartment, although how numerous these men were, or whether they paid Mlle Marchal for her services, was unclear. The article reiterated the basic facts of the story, before quoting the lead investigator, Philippe Lambert, to the effect that the police were currently pursuing a number of leads and that he would inform the press of developments in due course. Gorski understood exactly what such a line meant: Lambert had nothing. The woman's body had not been discovered until the following morning, and as such the time of death could not be precisely pinpointed, but it was certain that the murder had occurred sometime in the evening of the 14th of November.

Gorski sat back on the banquette. He swallowed the last of his hotdog and wiped his fingers on the paper napkin provided.

Then he read the final lines of the story again. He was not mistaken. The murder had taken place during the unaccounted hours before Bertrand Barthelme's death. Gorski's first thought was to ask Yves for a *jeton* for the phone and immediately call Lambert. However, aside from the fact that it would be indiscreet to make such a call from Le Pot, he should not rush to any conclusions. He folded the newspaper under his arm and made his way back to the police station. He took a cup of coffee to his office and re-read the article. Even allowing ninety minutes for the 130-kilometre journey to Strasbourg, it would have been perfectly possible for Barthelme to drive there and back in the available time. Perhaps the alcohol he had consumed had been to fortify himself for the murder he planned to commit. Gorski shook his head: he was trying to make the facts fit his theory. Other than the fact that he had been driving back from that direction, there was nothing to suggest that Barthelme had been to Strasbourg on the night in question. Besides, the idea that he had been involved in a murder did not fit with the theory that he had fallen asleep at the wheel. Had he been fleeing a crime scene, he would—unless he was the most cold-blooded of killers—be in a state of agitation rather than drowsiness. Alternatively, had he been the perpetrator, he might have become overcome with remorse and deliberately driven his car off the road.

It had to be at least worth putting a call into Lambert. He would make it sound casual. *I'm sure it's nothing, but I thought I should bring it to your attention. It's probably just a coincidence.* And it was true; it probably *was* nothing more than a coincidence. What, after all, did he have? A man had been driving south on the A35 at a time roughly fitting the time of the murder. So what? The fact that he had been killed in an accident was irrelevant. Gorski hesitated. He reminded himself that Barthelme had lied to his wife about his whereabouts and had been doing so for years. He had clearly been engaged in some kind of illicit activity. He remembered the phrase Lemerre had savoured so much: 'Was known to entertain frequent gentlemen visitors.'

Why should Barthelme not have been one of those visitors? He and his wife did, after all, keep separate chambers.

Gorski got up and paced around his office. He looked out of the window. The paint on the outer sill of the window was peeling and the wood beneath was beginning to rot. An old woman was walking slowly along Rue de Mulhouse pulling a little battered trolley of shopping behind her.

He sat down at his desk and lifted the telephone receiver from its cradle. It would be remiss not to call. If it were his case, he would want anyone with even the most tenuous lead to share it. And it was possible that Lambert, shrewd operator that he was, was withholding certain information from the press. Perhaps a man in a green Mercedes had been seen leaving the scene of the crime. Perhaps when confronted with Barthelme's photograph, neighbours would suddenly recognise him as the man who visited Mlle Marchal every Tuesday evening.

The receptionist at the station in Rue de la Nuée-Bleue asked who was calling in a bored voice and then dialled an extension without further comment. The call was answered on the sixth ring.

'Yes?' The man's voice was impatient.

'Lambert?' said Gorski. It would have been over-familiar to call him by his first name—he had only met the Strasbourg detective on a few occasions—but he would have felt obsequious addressing him as Inspector. In any case, whoever was on the other end of the line did not say a word. Instead, Gorski heard a muffled shout of: 'Phil. Call for you.' He must have placed his hand over the receiver.

A few moments later, Lambert came on the line. He sounded weary. Gorski wondered if it had been unwise to call.

'Inspector,'—he couldn't help himself—'this is Georges Gorski.'

'Ah, Georges, Saint-Louis.'

Gorski was pleased that he didn't have to remind Lambert who he was.

'So you cleared up the business with the missing waitress.'

'It cleared itself up,' said Gorski.

'A case closed is a case closed,' said Lambert.

There was a pause.

'Is there something I can do for you?'

Gorski understood the inference contained in the question. It would never occur to Lambert that there might be something that Gorski could do for him.

'Well, it's probably nothing, a bit of a long shot, but I thought—'

Lambert interrupted. 'Look, Georges, I'm a little pressed here, if you could cut to the chase.'

'Yes, of course,' said Gorski. 'I understand you're in charge of the Marchal case.'

'Yes.'

Gorski imagined him rolling his eyes impatiently. 'That's what I'm calling about.'

'Oh?' Lambert sounded a little more interested. 'You got something for me? Because if you do, I'll drive straight down to wherever Saint-Louis is and plant one on you.'

'Well, as I say, it's probably nothing, but I thought I should put it to you.'

'Uh-huh.' The irritation had crept back into his voice.

'On the night of the murder, a lawyer named Bertrand Barthelme was driving south on the A35. He crashed a few kilometres north of Saint-Louis some time around ten thirty.'

'And you're telling me this, why?' said Lambert.

'Well, it struck me—' Gorski began, suddenly aware of the flimsiness of what he was going to say. 'It struck me that he might have been driving back from Strasbourg.'

'He might have been. Him and ten thousand others. So what?'

'Well, yes, of course, but the reason I thought he might have been involved, or that it might at least be worth mentioning, was that he had lied to his wife about his whereabouts that night and that—'

Lambert let out a weary sigh. 'Sorry, Georges, I appreciate you calling, but I've got the press all over me here.'

'Yes, of course, I just thought it would be remiss not let you know,' said Gorski, but Lambert had already put the phone down.

GORSKI FOUND HIS MOTHER ASLEEP in the chair next to the fireplace. She raised her head at the sound of the closing door, blinking heavily. The room was stiflingly hot, from the convector heater that now occupied the hearth.

'Is that you, Georges?' she said, her voice fluttering. 'Where's Georges?'

Gorski placed the bag of shopping he had brought on the table by the window and sat down next to his mother.

'I'm here, Maman' he said, taking her hand. 'You were sleeping.'

'Your father is late for dinner,' she said. 'Everything will be ruined.'

Gorski did not bother to correct her. Such incidents had become more frequent of late. At first, he had put her comments down to dreams she had been having, but it had become clear there was more to it than that. He had gently suggested that his mother might see Dr Faubel, but she had insisted there was nothing wrong with her and would not hear of such a thing. In any case, Gorski feared that any diagnosis of mental decline would lead to the doctor suggesting that she should be cared for in a nursing home, something Mme Gorski would not countenance. *I would like to die here in my own home, thank you*, she would say cheerfully.

Gorski unpacked the shopping he had brought and prepared some tea. He took his time in the kitchenette. The time he spent with his mother was becoming less and less bearable. When he returned with the cups carefully laid out on the tray with a saucer of sliced lemon, his mother appeared to have fully returned to reality. He opened the window to let in a little air.

'You look tired,' she said. 'Your skin is grey. Is Céline not looking after you properly?'

Gorski had not told her that Céline had left. Despite the fact that his mother had never liked her, he felt that she would be disappointed in him. In any case, there seemed little point upsetting her when, for all he knew, the situation might be temporary.

He replied that he had been working too hard and stirred three spoonfuls of sugar into his mother's cup. She smiled her thanks as he placed it on the occasional table next to her armchair. He sat in his father's chair by the table and sipped his tea. The sweet lemon taste always transported him back to his childhood in the apartment. The room was entirely unaltered. Every surface was cluttered with knick-knacks culled over the years from his father's pawnshop. He cast his eyes to the door, as if he too expected to see his father appear from below in his brown store-coat. His eyes alighted on the mezuzah on the doorpost, which he had passed so many times without noticing.

'Maman,' he said, 'do you remember one evening when I was a little boy, two Americans called by?'

He and his mother generally confined themselves to small talk about Clémence or Mme Beck who now ran the florist's downstairs and who often brought his mother a little soup or some leftover casserole. Until the night of the accident, the visit of the two Mormons had not crossed his mind for years. Mme Gorski did not, however, appear the least taken aback.

'Oh, yes,' she replied, as if the event had occurred only the previous week. 'Nice young men. But curious. There were dressed identically. And the way they spoke French—' She started to laugh. 'I'm surprised you remember them. You were very young at the time.'

Gorski wanted to remind her of the words they had used: *of the Jewish persuasion*. He had not intended to bring up the incident, and if he did so now it was entirely on account of this phrase. Indeed, he was quite sure that this was the only reason he remembered the incident at all. No further reference had ever been made to the affiliation the Americans had alluded to. Was it his mother or father who was Jewish? Or was the little box by the door nothing more than an ornament, signifying no more than the English Toby jugs that bookended the mantelpiece? He had hoped to prompt his mother to say something on the subject, but it was clear that nothing was forthcoming. Perhaps she had simply forgotten the remark. Instead, he said only that it must have stuck in his mind because he had never seen an American before.

'Oh, they were *very* American,' she said with a little chuckle. 'Homosexuals, of course.'

Gorski smiled. He was pleased that she was at least able to recall the incident.

Ten

THE FOLLOWING DAY RAYMOND returned to Rue Saint-Fiacre. At dinner the previous evening he told his mother he had decided to return to school. In the morning, he ate breakfast as he always did, standing at the counter in the kitchen. When Thérèse went upstairs with his mother's breakfast tray, Raymond, still chewing a mouthful of bread, opened the stone jar in which the housekeeping money was kept. He took two 100-franc notes and replaced the stopper. When Thérèse returned a few minutes later, his heart was beating quickly, but he forced himself to remain in the kitchen. He even passed some remarks about the weather. It was, of course, quite pointless to act in this nonchalant way. As soon as Thérèse set off to do her morning marketing, she would realise the money was gone. And if for no other reason than to establish her own innocence, she would immediately report the theft to his mother. Naturally she would not accuse Raymond outright. It would be enough to say that the money had gone.

Raymond's act was not spontaneous. It had occurred to him as he rode the train back from Mulhouse the previous day. Perhaps even before that, at the very moment the philatelist had told him the price of the knife. He had resisted thinking through the consequences of the theft, knowing that this would act as a brake on his plan. As it was, he had found, somewhat to his surprise, that he had no difficulty behaving as if nothing was amiss. It even gave him a sort of pleasure to stand blithely talking to Thérèse with the banknotes nestling in the back pocket of his trousers.

Raymond arrived in Rue Saint-Fiacre at half past nine. It was no busier than it been the previous day. As it was set back was from the town's main thoroughfares, there was little reason for anyone who did not live there to pass along it. The philatelist's shop was not yet open. In preparation for his day's surveillance, Raymond had packed a notebook and pencil, half a baguette, his book and the cigarettes he had bought at the café at the end of the street. On one page of his notebook, he had sketched a map of the street, showing the positions of the various landmarks. On the adjoining page, he had drawn a diagram of the building, a rectangle divided four by two, each division representing an apartment. The previous evening, he had looked up the names he had been able to commit to memory in the telephone directory. There was no listing for Ziegler, but he was not even sure he had remembered the name correctly. He had found the other three: Abbas, Lenoir and Comte. He was not interested in Abbas. He could not imagine his father fraternising with anyone of Arab origin. France, he had always insisted, should be for the French. Raymond called the remaining numbers from the telephone in his father's study. A man's voice answered the first call with a curt 'Yes?' A child was crying in the background. Raymond said he had the wrong number and put down the receiver. In his notebook he summarised his findings next to the name Lenoir. His second call, listed as *Comte, I.* in the directory, was answered by a woman. Raymond spoke as firmly as he could:

'May I speak with Monsieur Comte?' he said.

There was a pause.

'There is no Monsieur Comte,' said the woman. 'May I ask who's calling?' Her voice was neither youthful nor old. It had a bright, friendly tone, but there was a nervousness, a slight quaver there as well. Raymond paused for a few seconds. He could hear the sound of the woman's breathing. Perhaps she was drawing on a cigarette.

She repeated her question.

Raymond returned the receiver to its trestle. A light sweat had broken out on his brow. He felt guilty, as though he had committed some minor act of violence. Next to the name Comte, he wrote: *Single woman, middle-aged.*

Raymond took up his vantage point in the archway opposite No.13. Somewhere in the building, he pictured Mlle Comte in her dressing gown, sitting by her kitchen table with a bowl of coffee, a cigarette burning in an ashtray. He supposed she was around forty. Perhaps a cat was rubbing itself against her legs. Maybe she was thinking about the disconcerting telephone call she had received the previous evening.

Around ten o'clock, the philatelist emerged from inside his shop. He was wearing carpet slippers and had a cigarette in his mouth. He must live in the apartment above. He proceeded to unlock the padlock that secured the metal shutter on the window. Raymond stepped back into the archway until he heard the shutter clatter open. He would wait a while before entering. If he wanted to haggle over the knife, his position would be weakened if it appeared that he had been eagerly waiting outside for the shop to open. It would be better if he gave the impression that he had only happened to be passing and it was neither here nor there to him whether he left with the knife.

Moments after he had lit his first cigarette—he had decided in advance that he would allow himself to smoke four—the door to No.13 opened and a man in his thirties hurried out. He looked harassed. His tie was not properly fastened and he was eating a croissant or *pain au chocolat*. He was carrying a briefcase. He got into a battered Renault and drove off. It seemed likely that this was the impatient M. Lenoir, who had answered the telephone the previous night. A few minutes later, a woman of a similar age emerged with two small children, the younger strapped into a pushchair. The elder child had a piece of bread in his hand. His anorak was hanging off one shoulder. They went off in the direction of the town centre. Raymond stepped back into the archway and wrote down his observations.

Nothing else happened for half an hour or so. Then a woman in her late twenties came out. She was dressed in a green belted raincoat. It was not raining, but she opened a transparent umbrella. Her hair was yellow-blonde and tousled. She too hurried off in the direction of town, her heels clacking on the pavement. As she passed, she glanced in Raymond's direction, but her face showed no curiosity. Might this be the woman he had spoken to on the phone? Raymond did not think so. There was a confidence in her stride that did not fit with the hesitancy he had detected in Mlle Comte's voice. Might either of these be the woman who once wrote her address on the scrap of paper that Raymond had now returned to his father's desk? There was no way of knowing. Nevertheless, Raymond felt that he was making progress. Counting the old woman from the previous day, and assuming that none of those he had seen were named Abbas, he could now account for the occupants of more than half of the apartments.

A mid-morning stillness fell over the street. This seemed as good a time as any to enter the building and make a note of the remaining names on the mailboxes. If questioned, he had decided that he would simply ask if a M. Dupont lived in the building. Perhaps he would pat his satchel to suggest that he had a delivery to make. He walked purposefully across the road, his notebook and pen in his hand. Despite his cover story, Raymond felt the same nervousness as he had when he entered the building the day before. He was still reluctant to turn on the light, though if his presence were as innocent as he pretended, why would he not do so? If questioned, he could hardly say that he had not seen the switch: it was right next to the mailboxes. He pressed the glowing button. To his relief, nothing happened. He set to work, scribbling down the remaining names on a blank page: Ziegler (he had been correct), Jacquemin, Duval and Klein. When he had finished, he found that he had the courage to progress as far as the apartment doors on the ground floor. On the door to the right was a plaque with the name Abbas engraved in an ornate script. A heavy bar secured the door to the apartment to the left. Raymond stepped outside and drew breath. He strode along Rue Saint-Fiacre, then doubled back along the almost identical parallel street and returned to his post in the archway. He was becoming quite familiar with this little patch of Mulhouse. He rewarded himself for his endeavours with a cigarette.

Just after half past eleven, a woman of around sixty emerged from the philatelist's. Raymond had not seen her enter the shop. She must be the stamp dealer's wife. She returned twenty minutes later with a baguette under her arm and went back inside. Raymond decided it was time to make his purchase, but when he approached the shop a sign had been hung on the inside of the door: *Closed for lunch*. The door, however, had not been locked. Raymond gently pushed it open, tinkling the bell. He stepped inside the empty shop and stood listening for sounds of movement above. He heard footsteps on the floorboards. A door, which must have led to the apartment, opened and the proprietor called down the stairs: 'Is anyone there? We're closed.' Raymond held his breath. His eyes were fixed on the knife, which was still sitting on the pile of battered suitcases towards the back of the shop.

The philatelist's voice came again. 'Is someone there?'

Did he always leave the door open during lunch or had it been an oversight? Perhaps both he and his wife thought the other had locked the door. Or perhaps they were the sort of trusting people who imagined that a *Closed* sign was sufficient deterrent to thieves. In any case, footsteps could be heard making their way down the stairs. Without further thought, Raymond stepped lightly towards the back of the shop, grabbed the knife and pushed it into his satchel. He bolted out of the shop. He ran into the courtyard behind the archway and pressed himself to the wall. He felt dizzy, almost nauseous. He lowered himself onto his haunches. What had possessed him to do such a thing? He had never, until that morning, stolen so much as a bag of sweets. The philatelist was sure to notice that the knife was gone and remember that the previous day a young man had enquired about it. Raymond could not say how long he remained squatting with his back pressed against the wall. He tried to assess his position. Anyone who happened to look out from the apartments surrounding the courtyard would think his behaviour highly suspicious. Perhaps someone had already seen him and called the police. The philatelist, too, might have called the police. Raymond tried to think clearly. Whatever happened, nobody had seen him take the knife. As long as he was not caught with it on his person, he could deny everything. Glancing round to check that he was not being observed, he took the knife from his satchel and secreted it among some weeds sprouting from the foot of a drainpipe. Then he straightened up and, with as much nonchalance as he could muster, made his way back through the archway.

He craned his head slowly into the street. The philatelist was nowhere to be seen. No police sirens could be heard. As he emerged onto the pavement, he pretended to adjust his flies, as if he had stepped into the alleyway to relieve himself. Then he walked briskly in the direction of the town centre. He took the first left turn and, only when he was sure he was not being observed, doubled back to the end of Rue Saint-Fiacre. He lit a cigarette. His hands were shaking. He exhaled a long stream of smoke. What an imbecilic thing to do! If he had stopped to think for even a fraction of a second, he would never have had the nerve. But he *had* done it, and he had not been caught. He felt exhilarated. It was not so much that he had stolen the knife, which he could in any case have purchased. An opportunity had presented itself and rather than be crippled by indecision, he had grasped it.

He need only wait long enough to be sure that the police had not been called before retrieving the knife from its hiding place. The shopkeeper had probably not even noticed that it was gone. Abandoning his self-imposed limit, he lit another cigarette. He had 200 francs in his pocket. He could buy as many packets of cigarettes as he liked. He had, for the time being, quite forgotten the real purpose of his mission in Rue Saint-Fiacre.

Some time later, Raymond returned to retrieve the knife from its hiding place. Crouching by the drainpipe, he slid it into its sheath. It fit snugly. He straightened up and resisted the temptation to look around to see if he was being watched. Doing so would only make him seem more suspicious than he must already appear. Instead he kept his eyes to the ground and passed through the passage that led back to the street. As he was about to step out, the door to No.13 opened. Raymond stepped back into the archway. A girl emerged. She was nineteen or twenty years old, wearing black jeans and boots laced halfway up her calves. Above, she sported a men's tweed jacket with patches on the elbows. Despite the dull weather she was wearing a pair of round sunglasses with green lenses. A pork-pie hat perched on the back of her head. She headed towards the town centre. She had a long, loping stride, at once languid and purposeful. Raymond moved off in the same direction. He could not be accused of following her. It was mere coincidence that she had emerged from the building as he was about to leave. Nevertheless, he kept on the pavement on the opposite side of the street and regulated his pace so that he did not overtake her. His satchel knocked against his hip. The thought of the knife nestling there pleased him. The girl reached the junction at which Raymond had parted company from the pockmarked man who had given him directions. He hung back a little.

The girl ambled through the traffic, appearing entirely indifferent to whether she was hit. A large truck obstructed Raymond's view. When it pulled away, the girl was gone. Raymond felt a pang of disappointment. He skipped through the lines of cars. Then, above the vehicles, he spotted her hat bobbing along Rue de la Sinne. He trotted a few steps to catch up. He could no longer pretend that he wasn't following her. The girl stopped to look in the window of a record store. Raymond ducked into a doorway. He was no more than twenty metres behind. Her profile was striking. She had a strong Roman nose and prominent cheekbones. She held her head tilted back, perhaps only to prevent her sunglasses slipping down her nose, but the posture gave her a haughty air. If she were to turn round now, she would certainly catch Raymond looking at her. Perhaps she had already noticed him when she left her apartment, or had seen him earlier from her window. Raymond could think of no reasonable explanation for his behaviour. But he could not bring himself to walk away. Part of him even wanted her to see him.

The girl continued along Rue de la Sinne and entered the bar outside which his chaperon had paused to greet an acquaintance. Raymond waited a couple of minutes then followed her inside. The place was quite cavernous, with a high ceiling and ornate cornicing. Two men perched on stools at the bar, one slowly turning the pages of a newspaper, the other with his chin on his chest as if he was asleep. The bartender greeted Raymond with an unsmiling upward nod of his head. Raymond took a seat on the green banquette that ran the length of the wall to the right of the door. The girl was nowhere to be seen.

High on the wall opposite was a large clock bearing the name of the bar: Le Convivial. The second hand ticked round at a stately pace. It was a few minutes before five o'clock. There were around twenty tables with mismatched wooden chairs arranged around the perimeter of the room. Roughly half of these were occupied by an assortment of old men, trousers hiked to their navels, arms folded over their bellies. They exchanged rounds of handshakes and greetings with each new arrival, but for the most part sat in silence. The walls were painted in a yellow wash and hung with framed Lautrec playbills. Two pillars were plastered with movie bills and photographs of Belmondo, Bardot, Gainsbourg and the like. On the far side of the room was a billiard table with two cues carelessly discarded on the baize. Near the centre of the table the cloth was ripped and had been repaired with a strip of black tape. Raymond had the impression that it was never used.

No one so much as glanced at Raymond. He began to wonder if the bartender had actually seen him at all. He was a stocky guy of about thirty, with sand-coloured hair, combed back from his forehead. He was wearing a short-sleeved blue shirt with *Le Convivial* embroidered on the pocket. Various rudimentary tattoos were inked on his arms. He was leaning on the counter, gazing at a spot somewhere above the door and did not appear to have any intention of serving Raymond or anyone else. He had a little beard under his lower lip, which he absentmindedly stroked with his thumb and forefinger. Perhaps it was the sort of place where one ordered at the counter. In any case, if the girl was not here, there was no reason to stay. He would look foolish, however, if he were to suddenly stand up and leave without ordering anything. He imagined the bartender calling after him: 'Hey, kid, what do you think this is? A waiting room?' to a chorus of laughter from the men gathered around the tables.

Then, at precisely five o'clock, the girl appeared through a door marked *WC Femmes*, a facility Raymond did not imagine was frequently used. She had changed into a white blouse and had an apron tied around her waist. She had taken off her hat, and her sunglasses were now propped on her head. Her thick brown hair was cut short above the nape of her neck and brushed forward into a quiff. Without a word to the bartender, she immediately set about clearing the empty cups and glasses from the tables, before vigorously wiping them down. The regulars had clearly been awaiting her arrival as they now barked their orders at her, none of which she wrote down. She dealt with them in an easy, familiar way, addressing the more elderly among them as *oncle*. One man patted her on the behind as she wiped his table, earning himself a stern reprimand that he clearly enjoyed. The tables cleared, she recited the orders mechanically to the bartender, who set to work. Only then did she turn her attention to Raymond, whom she had so far affected not to notice.

She stood in front of his table, her right hand on her hip. Her left foot rested on its heel, swivelling back and forth as if she was grinding out a cigarette.

'So, monsieur, what can I do for you?' she said with an ironic emphasis on the word *monsieur*. She had a pleasant low voice. Her eyes were large and hooded and so widely spaced that they appeared to point in opposite directions. Raymond wondered if she wore her little glasses to correct some defect in her vision, or because she was self-conscious about her squint. But she did not seem to be the sort of person that would be discomfited by anything.

'I'll take a tea,' he said.

'A tea?' the girl repeated. She tipped her head to one side as if his order amused or surprised her. He should, for appearance's sake, have ordered a beer, but before he had the chance to change his mind, the girl had shouted his order over her shoulder: 'Dédé, a tea for the young monsieur!'

This caused several of the other customers to look in Raymond's direction. He found himself blushing. The girl returned to the counter and began to distribute the drinks Dédé had been setting out. The orders were dispensed with a minimum of fuss. No money changed hands. The reckoning-up would no doubt come later. The girl placed Raymond's tea wordlessly on the table and left the chit on a pewter saucer. Raymond emptied his customary three sachets of sugar into the glass and stirred it absent-mindedly. He took his cigarettes from his pocket and lit one.

The girl, having completed her initial round of chores, was now leaning on the corner of the counter, exchanging a few words with Dédé. She tipped her head in Raymond's direction and whispered a remark, causing him to give a snorted laugh. Raymond directed his eyes to the display of posters on the wall and then to the clock, which now read ten past five. He reached inside his satchel for his book. His hand rested for a moment on the sheath of the knife and he ran the tips of his fingers slowly along the worn leather, past the hilt and onto the handle. He glanced around to see if he was being watched. A couple of tables along the banquette, two men were absorbed in a game of chess on a linoleum board. Raymond took out his book and pressed it open on the table. The spine was broken and some of the pages were beginning to come away.

An old man with a neck like a turkey's pushed open the door and walked tentatively to the counter. His trousers were too short and he was not wearing any socks. There were stains around the crotch of his trousers. He exchanged a limp handshake with the bartender, who placed a small glass of dark liquor in front of him. The man contemplated it for a few moments, both hands resting on the counter, as if gathering courage. Then he took up his drink and knocked it back. He rummaged in his trouser pocket for a coin and left at the same unhurried pace as he had entered.

A few minutes later, another man entered and nodded to the patrons sat around the tables by the door. He took a newspaper from the rack and sat down at an occupied table. It was the man who had given Raymond directions the previous day. He must have been a regular because, without having ordered, the waitress brought him an espresso and a glass of schnapps. As the man's eyes followed her back across the bar, his gaze fell on Raymond, who immediately hunched over his book. But it was too late. A puzzled expression passed across the man's face. When Raymond glanced up a few moments later, the man was still looking at him. He raised his hand in greeting.

'Did you find it okay?' he called across the bar.

Raymond glanced towards the counter to see if the waitress was listening. She was looking at him inquisitively. At least the man had not mentioned Rue Saint-Fiacre by name.

'Yes. Thank you,' he replied. He pointedly returned his gaze to his book.

Raymond did not know what, if anything, he wanted to happen. His instinct was to drink his tea and leave as quickly as possible. That was what the Raymond of a few days before would have done. But the Raymond of a few days before would not be here in the first place. The Raymond of a few days before would not have dared to steal 200 francs from Thérèse's jar in the kitchen. He would certainly not have stolen the knife that now nestled in his satchel. Nor would he have followed a strange girl through the streets of Mulhouse. If he left the bar now, that would be the end of it. But he did not want it to end. He did not even know the girl's name. Was it so out of the question simply to ask? It was true that he had gone into the philatelist's shop and stolen the knife, but the act had been entirely impulsive. Had it been premeditated, he would never have had the courage to go through with it. In a similar way, had he hesitated, even for an instant, before following the girl into Le Convivial, he would have come up with a hundred reasons not to do so. But now, having failed to ask the girl's name when she first came to take his order, the task was beyond him. It would lack all spontaneity. Aside from Yvette, whom—despite their sexual activities—he thought of as somewhat akin to a sister, Raymond never failed to become tongue-tied on the rare occasions when a girl spoke to him. And if the girl was attractive, he habitually found himself blushing. As a result, he avoided the gaze of girls at school, lest they take it as an invitation to address him.

The only feasible course of action was to wait and see what transpired. Raymond found himself smiling at the thought that by thus trusting to chance, he was, in a sense, exercising a choice. The idea reassured him. It was now twenty past five. He still had to find his way to the railway station, take a train back to Saint-Louis and be home in time for the evening meal with his mother. He decided he could remain for another forty minutes without having to field awkward questions about his whereabouts.

The chess players at the nearby table had reached the endgame. After each move, they struck the timer on the table between them with increasing haste. The older of the two men played at a more leisurely pace, but under the table his leg twitched nervously. He wore a pair of wire-rimmed spectacles on the very end of his nose. The younger man, playing black, continually ran the palm of his hand over his mouth and shook his head, as if resigned to defeat. His king was besieged in the corner of the board. White advanced a bishop to check. Black blocked with a pawn. The white bishop retreated, before the younger man advanced his rook to his opponent's back row, where his king was hemmed in behind three pawns. The older man took off his spectacles and resigned the game. No words were exchanged as they packed the pieces into a wooden box. The younger man then rolled up the board and replaced it, along with the box of pieces, in the pigeonhole of a dresser in which the cutlery was kept. They left, parting company on the pavement outside the bar.

Raymond had become quite engrossed in the game. It was clearly a daily or weekly ritual. Perhaps he and Stéphane would one day have their own table at the back of a bar in Saint-Louis.

Another ten minutes had passed. The girl showed no interest in Raymond. If anything, she actively averted her eyes whenever she passed his table. He began to doubt the wisdom of his plan to trust to fate. Perhaps, after all, he would have to take the initiative. He gazed down at the book, which he still held open on the table in front of him. His eyes rested on the underlined words: *The flesh was laid open from the ball of the thumb to the root of the little finger.* Raymond pictured himself taking the knife from his satchel, standing up and drawing it across the palm of his hand. He imagined the men by the door pointing towards him, the girl running over with a cloth and binding his hand. This would afford the ideal opportunity—spontaneously, it would seem—to ask her name. He was pondering this when the girl appeared at his table.

'Is there something wrong with your tea?' She was holding a tray under her arm. Her left foot swivelled on its heel as before, giving the impression that she was annoyed or impatient.

'My tea? No, it's fine,' Raymond replied. 'I prefer to drink it cold.'

Then, as if to prove his point, he raised it to his lips and drank with exaggerated relish. The girl rolled her eyes. Raymond cursed himself. There had been no real reason for the girl to come over. Her comment about the tea had been a mere pretext. And all he could think of to say was: *I like to drink it cold*. How idiotic! It wasn't even true, and now if he were ever to see her again, he would be condemned to drink his tea cold. Still, the girl did not move off. She jutted her chin towards the book on the table and asked what he was reading.

He raised the cover to show her.

'Ah,' she said in the manner of a doctor diagnosing a serious illness. 'Well, don't worry, I'm sure you'll grow out if it.'

Raymond gave a little laugh through his nose, but he could feel the colour beginning to rise to his cheeks as it always did. As a distraction, he lit a cigarette. To his surprise, the girl pulled out the chair opposite and sat down. The chair made an unpleasant grating sound on the floor. She took a cigarette from Raymond's packet and lit it.

She leaned in towards him. 'You know, I saw you outside my apartment.'

Raymond instinctively leant back on the banquette. His cheeks were by now quite crimson. Of course, it would be ridiculous to deny it, but that is what he did.

'So you know where I live,' the girl said.

'Of course not. How could I?'

'If you don't know where I live, then how do you know you weren't outside my apartment?'

Raymond drew on his cigarette and puffed out the smoke without inhaling. 'What I mean is that if I was outside your apartment, I didn't know I was. Obviously, in the course of the day I've passed some apartments. If one of them was yours, then, yes, I was there, but only by chance.' He was satisfied with this response. The heat in his face began to subside.

The girl adopted a puzzled expression, as if she was weighing up what to make of him. 'So do you admit you were there, or not?' she said.

'If you tell me where you live, then I can tell you if I was there.'

The girl took a long draw on her cigarette. She let the ash fall to the floor at her feet.

'This morning I saw you on Rue Saint-Fiacre looking up at the building. You had a notebook in your hand. Later I saw you hanging around in the archway next to the junk shop. Then, when I left this afternoon, you followed me.' Her tone was matter-of-fact, as if it was the sort of thing that happened to her every day. She raised her eyebrows questioningly.

Before Raymond could respond, Dédé called out in an exasperated fashion: 'Hey, Delph, are you planning on doing any more work today, or are we just going to close the place up?'

And there it was: without having to do anything, Raymond had learned her name. She swivelled to face Dédé, who was standing by the hatch in the counter gesturing towards the customers by the door. She broke into a wide smile, tipped her head to one side and gave him the finger. She turned back to Raymond.

'So?' she said.

'It's true,' he said. 'I was there. But I didn't follow you. We just happened to be leaving at the same time.'

'And I suppose you "just happened" to follow me into this charming establishment?'

Raymond looked at the table. 'I wasn't spying on you,' he said quietly. He glanced up at her. Despite everything, she did not seem in the least put out. Raymond had the feeling that she rather liked the idea of being followed, of being spied on. He smiled at her.

'So what were you doing?' she asked.

'That I can't say, at least not now.' He added the last words quite deliberately, to hint at the idea that they might see each other again.

The girl—*Delph*—gave a little shake of her head and tutted to herself. She slid back her chair with the same grating noise as before and stood up. Raymond sensed his opportunity slipping away. His heart was beating quickly. He was going to have to take matters into his own hands. 'Perhaps we could meet up again, somewhere else,' he said. The colour returned to his cheeks.

Delph laughed. Once, when he was six or seven years old, during a school trip to the Petite Camargue, a group of older boys had ambushed him from behind some trees and he had lost control of his bladder. As he waited for Delph to say something, Raymond now felt some of the same mortification. She shrugged, as if it was neither here nor there to her.

'I'll be at Johnny's on Saturday,' she said, before striding off to attend to the waiting customers. Raymond nodded to himself, solemnly committing Delph's words to memory. He had no idea where or even what 'Johnny's' was, but he could not prevent himself from looking around to see if anyone had witnessed his triumph. The pockmarked man gave him a wink and jerked his fist towards his cheek in a lewd motion.

Raymond counted out some coins into the pewter salver on the table and left, his satchel clattering against the back of the chair in which Delph had been sitting. She did not look up as he passed. It was not yet six o'clock.

Eleven

GORSKI WAS LEAVING THE police station. It was half past ten. He was meeting Céline that evening and had decided that the least he could do was go to Lemerre's for a haircut. Later he would return home to shower and change his shirt. Without looking up from his newspaper, Schmitt called him back: 'Oh, Georges, I almost forgot.'

Gorski turned round. An exhausted-looking woman of about thirty was sitting on one of the plastic chairs that lined the wall to the right of the door. A small boy, around four years old, was scribbling on scraps of paper at her feet. The woman looked from Schmitt to Gorski. Her presence deterred Gorski from taking the desk sergeant to task for addressing him by his first name.

'You had a call from Strasbourg. An Inspector Larousse, Lamour or something.'

'Lambert?' Gorski said curtly.

'That's it,' said Schmitt. 'Lambert.'

'When was this?'

Schmitt puffed out his cheeks, cast his eyes towards the ceiling. 'An hour ago. Maybe two.'

Gorski forgot the presence of the woman for a moment. 'You're an asshole, Schmitt.'

The boy looked up from his drawing. Schmitt looked at the woman with an expression of bemused innocence. Gorski shook his head and marched back to his office. He snatched up the receiver and then halted, halfway through dialling the number. He replaced the handset in its trestle. After their previous conversation, perhaps it was no bad thing to leave a little time before returning Lambert's call. He did not want him to think that he had nothing better to do than sit around like a lovesick schoolgirl waiting for his big-city colleague to call. Maybe he should even wait for him to ring again. That would be churlish, however. Lambert would not have called if it was not important, and a respectable amount of time had elapsed.

When he was put through, Lambert picked up on the first ring.

'Georges!' he said, as though they were suddenly great buddies. 'How are you?'

'Fine,' he replied coolly. 'What can I do for you?'

'I was thinking about this suspect you called me about,' he began.

'Suspect?' Gorski shook his head as he spoke.

'The fellow involved in the accident.'

'Ah, Barthelme,' said Gorski, as if he had forgotten all about it. 'I'm sure you were right. There's no reason to think he might have been involved.'

'All the same, there's no harm in eliminating him from our enquiries, is there?'

'I suppose not,' Gorski agreed.

'Good,' said Lambert. 'Do you think you could save me a trip down there and put a few questions to him?'

'I'd be happy to,' said Gorski, 'except that there's one small problem: he's dead. He was killed in the accident.'

'Ah,' said Lambert. He clicked his tongue while he absorbed this fact. 'Maybe this is all to the good. You said something about him having lied about his whereabouts?'

'He had told his wife he was dining with some business associates.'

'Hmm.' Lambert clicked his tongue some more, then asked if the funeral had taken place.

'The body's in the mortuary in Mulhouse. It's due to be released to the family in a couple of days.'

'I'll tell you what, Georges,' said Lambert. 'You'd be doing me quite a favour if you could get some prints and bring them up here to me.'

Aside from the pressing business of his haircut, there was nothing at all to prevent Gorski doing this. 'I'm pretty busy down here,' he said. 'But I suppose I could shift a few things around.'

'If you could, Georges. It would be much appreciated. I'll buy you lunch.'

Gorski agreed. If nothing else, Céline would be impressed to hear that he was working a murder case in Strasbourg.

'Good man,' said Lambert. 'And it might be handy if you could get your hands on a photograph of the suspect.'

'I'll see what I can do,' said Gorski. He couldn't help feeling some satisfaction that Lambert had been forced to ask him for a favour. He drummed his fingers on the desk. He hadn't finger-printed a suspect for years. Such mundanities were taken care of by Schmitt or whoever else happened to be working the desk. He fetched the necessary kit and left without telling anyone where he was going. The woman in the waiting area had gone, but her son's drawings and a number of crayons were still strewn across the floor.

GORSKI HAD TROUBLE FINDING A parking space in the narrow streets around Rue de la Nuée-Bleue. There was a car park in the basement of the Strasbourg station, but he did not know if he was permitted to use it. In the event, he had to walk four or five blocks. The sky was overcast and by the time he arrived he had worked up a light sweat. Lambert came down to the foyer and greeted Gorski with a vigorous handshake, before steering him along a corridor. Everyone they passed greeted him as 'Boss' or 'Big Phil'.

'You got the prints?' he asked.

Gorski nodded. He was surprised that Lambert was treating his visit with such urgency. The investigation must have been properly stalled. Lambert pushed open a door with a frosted glass panel and ushered Gorski inside.

He took the manila envelope Gorski was holding and handed it to a man of about fifty years old with a pallid complexion, uncombed hair and a week's stubble. Lambert introduced him as Boris. An ashtray spilled butts onto the desk in front of him. Boris was the best fingerprint man in France, Lambert explained. 'The best one I've come across at any rate.'

'And how many have you come across?' said Boris. He had put on a pair of reading glasses and was scrutinising Barthelme's prints a few centimetres from his face.

'Just you, my dear,' said Lambert.

Boris gave a weary sigh. Gorski hoped the prints were usable. It had been an awkward business taking prints from a corpse lying in a mortuary drawer. Rigor mortis had subsided, but without a firm surface on which to place the card it had been difficult to get a clean impression. The card Boris was holding represented Gorski's fourth attempt. The technician noisily cleared some phlegm from his throat and spat it into the wastepaper basket on the floor at his feet. He clicked on the light of the microfiche reader on his desk.

'I'll check them,' he said, 'but I wouldn't get your hopes up.'

'Indulge me,' said Lambert.

The prints on the microfiche were magnified to the size of a man's hand. Boris scrolled through them at great speed, holding Barthelme's prints to the left for comparison. The images resembled little more than smudges to Gorski. At one point, Boris paused and scrolled back a little. He drew the card closer to the screen, then cleared his throat again and scrolled on. Then, as abruptly as he had started, he clicked off the machine and proffered the card over his shoulder.

'Thanks for wasting my time,' he said.

'You're very welcome,' said Lambert. He did not appear unduly disappointed.

Ten minutes later, Gorski and Lambert were in a tiny corner bar a short distance away on Rue Marbach. It consisted of a narrow passage with a long zinc-topped bar. At the back were three booths almost in darkness. The windows were dressed with stained voile curtains. The sill below was littered with dead flies. A lethargic wasp picked its way through the corpses. A man wearing an oversized cap sat at the bar with his head slumped on his chest. Lambert kicked his stool as they passed and he woke up with a start. The bartender nodded to the detective and placed two marcs on the counter. Lambert raised his drink in Gorski's direction and knocked it back, bearing his teeth as the alcohol hit the back of his throat. Gorski followed suit and Lambert indicated that they would take two more. He steered Gorski to one of the booths at the back of the bar.

Lambert leant against the back wall and put his feet on the banquette. He was wearing light brown slip-on shoes and striped socks. Céline would approve. He lit a cigarette. It was around half past two, but in the semi-darkness of the rear of the bar it could have been midnight. Lambert seemed to have forgotten his promise to buy Gorski lunch.

'So, tell me what you know about this Barthelme character,' he said.

Gorski looked surprised. It seemed a pointless exercise given that the lawyer had just been eliminated from the investigation.

Lambert shook his head. 'Quite the contrary, my friend,' he said. 'Here's the thing. There are fingerprints all over the apartment: the victim's, of course, and we still don't know how many others. But'—he held up his forefinger to emphasise the point—'on the table in the living room there were two glasses, both with traces of whisky. One glass was covered in prints—the unfortunate Veronique's—on the other, nothing. Also, there were no prints on the inner handle of the front door and the armrests of the chair where whoever drank from the second glass sat.'

He paused to allow Gorski to absorb this information, then said: 'So the killer had the wherewithal—forethought, whatever you want to call it—to wipe his own glass and the other surfaces he touched.'

'Maybe he wore gloves,' Gorski suggested.

Lambert dismissed this idea with a shake of his head. 'They sat and had a drink together. It would have looked a little strange if he was wearing gloves. Also, if he had worn gloves, these other surfaces would still have had prints on them, but they didn't. They had been wiped down. Thoroughly wiped down. So if your Maître Barthelme's prints had been found in the apartment, *that* would have eliminated him as a suspect. Anyone whose prints are still there is in the clear.'

Gorski imagined the short shrift he would get from an examining magistrate if he proposed the idea that the *absence* of fingerprints constituted evidence against a suspect. And yet there was an undeniable logic to Lambert's thinking. The bartender approached the booth.

'Two more?' he said. The question was redundant, however, as he had already poured the drinks and placed them on the table.

'Good man,' said Lambert. He waited for him to retreat to the bar before continuing. 'So tell me about him.'

Gorski outlined what he knew, purposefully making Barthelme seem as reputable as possible.

'And this subterfuge with the wife, how long had that been going on?'

'From what I can gather, as long as they had been married.'

'And Madame Barthelme?'

'She's younger,' said Gorski. 'A good deal younger.'

Lambert frowned, as if this did not fit his expectations. 'Attractive?'

Gorski gave a little shrug. 'Well, yes, I suppose so.'

Lambert reached across the narrow table and nudged him on the shoulder.

Gorski ignored him. 'They seem to have kept separate rooms.'

This delighted Lambert. 'So the old dog had to empty his balls elsewhere! Now we're getting somewhere. You need to ply the widow for a bit more info. From what you say, it won't be too onerous a task.'

Gorski objected, saying that he had no legitimate reason to question her.

Lambert made a dismissive gesture. Such niceties were not his concern. Lambert finished his drink and stood up.

'Want to take a look at the crime scene? It's only a block away,' he said. 'I could do with a fresh pair of eyes.'

Gorski could not help feeling flattered. Lambert visited the WC. He emerged, still zipping himself up, and they left the bar without paying. It had started to rain lightly. Lambert strode through the streets so quickly that Gorski had to trot by his side to keep up.

Veronique Marchal's apartment was on Quai Kellermann. There was no concierge. Access to the building was gained via a set of buzzers on a brass panel in the street. The *gendarme* stationed at the ornately carved door stood aside. The apartment was modishly decorated: the lampshades were orange plastic domes; the walls hung with brown flock wallpaper; the sofas and chairs were white leather. The carpet was so thick that Gorski's shoes nestled in the pile. It was difficult to picture the ascetic Bertrand Barthelme in such surroundings. Lambert led Gorski into the living room. High windows gave onto a small balcony overlooking a canal. Lambert rattled off his version of events as if he was giving a soccer commentary: 'Mademoiselle Marchal lets our man in … She offers him a drink … She sits here, he sits there … They chat for long enough for her to finish her drink … They move to the bedroom …'

Gorski gazed at the smoked-glass coffee table, the surface of which was covered in a film of fingerprint powder. Lambert walked him into the bedroom. He pointed out the silk ties that had been used to bind Mlle Marchal's wrists to the posts of the bed. 'No sign of struggle, so we can assume that everything is consensual up to this point.' He came to a halt in the middle of the floor, gazing down at the crumpled sheets. 'Then he strangles her. No sexual act took place, so my guess is that the murder was premeditated, rather than as a result of their little game getting out of hand. That tallies with the fact that the perpetrator had the nous to wipe down the surfaces he had touched.'

He looked at Gorski. It was hard to argue with his conclusions.

'A place like this'—he gestured round the apartment—'doesn't come cheap. Mademoiselle Marchal had no bank account, but there were thousands of francs stashed in a jar in the fridge, more in the bathroom cabinet. But no little black book of clients or anything like that. Either she never wrote anything down or the killer knew where she kept her diary and took it with him. I don't suppose anything like that was found in Barthelme's car?'

Gorski shook his head.

They were back in the living room. Gorski would have liked to add some thoughts of his own, but Lambert's version of events was quite plausible. If he now stepped back into the bedroom, it was only to give the impression that he was deep in thought. He walked slowly round the bed, imagining the woman he had seen only in a blurred newspaper photograph trussed to the bedposts. He was conscious that Lambert was watching him through the doorway. He willed himself to come up with some original insight, but nothing came.

Back on the landing, Lambert rattled the knocker on the door of the apartment opposite. He asked if Gorski had brought a photograph of 'the suspect', as he was now calling him. Gorski took it from the inside pocket of his raincoat. It was a grainy blown-up image of the photograph on Barthelme's ID card. Lambert looked at it sceptically, then shrugged as if the quality of the image was of no consequence.

Gorski did not hear any footsteps inside the apartment before the door opened.

'Professor Weismann,' said Lambert in a jovial tone. 'I hope you'll forgive a further intrusion.'

'It's a pleasure to see you, Inspector. Please come in.'

Lambert introduced Gorski. Weismann looked at him suspiciously, before offering a limp handshake. He was in his mid-fifties, dressed in baggy corduroy trousers, a grubby collarless shirt and a green cardigan, the middle button of which was dangling from a single strand of wool. He was wearing felt slippers and smelled strongly of cologne. He showed them into a large and exceptionally untidy study. The largest wall was lined with books and beneath that sat an old-fashioned desk with a typewriter at its centre. Most of the floor was covered with cardboard boxes filled with journals and other papers.

Lambert turned to Gorski. 'Professor Weismann is a renowned historian,' he said.

'I'm afraid your colleague flatters me. I am no professor,' said Weismann modestly.

'Nevertheless, you are something of an expert in your field, are you not?'

'Well, I daresay,' he said. 'Are you interested in the period of the Reformation, Monsieur Gorski?'

Gorski smiled non-committally.

'My contention is that despite the failure of Lutherism to truly take hold in—'

'It's fascinating stuff,' Lambert interjected. As there was nowhere to sit down, the three men had settled in an awkward triangle in the middle of the room. Lambert asked the historian if he would mind taking a look at a photograph.

'Another of your suspects, Inspector?'

'Just someone we'd like to eliminate from our enquiries,' replied Lambert.

He handed him the photograph. Weismann held it close to his face and squinted at it.

'You have problems with your eyesight, monsieur?' Gorski asked.

'Only for reading,' he replied curtly.

'Professor Weismann often passed men in the stairwell or happened to observe them on the landing,' explained Lambert.

'Sometimes, if Mademoiselle Marchal had a visitor, I would mistake her buzzer for my own, you see,' Weismann added.

Gorski smiled thinly at him. He had noted the stool positioned behind the door to the apartment when he came in. 'And did you see anyone enter Mademoiselle Marchal's apartment on the evening of her murder?' he asked.

'Regrettably, no,' said Weismann with a slight bow of his head.

Lambert gave him a few moments to study the photograph before asking if he recognised the man. Weismann pursed his lips and shook his head slowly.

'It's not a very clear photograph, but I don't believe so, Inspector.'

'But if you only saw the men entering Mademoiselle Marchal's apartment from behind, you couldn't say for sure that you *didn't* see this man, could you?'

Weismann conceded the point.

Lambert addressed Gorski. 'How tall was Maître Barthelme?'

'One metre eighty-five.' Barthelme's height had been recorded in the post-mortem report.

'Were any of the men you saw of around that height, Monsieur Weismann?'

'Well, yes, I would think so.'

'And were any of the men you saw bearded and well dressed?'

'Oh, all the gentlemen Mademoiselle Marchal entertained were well dressed. There was no riff-raff.' He seemed to take a vicarious pride in the quality of her clientele.

'And I imagine,' went on Lambert, 'that if you passed any of these men on the stairs, they would hardly be likely to stop to pass the time of day, given the purpose of their visit. In fact, they would be more likely to hurry past with their heads down.'

'Indeed, Inspector,' Weismann agreed with a complicit laugh, 'you are entirely correct.'

Gorski observed the scene with a mixture of admiration and dismay. It was clear that within moments Lambert would have convinced Weismann that he had indeed seen Barthelme.

'So you couldn't say that this was not one of the gentlemen you saw?'

He handed the photograph back to Weismann. This time the historian retrieved a pair of reading glasses from his desk and put them on. He adopted a sombre expression, as if a great deal rested on his verdict.

'He's certainly a distinguished-looking fellow.' He nodded slowly to himself, then tutted as if he could not believe his previous error. 'Now that I look again,' he said, 'there *is* a certain resemblance to a gentleman I saw once or twice.'

'Someone you saw entering Mademoiselle Marchal's apartment?'

'I couldn't say for sure that it's the same person, but, as I say, there's a certain resemblance. It's not a very good picture.'

'And this gentleman you saw,' said Lambert, 'how would you describe him?'

Weismann cast his eyes towards the ceiling, before earnestly enumerating his characteristics: 'Tall, well dressed, bearded. Somewhat older than the man here. But perhaps the photograph is a little out of date.'

Gorski was about to intervene, but Lambert silenced him with a curt shake of his head. Instead, he apologised for interrupting Weismann's work and led Gorski towards the door. Weismann apologised for not being of more assistance and assured Lambert that he was most welcome to return whenever he wanted. 'Next time I must offer you a glass of schnapps.'

Lambert promised that he would look forward to that.

On the landing, Lambert gave Gorski a wink and put his finger to his lips. Only when they were outside on the pavement, did he declare: 'I think this calls for a drink.'

They strode back to the little bar on the corner of Rue Marbach. The man in the cap had been replaced by a tiny man wearing a suit several sizes too big. He had a glass of white wine in front of him.

'Afternoon, Inspector,' he said as Lambert entered.

'Glad to see you're keeping out of trouble, Robideaux,' Lambert said as he passed.

They sat down in the same booth as before. The bartender appeared at the table.

'A bottle of red, Karl,' said Lambert. 'Something decent.'

There was an art deco clock on the wall opposite the counter. It was quarter past four. Gorski was not due to meet Céline until eight. He would have to forgo his haircut, but he had plenty of time. If necessary, he did not even need to go home to change his shirt. The future of his marriage did not depend on what shirt he was wearing.

They touched glasses. '*Salut*,' said Lambert. 'And congratulations!'

Gorski was not sure why he was being congratulated, but he accepted with a nod of his head. The two men drank.

'Not bad,' said Lambert approvingly. 'White gives me heartburn.'

Gorski had only taken a small sip of his wine, but Lambert topped up his glass. He loosened his tie and undid the top button of his shirt. He was wearing a heavy gold watch on his wrist. He leaned across the table, as if he was about to share a confidence.

'You know, to be honest, Georges, I had you down as a bit of a plodder. One of these provincial by-the-book types, but I'm the first one to hold my hands up when I'm wrong.'

Gorski did not say anything.

'We could do with more guys like you up here. There are too many college boys with their law degrees these days. You've learned your trade the proper way.'

'I wouldn't say that,' said Gorski.

'And that's your problem, right there. You're too modest. Tell me this: what made you call me about Barthelme? Procedure?' He shook his head theatrically. 'No, this!' He tapped the side of his nose. 'You can't learn that from a textbook.'

Gorski made a self-effacing gesture, but he had no wish to

disavow the Strasbourg cop of his favourable view of him. He took a good swallow of wine. It felt good to be in this grotty bar with this big shot who had not once looked at his watch or suggested that he needed to be elsewhere.

Either on account of the wine or Lambert's praise, he began to feel more comfortable. 'Even so,' he said, 'I doubt if Monsieur Weismann will be quite so sure about having seen Barthelme tomorrow.'

Lambert held up a finger. 'That's where you're wrong, Georges. When Weismann wakes up tomorrow, he'll be more convinced than ever about what he saw. That's why I backed off. Never push a witness. Maybe I planted a seed in Weismann's head, but the more he thinks it was his own idea, the more adamant he'll be.'

'But it wasn't his own idea.'

'That's neither here nor there. The point is that he *believes* it was his idea. If I go back tomorrow and say: "Oh, Monsieur Weismann, I think you were mistaken about what you told me yesterday," then I guarantee you he'll insist that he saw Barthelme numerous times and even, now that he remembers, spoke to him occasionally. It's human nature,' he said with a laugh. He knocked back his wine and refreshed the glasses.

Gorski had no time for the idea of human nature. It was a meaningless idea people used to absolve themselves of responsibility for their own actions. He kept this thought to himself, however, stating only that it would be difficult to convince an examining magistrate of the soundness of such testimony.

Lambert waved his hand dismissively. 'I'm sure you don't need me to tell you that it's always worth cultivating a few friends on the other side.'

Gorski had never thought of examining magistrates as being on 'the other side', but again he kept his counsel.

'Still, you're right about one thing,' Lambert went on. 'We will need some kind of corroboration. Mademoiselle Marchal wasn't living on fresh air.' What they needed, he said, was to have a look at Barthelme's financial records. 'Think you'd be able to take care of that?'

Gorski stared at him blankly. He had a sinking feeling in his stomach. 'It might be tricky to get a warrant,' he said.

Lambert tucked his chin into his chest. 'Georges, that's the sort of thing I'd expect from one of the college boys. You're in with the widow. I'm sure you can charm her a little?'

Gorski lit a cigarette. Lambert's view of him was correct. He *was* a plodder, a provincial plodder. And now, when against his better instincts he had followed a hunch, he had found himself drawn into a situation he wanted no part of. He should never have called Lambert in the first place.

Lambert began to tell the story of a teenage boy who had stabbed his mother. Gorski was relieved that the conversation had moved on, but he was barely listening. He looked at the Strasbourg cop's wide, handsome face. At the station, everyone called him 'Boss'. But there was an edge to him. He well understood Weismann's compliance: Lambert was the sort that people gravitated towards; they wanted to please him. And Gorski was no better. Was he not also acquiescing because he felt grateful to be sharing a bottle with 'Big Phil', to feel that he was part of his circle.

'The kid got off with five years,' Lambert was saying. 'Mitigating circumstances, apparently. Fuck mitigating circumstances. There's no such thing.'

Gorski nodded obediently.

'You should get yourself a transfer up here, Georges,' Lambert went on.

Gorski gave a dismissive laugh. Years ago he would have jumped at such a proposition, but he had long since given up on the ambition to test himself in a more challenging environment. Saint-Louis might not be much, and the role of chief of police might not be unduly demanding, but it was his domain. He had no desire to involve himself in the grubby practices of his big-city counterparts. Nevertheless, it was he who insisted on the second bottle.

Twelve

SINCE THE ACCIDENT, RAYMOND and his mother had eaten their evening meals in near silence. Naturally, they sat in the same places as before. It would have been unthinkable for Raymond to take over his father's place at the head of the table, but the unaltered seating arrangements only emphasised his absence. And perhaps because of this, they had become locked into a certain way of conducting themselves. They kept their eyes downcast, ate with little appetite and made only the most mundane remarks. Certainly no mention of the accident passed between them. They had achieved a near-perfect imitation of a solemn, grieving family. Raymond wondered if this charade was for the benefit of Thérèse, who would undoubtedly frown upon any merriment. It might, on the other hand, be that the two of them simply had little to say to each other and it was easier to blame the presence of the housekeeper than admit this.

This evening, however, Lucette seemed determined to dispel the gloomy atmosphere. She was dressed in a light skirt and a yellow blouse and had even, Raymond discerned, applied a little make-up to her cheeks. When Thérèse brought in the soup, Lucette asked in an excessively jovial manner if she wouldn't mind turning up the heating. She even affected a little shiver to give credence to her request. In most households, this would have been a matter of no significance, but at the Barthelme's it amounted to a minor mutiny. Previously, if she had been chilly, Lucette would have gone upstairs to fetch a cardigan. On the rare occasions that the heating was turned up, it was only at the behest of the head of the household, and then only when it had reached the point that the occupants of the house could see their breath. It was not unusual during the winter for Maître Barthelme to wear a scarf and gloves in his study to set an example to the other members of the household.

Thérèse responded to Lucette's request only with: 'Of course, Madame.'

As she left the room, Lucette shot her son a complicit smile. When they were alone, she took a deep breath. It was obvious to Raymond that she had rehearsed whatever she was about to say. He assumed it would be about the 200 francs he had stolen. After first wishing him *bon appétit* and taking a spoonful of soup, she began: 'I'm pleased that you decided to go back to school, Raymond. We mustn't mope around the house feeling sorry for ourselves.' This was the closest either of them had come to alluding to his father's death. 'Was everyone kind to you?'

Raymond took a spoonful of soup. It was cauliflower. It had not occurred to him that his mother would ask about his day at school. But he was glad she was making this effort to lighten the atmosphere, and he was proud of her rebellion over the heating.

'I'm glad I went too, Maman,' he said. 'Of course, everyone knows what happened.'

'Tell me all about it.' Lucette's manner was rather forced. Perhaps she already knew he had not been to school and wanted to see how long he would keep up his pretence. But Raymond could not imagine his mother engaging in such subterfuge. He had never known her to be anything other than ingenuous. It was this that made her so easy to deceive. His father, on the other hand, immediately saw through the pettiest of lies, and even when Raymond had been a small boy, he had been quite prepared to utilise his armoury of lawyer's tricks to get the truth out of him. It was impossible to imagine Lucette having an ulterior motive, however. She was merely trying to shake off the grip that Bertrand continued to exert over them.

So Raymond played along: 'Mademoiselle Delarue kept me behind and asked if I was all right. She said that if I needed to leave suddenly, or whatever, I was just to do so.' Then to embellish the lie—which had, in any case, come easily to him—he added: 'She seemed a bit embarrassed. The whole time she was talking to me, she kept looking at her fingernails. But she was nice. Everyone was nice. And everyone asked me to pass on their condolences.'

He glanced up from his soup. Lucette looked pleased with him.

'I'm very proud of you, Raymond. And I'm sure your father would be as well.'

Raymond gave a derisive snort.

'What else?' she persisted, fearing that silence would envelop them again.

Previously, Raymond might have answered such an enquiry monosyllabically, but now, feeling that they had entered into a kind of pact, he embarked on a long speech about how he was finding his French class quite demanding. The novel they were studying was dreadfully boring, and of course missing a week's classes hadn't helped. He even, out of sheer bravado, kept his monologue going when Thérèse came in to clear away the soup bowls. The problem with Zola, he found himself saying, is that he's so judgemental about his characters, it's hard to form an opinion of one's own. He paused to draw breath.

Lucette nodded seriously. 'I always struggled with Zola at school. Those endless descriptions!'

'Exactly!' said Raymond. They smiled at each other, pleased to establish this point of commonality. Thérèse entered with the main course. It was lamb casserole. As she put the plates in front of them, she wished them *bon appétit*, but she imbued the phrase with such sourness that it was less an invitation to enjoy their food than to stop chattering like children.

Lucette ignored or failed to notice her tone. With a glance towards Raymond, she said: 'Is there no wine tonight, Thérèse?'

Thérèse's only reply was to incline her head and return to the kitchen to fetch a bottle. It fell to Raymond to open it. He took the corkscrew from the drawer of the sideboard and replicated the actions he had seen his father perform so many times. The task accomplished, he poured a glass for his mother and then, at her invitation, for himself. Thérèse left the room. She had a way of making her disapproval apparent with the smallest adjustment of her gait.

They ate in silence for a few minutes. Thérèse had succeeded in dampening the convivial atmosphere they had conspired to create, and Raymond could not think of anything other than the most banal of remarks.

Eventually, Lucette said: 'Yvette rang.' She tried to make it seem as if she had only just remembered, but she was no actress. Raymond wondered if this was her way of telling him that she had known all along that he had not been at school. Yvette would have had no reason to call if he had been. His mother liked Yvette, and it irked Raymond that they got on so well. His mother affected an irritating girlishness in her company, while Yvette talked to Lucette unselfconsciously as if they were two friends, rather than members of different generations. It was likely that they would have talked for some time.

'She did?' Raymond replied. 'When was that?'

'Around four.'

'I'll call her back later,' he said.

'I thought you would have seen her at school,' Lucette said.

'We missed each other,' he said. 'We didn't share any classes today,' he said.

'I see,' she said sadly. It was clear that she knew Raymond was lying. She attempted to conceal her embarrassment by asking Raymond to replenish her wine.

She made an effort to brighten her tone. 'In any case, you must invite her round for dinner now that—' She had been on the brink of referring to her husband's death. She looked down at her plate. She had only taken a few mouthfuls of her lamb.

'I will,' said Raymond.

The conversation petered out, and it was a relief when Thérèse returned with dessert.

At this point, Lucette asked the housekeeper to join them at the table. She sat down opposite Raymond and folded her arms. Lucette became quite agitated. She fidgeted with her hair and took a sip of wine, before explaining that Thérèse had brought a certain matter to her attention and that all she required from Raymond was an honest answer. Raymond adopted an expression suggesting that he had no idea what she was talking about.

'Apparently, this morning a certain sum of money went missing from the jar in the kitchen.'

'I see,' said Raymond. Thérèse was staring fixedly at him across the table, her folded forearms pushing up her bosom. Raymond had assumed that she would tell Lucette about the missing money and that his mother would, in turn, feel obliged to raise the subject with him. He had planned to say that he had needed the money for a project at school and that he hadn't wanted to disturb her first thing in the morning. *I'm sorry, Maman,* he had imagined himself saying, *I quite forgot to mention it.* Lucette would not trouble to ask for details about the project. But he had not reckoned on his mother questioning him in Thérèse's presence. They must have cooked up this little plan to confront him during the day. It crossed his mind to suggest that Thérèse might be mistaken, but given her scrupulousness over the tiniest sums of money, that would have been implausible.

Instead, with an air of defiance, he said: 'And I sense that she has accused me of taking the money.'

'Nobody is accusing you,' said Lucette. She fidgeted with the stem of her glass. 'But we thought that as you were in the kitchen this morning, you might be able to shed some light on the matter.'

It was clear that all he had to do was admit that he had taken the money and that would be the end of it, but he did not want to concede defeat to Thérèse.

He shrugged. 'Well, I can't,' he said.

Lucette looked quite distressed. She glanced in Thérèse's direction, but the housekeeper kept her eyes on Raymond.

'If you need money, Raymond,' she continued, 'you need only ask. But we can't have you stealing.'

There was no other course of action available. 'I didn't steal the money,' he shouted. Then he pointed a finger across the table at Thérèse, aware as he did so of the silly theatricality of his gesture. 'Maybe it's her you should be accusing instead of me!'

Lucette burst into tears and hid her face in her hands. Raymond regretted upsetting her, but there was no question of backing down. He stood up and threw his napkin on the table, spilling the remains of his wine. Then he strode out of the room. He did not have the heart to slam the door, but he stomped noisily up the staircase. He was angry with his mother. She had given him no choice but to act as he did.

Raymond prowled the perimeter of his room for some minutes. He thought of punching the wall, but did not do so for fear of hurting his hand. There was, in any case, little point in doing so if there was no one there to witness the act. When he had calmed down a little, he sat on the edge of his bed. The straight-backed chair had been pushed neatly under his desk. It was a sign that Thérèse had been in to tidy his room. Raymond wondered if she had taken it upon herself to go through his things. He got up and opened and closed the drawers of his desk, but there was no sign that anything had been disturbed. It crossed his mind to sneak into Thérèse's quarters and secrete the money somewhere. The thought made him smile, but it would be impossible to convince his mother to search her rooms. Instead, he resolved to buy a padlock for his bedroom door. He got up and pressed his ear to the back of the door. He could hear the sound of dishes being washed in the kitchen below. He fetched his satchel from the back of the wardrobe and took out his new knife. It was the first opportunity he had had to properly examine it. He pulled it out of the sheath and weighed it in his hand. It felt good. He ran his finger along the blade. It was not particularly sharp. He pressed it tentatively against the fleshy part of his hand. It did no more than leave a pale line on the skin. One day, when Thérèse was out, he would borrow the steel from the kitchen and sharpen it. Not that he had any intention of ever using it. He stood in front of the mirror on the inside of the wardrobe holding the knife casually by his side. He imagined being confronted by two older boys, like the ones he had seen in Mulhouse. He smiled, then returned the knife to its sheath. He looked around for a suitable hiding place, but there was nowhere that Thérèse might not find it. Until he procured a lock for his room, he would have to keep it with him at all times.

He went into his father's study and sat at the desk. He already felt more comfortable there. He picked up the telephone receiver and dialled Yvette's number. Madame Arnaud answered. She was a diminutive woman in her late thirties, with the same neat features as her daughter. She was a teacher at a local elementary school and often spoke to Raymond as if she was addressing one of her pupils. Early one Sunday afternoon, when Raymond had called for Yvette, she had answered the door while pulling on her robe. He had been surprised that she had been in bed so late.

On the phone, Madame Arnaud expressed her condolences and asked how his mother was. Raymond did not know what to say. Lucette did not seem particularly upset. If she had been more subdued than normal, he assumed that that was only because she was expected to act that way. Certainly until the incident at the dinner table, he had not seen her crying.

'I think she's coping,' he replied.

'If there's anything we can do,' she said.

This struck Raymond as odd, since as far as he knew the two women had never met.

'Thank you,' he said.

Yvette came on the line.

'Hello, Raymond,' she said.

'Hi.'

Raymond disliked talking on the telephone. There was something about speaking into the plastic handset that made the conversation feel fake. And he always imagined that Thérèse was listening on the other line. In any case, as he saw Yvette every day at school they rarely had cause to talk on the phone. Despite the fact that it had been he who had called her, he waited for Yvette to say something. She asked how he was.

'I'm fine,' he said. 'A little bored.'

'When will you be coming back to school?'

'I don't know,' he said. 'After the funeral, I suppose.'

'Why don't you come over? I could fill you in on what you've missed.'

'I don't think I can,' said Raymond. 'Maman is upset.' In truth, he would have liked to see her. Yvette's parents never objected to Raymond spending time in their daughter's bedroom. But he felt that in some way, although nothing meaningful had occurred, he had already betrayed her with Delph.

'I'm sitting in my father's study,' he said, by way of changing the subject. 'At his desk.'

'How does that feel?'

'Weird. Like I've ascended to the throne.'

He could hear Yvette's breathing. 'What about Saturday?' she said.

'Saturday?' said Raymond. He thought of his assignation with Delph. 'I'm sorry. I have to help Maman. Funeral arrangements and all that.'

'In the evening, then?'

'No,' he said too quickly. 'I can't. Maman will need me.'

Yvette said goodnight. She sounded disappointed. She hung up. Raymond turned off the lamp on his father's desk and sat in the dark for a few minutes. He could hear Thérèse moving around downstairs.

Thirteen

GORSKI AWOKE WITH A FEELING of dread. The curtains were open. The sky outside was a yellowish-grey and seemed to be pulsating slightly. He raised his head from the pillow. His clothes were strewn across the floor. The bedroom door was wide open. There was an acrid taste in his mouth. He looked at the clock on the bedside table. It was 10:25. He swung his legs out of bed and sat for some time with his forehead in his hands. He felt nauseous. He forced himself off the bed and got into the shower.

The previous night began to come back to him. After the bar with the zinc counter, he and Lambert had eaten *steak-frites* in a brasserie on Place Kléber. The Strasbourg cop had then insisted on taking Gorski to what he called a 'special little place'. Gorski had put up no resistance. He was already drunk and had lost his bearings in the winding streets. Lambert's special little place was located in an alleyway basement. It was a tiny establishment with nine or ten tables, half of them unoccupied. The room was illuminated only by the candles on the tables and the backlit bottles of liquor behind the bar. A soundtrack of *chansons* was loud enough to drown out the murmur of conversation from neighbouring tables. The place was presided over by a gaunt woman in her fifties perched on a high stool at the end of the bar. When she saw Lambert, she wafted across the room and greeted him warmly. She led him by the arm to a table, around which there was a semi-circular velvet banquette. Lambert introduced

Gorski, and—he was embarrassed to recall—he had made a little bow and kissed her hand. Lambert made a remark about him being from the provinces.

'I think it's charming,' the *patronne*—Simone—had responded. 'So few people have any manners anymore.' She gave Gorski a wide smile. Her eyes were heavily made-up, and she had a large, hooked nose. Her profile reminded Gorski of a figure from a book of Egyptian pictograms he had had when he was a boy.

A bottle of champagne was brought to the table and they were joined by two girls, one of whom appeared barely older than Clémence. Lambert took it upon himself to make the introductions. Gorski did not catch either girl's name. At some point—either in the bar with the zinc counter or at the brasserie—Gorski had made the mistake of telling Lambert that Céline had left him. Lambert cheerfully relayed this information to the girls and instructed them to be nice to him. Gorski smiled apologetically. Lambert carelessly filled their glasses, splashing champagne over the table, and toasted Simone, who had returned to her perch by the bar. She inclined her head in acknowledgement. Gorski's head was spinning. He placed his glass on the table.

Lambert leant in towards him. 'Come on, Georges, you're a free man. Drink up! It's on the house. Everything's on the house.' He tipped his head towards the girl sitting next to Gorski and elbowed him in the ribs. The girl was drinking her champagne through a straw. She did not make any attempt to take part in the conversation. She looked bored but did not seem to be ill at ease.

A second bottle of champagne arrived. Lambert demanded a bottle of whisky also be brought. Gorski realised he was required to do little more than laugh at Lambert's jokes and appear to be drinking his share. New arrivals frequently paused at the table to greet Lambert. They were cops, journalists, or perhaps politicians, local or otherwise. No one seemed in the least concerned about being seen in such an establishment.

A little later, Lambert nudged the girl next to him off the

banquette and they disappeared through a door to the rear of the bar. Gorski assumed they were going to the WC, but they were gone too long for that. He took a sip of his champagne and filled his companion's glass. She was a pretty girl, with yellow-blonde hair and a down-turned mouth. Even in the warm glow of the candlelight, her skin seemed exceptionally pale. Without Lambert's stream of anecdotes, the silence between them was uncomfortable. Gorski asked where she was from. He did not hear her reply, but her French was heavily accented. Gorski nodded as if he had understood her perfectly.

'What brings you to Strasbourg?' he asked.

The girl rolled her eyes to indicate that the answer was self-evident. Gorski nodded. 'Of course,' he said, embarrassed by the naivety of his question.

'I'm from Saint-Louis myself,' Gorski said for the sake of something to say. He was aware that he was slurring. The girl gazed blankly around the room and he made no further attempt at conversation. Lambert reappeared a few minutes later, wearing a roguish grin. The girl was not with him. He slid back onto the banquette.

'Your turn,' he said.

'I'm sorry?' said Gorski.

'Your turn,' Lambert repeated. He jutted his chin towards the girl. 'I told you, everything's on the house.' He then addressed the girl: 'Hey, whatsyourname, take our friend through the back, will you?'

The girl shrugged and stood up, waiting for Gorski to follow her.

'Really, I'd rather not,' he said, before adding lamely: 'I'm feeling a little nauseous.'

The girl looked at Lambert, who shook his head in exasperation. To Gorski's relief, the girl resumed her seat. Lambert leaned into his ear. 'Freedom's wasted on you, chum,' he said.

In an attempt to prove that he was not a stick-in-the-mud, Gorski ordered another bottle of champagne. Lambert's girl reappeared. She had changed her blouse. Lambert put his arm round her shoulder and playfully bit her on the neck, making a noise like a big cat. The *patronne* joined them at the table. She smiled charmingly, but Gorski had the feeling she did not like Lambert. Gorski found himself telling her about Céline. She appeared to listen intently, but after a few minutes she slipped silently away to welcome some new guests. She must have heard a thousand such stories.

Gorski could not recall how many more bottles were brought to the table. At a certain point, he stumbled into the WC and vomited, disinterestedly noting his tie dangling in the pan as he did so. He took it off and attempted to flush it away, but it floated there like a malevolent snake. He fished it out and stuffed it behind the pipes of the wash-hand basin. Céline had bought it for him.

Gorski did not remember driving home, but when he had showered and made some coffee, he looked outside. His car was in the drive.

Shameful though it was, it was not the memory of his evening with Lambert that now filled him with dread. It was the fact that he had missed his dinner with Céline.

THE HOUSEKEEPER SHOWED GORSKI into a drawing room at the back of the Barthelme house. It was a large room, old fashioned and over-furnished. Barely a foot of floor space was not occupied with a chair, occasional table or a large urn filled with dried stalks. The walls were decorated with murky landscapes in ornate gold-leaf frames. The French windows were hung with velvet drapes secured with gilt cords. Gorski disliked such rooms. The accumulation of generations of junk was not as haphazard as it might appear. It served to remind visitors of the unassailable permanency of old money.

Despite the fire burning in the hearth there was a chill in the room that Gorski suspected never lifted. Lucette Barthelme was standing with her back to the fireplace, a cigarette in her right hand. Gorski had the impression that she had lit the cigarette only when she had heard the doorbell and adopted this pose quite knowingly. She was dressed in a white silk blouse and beige knee-length skirt. He noted, with pleasure, that she had applied a little make-up in anticipation of his visit. In order to avoid the embarrassment of again being received in her bedroom, Gorski had disregarded Ribéry's dictum and telephoned in advance of his visit. There was, in any case, no reason not to do so. Lucette Barthelme was not herself suspected of any wrongdoing.

She crossed the room to shake hands and thanked him for coming. They stood looking awkwardly at each other for a few moments. Lucette invited him to take a seat. Gorski sat on a brocade chaise longue in the centre of the room. She sat at the opposite end. She stubbed out her cigarette in an ashtray that already contained several butts. Gorski did not have the impression that this was the sort of household where the ashtrays would go unemptied overnight.

'Perhaps you would like some coffee?' she said. 'I could ring for Thérèse.'

Gorski shook his head.

She was then struck by another idea. 'Perhaps a brandy then?'

Gorski did not refuse. It was just what he required to clear his head. He had spotted the decanter on the sideboard as soon as he had entered the room. Lucette got up and poured two large measures. There was something in her gait that made her seem out of place in the grand surroundings. She stepped lightly— tentatively even—around the room, as if she was afraid of being detected. It was clear that nothing in the room had altered since her arrival in the household. Even after twenty years of marriage, she was more akin to a lodger than the mistress of the house. She was the sort of woman Gorski should have married. She would have been comfortable in the modest apartment above the shop in Rue des Trois Rois. Gorski found himself picturing them there, sitting in the evening light, reading or playing a hand of cards at the table by the window.

She handed him the glass, then resumed her seat. They drank. The spirit caused her to give a little cough.

'Perhaps it's a little early for brandy,' she said. Then she gave a silly, schoolgirlish laugh, which Gorski found at once affected and endearing. She brushed a strand of hair from her cheek.

'So, Madame—'

She interrupted to ask him to call her Lucette, as he knew she would.

'Of course,' he said, repeating her name.

'And I shall call you Georges.' She seemed pleased to have established this intimacy between them.

Gorski cleared his throat. He adopted a more formal tone. 'As requested, I have made some enquiries about your husband's movements on the night of his death. Of course, these enquiries have been of an informal nature.'

'You make it sound so grave, Georges,' she said.

'It seems that your husband did not, as he told you, have dinner with Maître Corbeil, or any of his other associates. He left his office around four o'clock and, as yet, his movements between then and the time of his death are unaccounted for.'

'I see.'

'I'm afraid this club he spoke of appears to have been no more than an invention.'

Lucette did not say anything. She reached for a carved wooden box of cigarettes on the coffee table and lit one.

'Please go on,' she said. 'Don't feel that you need to spare my feelings.'

Gorski explained as delicately as he could that the most obvious explanation for Barthelme's duplicity was that he kept a mistress. 'Did you ever suspect that your husband might be deceiving you?'

Lucette gave another silly laugh. She glanced at the brandy glass she was cradling in her lap, then said quietly: 'My husband did not have much interest in such things.'

'I could not help but notice when I called on the night of the accident,' said Gorski, 'that you and your husband kept separate chambers.'

'Yes.' She glanced up at him.

'May I ask how long this arrangement had been in place?'

'Since the beginning of our marriage. We never shared a bedroom.'

'But you—?' Thankfully he did not need to complete the sentence.

'At first, of course, but my husband did not think it convenient to share a bed. He was a light sleeper and said we would only disturb each other. He was very practical.'

Gorski nodded. He noted that Mme Barthelme never used her husband's name. She put her cigarette to her lips and exhaled a stream of smoke.

'And did you ever have any suspicion that Maître Barthelme might be satisfying his needs elsewhere?'

'My husband did not give the impression of having any sexual needs. Even when we were first married he treated the act as an obligation, rather than as'—she glanced bashfully towards the fireplace—'rather than as a pleasure.'

A little colour rose to her cheeks. Gorski thought of the modish apartment in Strasbourg and of the silk ties that were still fastened to the bedstead there. Lucette brushed a little cylinder of ash from her skirt. And suddenly she seemed the betrayed wife. Gorski felt that he was being cruel. No matter how chilly the couple's relations, it must have been preferable for Lucette to believe that her husband had no interest in sex, rather than that he indulged himself with a mistress.

He had liked the gay Lucette Barthelme, no matter how put-on her breezy demeanour had been. And what if the tables were turned and his own marriage was placed under similar scrutiny? Even as his marital relations with Céline had dwindled, he had never suspected her of having a lover. She would have had no end of opportunities. As she had grown older, she had only become more attractive. She had retained her boyish, willowy figure, but her face now had more character. The little lines around her eyes only had the effect of drawing one's gaze towards them. And she was charming. Gorski had often observed how men looked at her. They liked to be in her company. It did not make him jealous. Céline enjoyed the attention of other men, and Gorski enjoyed observing her. It was often after they had attended a social event together that their lovemaking was most passionate. If Céline was aroused by the attentions of other men, what did it matter if he was the beneficiary? And if their sex life had waned a little in recent years, was that not the case with all couples? Or was it that, like Maître Barthelme, Céline had taken to satisfying her needs elsewhere? It was perhaps only because he had never himself been tempted to stray that the thought had not crossed his mind.

Lucette rose and fetched the decanter of brandy. She topped up his glass.

'I sense your marriage was not a happy one,' he said.

She sat down, a little closer to him this time. She had not replenished her own glass.

'It was not unhappy,' she said. 'I don't suppose it was a great love affair, but I'm not sure such things really exist, do they, Georges? My husband was a very busy man. He hadn't time for romantic gestures. And I was a disappointment to him. He should have married someone more forceful. I suppose it shouldn't come as a shock to hear that Bertrand had a mistress. You men have your needs, don't you?'

'And you?' said Gorski.

'Me?'

'You must also have needs.'

Lucette did not appear to object to this impertinent question. It was almost as if she relished having Gorski delve into the intimate details of her marriage. 'Oh, we girls can be quite creative, Georges,' she said.

It was Gorski's turn to blush. He took a sip of brandy, then leant forward to take a cigarette from the wooden box on the table. Lucette observed him.

'And you?' she said.

In the course of a normal investigation, Gorski would never have tolerated the tables being turned in this way.

'Is your marriage a happy one?'

He instinctively fingered his wedding band.

'Actually, my wife and I are separated.' Aside from his drunken ramblings the previous night, this was the first time he had admitted it to anyone.

'Oh, I'm sorry,' Lucette replied. But a little smile played across her lips.

Gorski was tempted to tell her the whole story there and then, but it would have been wholly improper. He had quite forgotten that since his ill-advised trip to Strasbourg, his enquiries had taken on a more official character. He stood up, cigarette in hand, and took a turn around the room. The French windows looked out onto a sloping lawn, which in turn gave onto a copse of trees. A gardener was raking leaves from the grass, a cigarette dangling from his mouth. Gorski turned and stood with his back to the windows.

'If you wish me to continue with my enquiries, it might be beneficial to inspect your husband's financial records,' he said.

Lucette looked questioningly at him.

Gorski explained that withdrawals Maître Barthelme might have made could indicate his movements. 'Of course, perhaps you would prefer not to know,' he said.

She gave a little sigh. 'No,' she said. 'But you will have to see Maître Corbeil about anything like that. He removed my husband's papers from the house.'

'When did he do that?'

'The day after my husband's death. He said they were required to conclude my husband's will.'

Gorski nodded. It was inconceivable that Maître Corbeil

would allow him to see Barthelme's accounts in the absence of the appropriate paperwork. He waved his hand casually in the air, suggesting that it was a matter of no importance. There was nothing more to say. He approached the table and stubbed out his cigarette in the ashtray.

'Perhaps you would like to stay to lunch,' said Lucette. 'I need only tell Thérèse to set another place.'

Gorski would have liked nothing more than to have lunch with Lucette Barthelme, but not there in the dead atmosphere of the house on Rue des Bois. Not under the disapproving eye of the housekeeper. He would have liked to drive Lucette to a little country inn, or to take a turn around the lake in the Petite Camargue. He politely declined the invitation. Afterwards, he reflected that he should have suggested lunch another time, but the moment had passed. Lucette stood up and they shook hands with awkward formality. He showed himself out. Thérèse observed his departure from the kitchen doorway, as though she expected him to pilfer a candlestick.

By the time Gorski arrived at the Restaurant de la Cloche, lunch service was winding down. The *pot-au-feu* was finished. Gorski ordered the lamb cutlet and followed it with a slice of apple tart. He drank the glass of wine that was included in the *menu du jour*, but resisted the temptation to order a second with his dessert. He had decided that he would go directly to see Céline at her boutique. Then, when he was settling his bill at the counter, he asked Pasteur for a marc. The proprietor placed the little glass on the counter.

'That's on the house, Inspector,' he said.

Gorski did not demur, but he left a gratuity large enough to cover the cost of the drink.

Céline's shop was a two-minute walk from la Cloche. He loitered in the little park outside the Protestant temple for a few minutes. The leaves of the chestnut trees had started to fall and the November drizzle had made them slippery underfoot. There was a single customer in the shop. Céline was standing at the counter, turning the pages of a magazine. The customer left without making a purchase. Gorski stepped over the low perimeter wall of the park and entered the shop. Céline looked up when the little bell sounded above the door. She gazed at him impassively.

'Hello, Céline,' he said.

'Hello, Georges,' she replied in a weary tone.

She allowed him to kiss her on both cheeks.

'Have you been drinking?' she said.

'Just a glass of wine with lunch.' But he took a step back from her.

She folded her arms. 'Your eyes are bloodshot,' she said.

Gorski explained that he hadn't been sleeping well. He could not help recalling how, when they had first met, they had often gone into the back of the shop to have sex.

'I wanted to apologise,' he said.

'It's a little late for that, don't you think?' She returned her gaze to the magazine on the counter.

'All the same,' he said, 'it was inexcusable.'

'Don't worry,' said Céline drily, 'no one's about to excuse you.'

The remark almost constituted a joke and Gorski took a little encouragement from it.

'I was in Strasbourg. I'm working a murder case up there.'

Despite herself, Céline's eyes betrayed a flicker of interest.

'It was impossible to get away,' he continued.

'I suppose it would have been too much to ask to call the restaurant?'

Gorski had tried not to picture his wife sitting alone in the draughty surroundings of the Auberge du Rhin, nursing a vodka tonic and ignoring the pitying looks of the waiters. If he had set out to humiliate her, he could barely have come up with a more apposite scheme. And of course it was true, it would have been a simple enough matter to call. He had known as soon as he ordered the second bottle in the little bar with the zinc counter that he would not be keeping their date. And as the alcohol had exerted its grip, he had become bloody-minded: it was Céline who had left him. It was not for him to go running after her. It was she who should be making amends with him. But he did not really believe that. If he had not telephoned, it was not out of bravado. It was because he could imagine the derision Lambert would heap upon him. The truth was, he had not called because he had not wanted to look spineless in front of his colleague.

Of course, he did not say any of that. He merely repeated that it had not been possible to call. He explained vaguely that he and Lambert had been in the midst of an interrogation.

Céline exhaled wearily. It was impossible to tell if she believed him or not. If he expected a tirade, it did not come.

'To tell you the truth, Georges, I only agreed to meet you to please my mother,' she said.

'Even so,' said Gorski, 'there are things we need to discuss.'

'Are there?'

'Well, yes,' he said. 'Clémence for one.'

'What about her?'

'We'll need to come to some agreement about… access.' He hated even using such a bureaucratic term.

'You've had access to her for the last seventeen years. You never seemed so concerned about it then.' She looked at him, defying him to disagree.

Gorski ran his palm over his brow. It was prickled with sweat.

'All the same,' he said.

He took a step closer to her. She turned her head to avoid the smell of his breath. Gorski could see her clavicles beneath the collar of her blouse. It was true that they would have to make certain arrangements, Céline agreed with an air of resignation, 'but I'd prefer to do it when you don't reek of stale booze.'

Gorski assured her that he would not be late next time.

Céline turned to face him. 'I'm sure you won't,' she said. She ran the tips of her fingers along the line of the clavicle he had been staring at. He left without attempting to kiss her goodbye.

MADAME GORSKI WAS ASLEEP. The room was overheated and stuffy. Gorski turned down the convector heater that his mother had used since her arthritis had made it impossible for her to set a fire. He opened the casement to let in a little air then unpacked the shopping he had brought. Mme Gorski's hands were too weak to grip a knife, so he had taken to bringing her powdered soups. Her favourite was asparagus. His mother insisted that it was every bit as good as her own soup. Why go to all the trouble of chopping vegetables, when one need only boil up some water? But Gorski missed the smell of simmering stock that used to waft down to the pawnshop below when he was helping his father after school.

Returning from the kitchenette, he sat down in his father's chair at the table by the window. It was dark outside. He looked at his reflection in the window, disfigured by the condensation that had formed on the glass. He closed the window then got up and sat in the armchair opposite his mother. His mother's chin rested on her chest, her hands clasped across her bosom. Her breathing was even and peaceful. One day, he would come to the apartment and find her in exactly that repose, her chest still and her skin cold. Gorski felt his own eyes become heavy. He let his head fall forward. It was, after all, quite pleasant to surrender to the warmth.

When he woke up, his mother was standing by the stove.

'Tell your father the soup's ready,' she said.

Gorski ran the palm of his hand over his eyes then massaged his temples. His mouth was dry. He looked at his watch. He had been asleep for over an hour. He got up and walked to the door. He called down the stairs towards the shop. There did not seem any harm in it. It seemed less cruel than reminding his mother for the umpteenth time that his father was no longer with them.

By the time they sat down to eat, she would have forgotten all about him. Gorski fetched the placemats, napkins and cutlery from the sideboard and arranged them on the table. He then fetched two glasses and a carafe of water. There was little by way of conversation over dinner. Mme Gorski chewed each mouthful of bread for an inordinate length of time. Gorski was aware of the quiet smacking of her lips.

'And how is Céline?' she asked.

'Fine,' Gorski replied. 'Busy at the shop, of course.'

'And Clémence?'

'The same. Busy with her schoolwork, I mean.'

'I'd like to see her,' she said.

'Yes, I'll tell her to stop by.'

Mme Gorski turned and looked towards the door.

'What's happened to your father?' she said with a little shake of her head. When she turned back, she started a little. 'Ah, there you are,' she said. 'I was just going to call you again.'

Gorski smiled at her. He had always shared some of his father's mannerisms and patterns of speech, but now that his own hair was grey and his face had grown gaunt—he had recently lost a few kilos—he had started to resemble his father physically.

Gorski cleared the table and washed up. There was enough soup left for his mother's lunch the following day.

Fourteen

JOHNNY'S WAS TUCKED BETWEEN two other bars on a narrow
street called Rue de la Loi. Raymond had been loitering on
the pavement outside for half an hour. It was raining lightly.
Johnny's had no windows, so he could not see if Delph was
inside. There was only a door, above which was a wooden sign in
the style of an American saloon. A few people had entered or left
the premises, but from the pavement opposite Raymond could
see only into a dimly lit passage. Whenever the door opened, a
burst of rhythmic music issued from within.

Raymond had gone over and over Delph's words. *I'll be at
Johnny's on Saturday.* At least, that was what he thought she
had said. There had been no mention of whether she would be
there in the afternoon or evening, certainly not of an actual time.
Still, there was no question of not entering. If she was not there,
he could drink a beer and leave. What was the worst that could
happen?

He walked to the end of the street, doubled back and then,
when he reached the door of the bar, went straight in as if he
had just happened on the place. The first thing that hit him was
the music: all percussion and double bass, a deep semi-spoken
baritone. The passage opened into a dark barroom. Raymond
scanned the room for Delph. To the right of the room was a
raised area separated by a balustrade and reached by two wooden
steps. A group of students was gathered round a table there,

deep in conversation. Delph was nowhere to be seen. Directly ahead was the bar. Raymond spotted an unoccupied table in the corner. He hung his satchel over the back of the rickety wooden chair and sat down. He removed his scarf and hung it next to his satchel, this done with the intention of giving the impression that he was entirely at ease. It was only then that he was able to properly take in his surroundings.

Above the bar was a Confederate flag and a number of signs: *Please use the spittoons provided—No cussin'—Kindly refrain from brawling*, none of which Raymond understood. Every inch of wall space was covered with Johnny Cash record sleeves, playbills and photographs. Some of the posters were plastered directly onto the walls, others had been hung in mismatched frames. To the right of the bar was a pair of swing doors marked *Restrooms*. Next to that was a 1950s jukebox, its display of lights illuminating a patch of wooden floor in front of it. Leaning on the end of the bar was a short, stocky man of around fifty, dressed in a black suit, wing-collared white shirt and Cuban-heeled boots. His jet-black hair was swept back into an impressive quiff. He had a thin cigar clamped in the corner of his mouth. This, Raymond supposed, was Johnny. Aside from the table of students, the only other customers were two burly, shaven-headed men in leather motorcycle jackets standing at the bar drinking tankards of beer. On the back of one of the men's jackets the motto *Born to live, Live to die* was picked out in metal studs. Once Raymond was settled at his table, the little man in the black suit walked over with a rolling gait.

'Whaddaya drinkin', buddy?' he said in American-accented English. Even in the dimly lit bar, it was obvious that his hair was dyed.

Raymond asked for a beer. Johnny communicated his order to a woman behind the bar with a large, placid face and long, grey hair tied in plaits at the sides of her head. His wife, Raymond assumed. She unhurriedly pulled the beer and the proprietor brought it over.

'Your first time in Johnny's?' he asked as he placed it on the table. It was smaller than the ones the men at the bar were drinking.

Raymond nodded cautiously.

'Tell me, *mon fils*, who is the king?'

'The king?' Raymond repeated.

'Yes, the king. Who's the king?'

'I don't know, monsieur,' said Raymond. 'You?'

The little man took his cigar from the corner of his mouth. His fingers were adorned with a number of oversized signet rings. He shook his head and tutted his disappointment. He gestured round the walls of the bar.

'Now,' he said with weary patience, 'let's try again. Who is the king?' He enunciated the question as if each word was an entire sentence.

Raymond cottoned on. 'Johnny Cash?' he said doubtfully.

'Johnny Cash! Correct answer.' He took a step back from the table, replaced his cigar in his mouth and gave a slow handclap. 'Fuck Elvis. Fuck Hallyday. Fuck Gainsbourg. Johnny Cash is the king.'

The bikers at the bar looked over, no doubt having witnessed the routine many times before. The proprietor shouted to them: 'The kid didn't know who the king was.' Then he turned back to Raymond. 'First drink's on the house, buddy.'

He strutted back to his post at the corner of the bar. Raymond did not know what to make of the exchange. Any hope he had of passing unnoticed in the corner had gone. And now, if Delph did not show up, he could hardly just leave as if he had casually dropped in with no ulterior motive. *First drink's on the house*. The statement clearly implied that the first drink would be followed by a second and probably by a third and fourth drink. You could not accept a drink on the house and then leave. Perhaps he should have insisted on paying, but Johnny would no doubt have taken such a suggestion as a grievous insult.

Raymond took his book from his satchel, but there was barely enough light to read by. He took out his cigarettes and lit one. The act of smoking put him a little more at ease. The music battered on at a relentless pace. With each new song Raymond grew more accustomed to Johnny Cash's voice and the clanking train-track rhythm. He tried to relax.

From where he was sitting he could not see the door, but he did not want to give the impression that he was waiting for someone. He drank some beer. His father always insisted that beer was a drink for ruffians. He took a second swallow and then drained the contents. He stared at the empty glass on the table in front of him with satisfaction. Perhaps *he* was a ruffian. Johnny appeared at his table and placed a second beer in front of him.

'You're thirsty,' he said. It was a statement rather than a question.

Raymond folded open the pages of his book. He rested his elbow on the table and placed his left hand on his forehead, as if he was reading. But through his fingers he watched the group of students around the table on the platform. There were two girls and three boys. The music was too loud to hear what they were saying, but their conversation was animated. The focal point of the group was a guy in a black leather jacket who kept a cigarette pinched between the thumb and middle finger of his left hand. His chair was pushed a little back from the table and his right arm was draped around the back of his neighbour's seat. He did not take much part in the discussion, but he seemed to exert a pull on the others. When he took a draw on his cigarette, he tipped his head back and exhaled a stream of smoke directly above him. Raymond found him loathsome.

At one point, he looked directly across the room at Raymond. Raymond immediately lowered his eyes, but he felt that he was being scrutinised. He turned a page of his book and forced himself to read a few lines. When he glanced through his fingers a few moments later, the guy had turned to the girl on his left and was whispering something in her ear.

Two or three of the other tables were now occupied. Johnny greeted each new arrival with something from his repertoire of American greetings. It was half past eight. As the bar filled up, Raymond began to feel less conspicuous. So what if Delph did not appear? He could drink a few beers and get the train home. *I'll be at Johnny's on Saturday.* It was a statement of fact rather than an invitation. Still, why would she have told him she would be there if she did not want to see him? Johnny had brought him a third beer. Raymond decided he would drink it slowly, then perhaps a final one, and leave. The last train to Saint-Louis was at 23:25. He had plenty of time.

He was halfway through this third beer when Delph walked in. She was wearing the same men's jacket, pork-pie hat and sunglasses as before, but now with a short skirt and green and black striped tights. Her boots reached to just below the knee. Despite the darkness, she kept her sunglasses on. She walked straight to the group of students and greeted each of them in turn; a process that, due to the cramped space, took some time and was not achieved without logistical difficulty. A drink was upset, but this caused no particular consternation. Delph pulled up a chair, turned it so that the back was to the table, and strad-dled it. The centre of gravity of the group immediately shifted towards her. Johnny strolled over to the table, cloth in hand to mop up the spilled drink. Delph rose and greeted him with a kiss on both cheeks. He stood back to admire her outfit. Beneath her jacket, she was wearing an oversized men's shirt, the cuffs of which hung loosely around her wrists. He took their orders and returned to the bar.

Raymond moved his chair around the table so that he was no longer facing Delph's group. He hunched over his book. Clearly, Delph had entirely forgotten about him. She had not so much as glanced around the bar to see if he was there. If she did spot him, he would pretend he had been so immersed in his reading he had not seen her come in. He resolved to finish his beer, pay up and make his exit when the opportunity arose. After a few minutes he gestured to Johnny that he would like to settle his bill. To his dismay, however, the proprietor instructed his wife to pour another beer and brought it over. At this moment, Delph looked up from her conversation and followed Johnny's progress across the room. Raymond stared fixedly at his book. Moments after Johnny had placed the fresh beer on the table, Delph made her way across the bar. Raymond feigned surprise at seeing her. She stood at his table with one hand on her hip, a puzzled expression on her face. She was wearing black lipstick.

'So you came?' she said. She did not seem displeased.

'Yes,' said Raymond.

'What are you doing sitting over here? Why didn't you join us?'

'I didn't see you.' He brandished his book as though it was an exhibit in a trial.

Delph rolled her eyes. 'Are you going to grace us with your presence or not?'

'Sure,' he said, as if the idea had not previously occurred to him. He gathered up his scarf and satchel. She took him by the wrist and led him across the bar. He was a little unsteady on his feet. He had never drunk three beers before. When they reached the table, Delph instructed her friends to shove up.

'Everyone,' she said, 'this is—' She then realised that she did not yet know his name. Raymond told her.

She then gestured vaguely towards the group. 'This is ... everyone.' No one was the least bit interested in him. A girl reluctantly shuffled along. The sides of her head were shaved and she had a stud through her lower lip. Raymond thanked her and perched one buttock on the end of the bench. She smelled of patchouli.

'I'm Raymond,' he said.

The girl looked at him with a bored expression and returned to her conversation with her neighbour. She had a series of rings from the lobe to the top of her ear. Delph resumed her seat at the end of the table. She gave Raymond a look, intended to convey that he should not be perturbed by her friends' rudeness.

Raymond found himself opposite the guy in the leather jacket. He had studiously dishevelled black hair and dark, hooded eyes.

'So this is the guy that's been following you?' he said to Delph.

'The very one,' she replied.

Raymond did not know whether to be offended or pleased that he had at least merited mention.

'This is Luc,' said Delph.

Luc leaned back on his chair, so that the front legs tipped off the floor, and appraised Raymond. 'He looks like a girl.'

'I know.' Delph seemed pleased by Luc's observation. 'A pretty girl.' She reached out and stroked Raymond's hair, before letting her hand rest on his shoulder. Raymond felt a frisson of excitement. Luc stared at him with an antagonistic expression. Raymond forced himself to hold his gaze. He took out a cigarette and lit it. Luc reached across and shook out a cigarette without asking. There were only four left.

Johnny appeared at the end of the table. He slapped Raymond on the shoulder. 'Why didn't you say you were a friend of Delph's?' He seemed offended by Raymond's omission. He cleared the table. 'Same again?' he said.

'Of course,' said Delph.

Johnny nodded and returned to the bar.

'Can you see anything through those glasses?' Raymond asked.

'Not much,' said Delph. 'They're an affectation.'

She took them off and handed them to him. He put them on. The room darkened.

'They suit you,' said Delph.

He felt queasy, but the glasses allowed him to study Delph more closely. Her features were sharp and angular. Her eyes were thickly rimmed with mascara. He could see her clavicles where her shirt was open at the neck. She was almost completely flat-chested.

'I like your shirt,' he said.

Delph glanced down. 'It belonged to my father,' she said.

152

'Oh, yes?' said Raymond, but Delph responded only with a series of unhurriedly blown smoke rings.

Johnny returned and placed a tray of drinks on the table. 'Six *tomates*,' he said as he passed them out.

Raymond lifted the spectacles to examine the contents of his glass. It was a lurid red. The group raised their drinks to the centre of the table. Someone made a toast to Johnny. The rhythm of the music seemed to be gathering pace. Raymond recognised the aniseed flavour of *pastis*.

'Ricard and grenadine,' said Delph, seeing him screw up his face.

'It's good,' said Raymond. He took another sip to prove the point. His eyes lost focus for a few moments. He handed Delph's glasses back to her. She folded them up and hung them on the cleft of her shirt. After the toast, there was a lull in the conversation. Delph announced to the company: 'Raymond here is a disciple of Monsieur Sartre.'

Raymond protested that he was not a disciple of anyone, but no one seemed to hear him.

'Ah, the squat toad of existentialism!' declared Luc. He made himself go cross-eyed and puffed on an imaginary pipe. 'Would you mind terribly, my dear Beaver, if I fucked your girlfriend?' he said in a comic voice.

The girl next to Raymond laughed.

Luc leaned across the table. 'But really,' he said, 'all that quest for freedom stuff's a bit old hat, isn't it?'

Raymond looked at him. The simplest thing would be to agree, to make some dismissive remark. But Delph was looking at him, expecting him to mount a defence. It was a test. 'So you don't want to be free?' he said.

Luc shook his head. 'That's not the question,' he said. 'You're either free or you're not. Whether I *want* to be free has no bearing on the matter.' He leaned back in his chair, as if this was the definitive statement on the matter and no argument could be entertained.

Delph cupped her chin in her hands. Because of her squint, it was difficult to tell whether she was looking at Raymond or Luc.

'Tell me,' she said to Raymond, 'which character in your beloved book is the most free?'

'Mathieu, I suppose,' he said. He was about to explain his answer, but Delph was already shaking her head. Raymond felt like he had flunked a test at school.

'Mathieu is the least free,' she said. 'He's so busy analysing what it means to be free, he's entirely enslaved.' She held up a long index finger. 'No, the freest character is Lola.'

'Lola?' Raymond repeated. Lola, the heroin-addicted night-club singer.

'Of course,' said Delph. 'She's free because she makes no effort to be free.'

Raymond nodded earnestly. 'I hadn't thought of it like that,' he said.

'Looks like you're going to have to read it all over again. In the meantime,' she said, reaching for her glass, 'I myself am free to drink as many *tomates* as I like.'

'And you,' Luc said to Raymond, 'are free to clear off.'

'Why don't *you* clear off,' Delph said to Luc.

Raymond, emboldened by the alcohol he had consumed and by the fact that Delph appeared to have taken his side, pointed across the table at Luc and said: 'You, sir, are a second-rater!'

The six faces around the table stared at him blankly. The girl next to Raymond started to laugh, followed by Luc. Raymond felt the colour rise to his cheeks. It was a routine he had with Stéphane, who would retort: *And you, sir, are a man of no account!* But Raymond would only make himself seem more ridiculous if he explained that it was a snatch of dialogue from the very book they had ridiculed. Nevertheless, his silly comment served to lighten the atmosphere around the table.

Johnny arrived with another round of *tomates*. Delph leaned in close to Raymond. 'Don't worry about Luc,' she whispered. 'He's always like that when he's jealous.'

'Jealous?' said Raymond. The idea that he might be worthy of provoking jealousy in Luc thrilled him.

'Well, he's not as pretty as you, is he?' she said. 'And he's never actually read a book in his life.'

Luc was watching them from across the table. Delph flashed him a smile, before turning back to Raymond. She was leaning in so close he could smell a faintly musky odour from her skin.

'So what do you think of Johnny's?' she said.

'It's cool,' he said.

She asked why she hadn't seen him there before.

He was pleased that he might seem like the kind of person who would frequent such a place. 'I'm not from here. I'm from Saint-Louis,' he said by way of explanation.

Delph looked shocked. 'Saint-Louis?' she said. 'I didn't know anyone actually came from Saint-Louis. I thought it was some sort of transit camp.'

'I am one of those unfortunates,' said Raymond.

'We're all unfortunates here,' she said.

Then she leant forward and kissed him on the mouth. Raymond did not resist, but he fully expected Luc to reach across the table and thump him at any moment. Delph clasped her hand around the back of his neck and angled her head so that their mouths were perpendicular. Raymond could taste the grenadine on her tongue. She smelt familiar, like his own sweat. The embrace lasted thirty seconds or a minute. When Delph released him, her lipstick was smudged around her mouth. Raymond wiped his own mouth with the back of his hand. It was smeared with black. He felt like he had emerged from underwater.

'Later, we'll go out the back,' Delph whispered. Raymond swallowed hard. He tried not to think about what 'going out the back' might entail.

'I should probably be going,' he said. 'I have to catch my train.' He looked down at his watch but was unable to focus on the face.

'Forget your train,' said Delph. She stood up, tugging the hem of her skirt around her thighs as she did so. 'I need to pee,' she said.

Raymond nodded dumbly. He watched Delph make her way across the bar with her loping gait. She greeted a few of the other regulars as she passed. All the tables were now occupied, and a dozen or more men dressed in leather jackets were now standing around the bar. The hubbub of conversation competed with the music. Raymond swivelled on the bench to face the table. The motion of turning his head made him dizzy. He did not know if he could drink any more. The rest of the group were engaged in an argument about a musician he had never heard of. Luc was of the opinion that the person in question was a phoney.

'You're the phoney,' said the girl with the heavily pierced ears.

'I *am* a phoney,' said Luc indifferently. 'And so are you. We're all phonies.'

Raymond held his watch in front of his face and screwed up one eye to read it. It was almost ten o'clock. He still had an hour or so. *Forget your train*, Delph had told him. It was easy to say, but he had no other way to get home. The idea of telephoning his mother and telling her he was drunk and stranded in Mulhouse was unthinkable, particularly as he had told her that he was spending the evening at Yvette's. He clumsily grasped the glass on the table in front of him and took another sip of his *tomate*. It wasn't so bad. Perhaps he *should* forget his train. He should abandon himself to whatever was to occur. That was what Lola would do.

Delph returned. She had repaired her smudged lipstick. Raymond also needed to use the WC, but he did not want to relinquish Delph to the general company. He started to say something but lost his thread after a few words. Delph did not seem in the least bit fazed by his inebriated state.

'So, monsieur,' she said, 'you still haven't told me what you were doing in Rue Saint-Fiacre.'

The question brought Raymond to his senses a little. He had quite forgotten the circumstances of their meeting. Perhaps he should simply tell her the truth. The story might make him seem interesting, intrepid even. Certainly a good deal more interesting than he actually was. But the truth would only invite questions about the circumstances of his father's death, and Raymond had no more desire to discuss this than he did to telephone his mother.

All he could think of to say was: 'I can't tell you.'

'So you're just a guy who likes to follow strange girls in the street.' She didn't seem to particularly disapprove of such an activity.

Then he hit on what, at that moment, seemed a very reasonable explanation. He rummaged in his satchel and then, without raising it above the level of the table, brought out the knife. He pulled it slowly from its leather sheath. He glanced from the knife to Delph. Her eyes had widened. Raymond leaned in and whispered in her ear: 'I stole it from the philatelist's shop opposite your apartment.'

When he leaned back, Delph was wearing an expression of distaste. Luc was straining to see what they were looking at beneath the table. Raymond suddenly felt himself to be a wild and dangerous character. He grinned stupidly at her.

'Why would you do something like that?' she said.

Raymond was pleased that he had shocked her. 'I don't know,' he said. He shrugged, as if to suggest that it was the sort of thing he did all the time. 'It was a spur-of-the-moment thing.'

Luc stood up and craned his head across the table. With a rapid movement of his arm, Raymond brought the knife into view. Luc recoiled. He glanced around the room. People at other tables had looked up from their conversations. The music clattered on relentlessly. Raymond moved the blade to and fro so that it caught the light. He felt the need to do something dramatic. He remembered the scene in the Sumatra, Ivich's hand laid open from the ball of the thumb to the root of the little finger.

He stood up clumsily and pushed the blade against the heel of his left hand. A look of excitement passed across Delph's face. Thankfully the blade was too blunt to pierce the skin. Raymond hesitated. Delph was staring at him, her mouth slightly open. He did not really want to cut himself, but he would look ridiculous if he did not go through with it. He felt a sudden grip on his wrist.

With a rapid movement Johnny twisted Raymond's arm behind his back. Raymond thought for a moment he might break his arm. The knife dropped to the floor. Johnny drew his face close to Raymond's. He was surprisingly strong.

'We don't like that sort of thing in here,' he said. He released Raymond's arm.

'I'm sorry,' said Raymond. Johnny gave a sharp nod, to indicate that this was an acceptable response. Then he returned to his post at the end of the bar. The other patrons had already returned to their conversations. The little incident did not seem to have aroused any great interest. Raymond sat down on the bench and massaged his wrist. He glanced up at Delph. She did not seem troubled by what had occurred.

Luc called him an asshole. Raymond looked at him evenly, then picked up the knife and put it in his satchel. He got up and walked unsteadily across the bar to the WC. He pushed through the swing doors and found himself in a passage that smelt of mould. A man in a sleeveless T-shirt with heavily tattooed arms was waiting for the toilet to be vacated.

'You'll get yourself in trouble waving knives around like that, kid,' he said.

Raymond shrugged. A woman in her thirties came out of the WC. She gave Raymond a disapproving shake of her head as she squeezed past to return to the bar. The tattooed man went into the lavatory and urinated noisily without closing the door. At the end of the passage was a room stacked with crates of bottles and metal kegs. When the man had finished, Raymond went in and shut the door. It was secured by means of attaching a loop of string round a bent nail. He urinated, placing his hand on the wall to steady himself. Then he splashed cold water on his face and dried it with a filthy towel he found hanging on a hook by the toilet bowl. He pushed his hair behind his ears and looked at himself in the mirror above the basin. He felt strangely pleased with himself. Even Johnny had not seemed unduly put out by his behaviour. He would have been quite justified in throwing him out, but he had not even threatened to do so. When he unhooked the string on the door, Delph was standing in the passage smoking.

Fifteen

RAYMOND DID NOT WAKE UNTIL early on Sunday afternoon. There was a sour taste in the back of his throat. His head hurt. He was still wearing his shoes and trousers, but he was naked from the waist up. The curtains were not closed and weak sun filtered through the window. The remains of a packet of cigarettes were strewn across the floor. He pulled the blanket over his head. He remembered nothing of the journey home from Johnny's. Neither did he know if Thérèse had been up when he returned. His mother would certainly have been in bed. The best thing to do would be to get up and act as if nothing out of the ordinary had occurred.

Raymond threw off the blanket and lay on his back for a while staring blankly at the ceiling. The swaying motion of the train journey home returned to him. Had there been some incident with the conductor? He closed his eyes to stem the memory. In preparation for leaving the bed, he turned on his side. He must have tried to smoke a cigarette, because an end had burnt itself out on the carpet. Slowly he lowered his feet to the floor. When he leaned over to untie his shoelaces, he felt a convulsion and retched into his mouth. He straightened up and took a series of slow breaths. He prised off his shoes with the toes of the opposite foot. He walked bare-chested to the bathroom and drank two glasses of water. There were some painkillers among the bottles in the cabinet and he took three. He examined his face in the mirror. His skin was pasty, almost yellow, and his eyes bloodshot. He brushed his teeth thoroughly then removed his trousers. His underpants were crusted with semen. He got into the shower. The hot water was reviving. He turned his face towards the showerhead and pushed his hair back from his forehead, then soaped his armpits and private parts. An image of Delph flashed into his mind. A certain odour that he could not quite place. He exhaled slowly, allowing the memories to seep back into his mind.

When he had emerged from the WC at Johnny's, Delph had indicated with a motion of her head that she should follow him. The room at the end of the passage was dark and smelled of drains. It was cold. Without ceremony, Delph pulled down her tights and underwear and perched on a pile of crates. It was too dark for Raymond to see between her legs. Once or twice, when his mother had got out of bed carelessly, he had glimpsed her sex, but other than that, and his inept fondling of Yvette, his knowledge of female anatomy was vague. Delph unbuttoned her shirt. She was not wearing a brassiere. Her chest was as bony as a pubescent boy's. She suggested he take down his trousers, and he did so. She motioned him towards her. She took his penis in her hand and attempted to guide it into her sex, but he spent himself on the inside of her thigh as soon as she touched him. He attempted to disguise this by thrusting his hips between her legs in the way that he had seen actors do in certain films, but his erection quickly subsided. Delph made it clear that she found his efforts unsatisfactory. She pushed him away and slipped off the crates. Having first wiped the semen from her thigh, she pulled up her tights and fastened her shirt. Raymond zipped up his trousers. Delph's hat had fallen off. He retrieved it from the floor and handed it to her, mumbling an apology.

'Don't worry about it,' she had said. 'Luc will sort me out later.'

She put her hat on, fixed it at a jaunty angle, and retraced her steps along the passage. A man waiting outside the WC had observed the whole episode. He was laughing. Raymond waited until he had gone into the toilet before making his exit.

In the shower, Raymond became aroused as he recalled the incident. He masturbated rapidly, one hand steadying himself against the tiled wall. As he caught his breath, he watched his emission form a tiny vortex before being sucked down the plug-hole. He resolved to push things forward with Yvette so that he might perform more satisfactorily next time. If there was to be a next time.

Raymond returned to his room and put on clean clothes. He was glad he had slept through lunch. He did not wish to face his mother. It was not that she would scold him. She would simply look forlorn, and Raymond could not bear to see her look forlorn. He put his baseball boots in his satchel and padded quietly down the stairs. Despite his efforts, his mother called out to him from the drawing room. She must have been listening out for him. Her tone was light, as if she wanted to make clear that he was not in trouble, but he continued to the front door and trotted down the drive, pausing only when he reached the pavement to put on his shoes.

Saint-Louis seemed even drabber than usual. The mid-afternoon light was flat and seemed to drain the colour from everything. The shops along Rue de Mulhouse had the air of being abandoned, rather than merely closed. Aside from the occasional passing car, the streets were deserted. Raymond felt queer. He could feel every contour of the pavement through the soles of his shoes. Buildings he had barely noticed before now seemed offensive in their ugliness. He was conscious of a moment of blackness every time he blinked and felt a momentary relief that the world was still there when he opened his eyes. He walked slowly past the *gendarmerie*. Perhaps the little cop was in there now, sitting in an office with a grey linoleum floor and a dying pot plant on the window sill. Raymond paused by the noti-ceboard at the foot of the steps up to the entrance. Behind the scratched perspex was an appeal for information about a missing person, Artur Kuper, with a photograph and a description of the clothes he had been wearing. He was an ordinary-looking man, with a scruffy moustache and a receding hairline. The poster was three years old. Next to the announcement was a faded advertisement for the Foreign Legion. It was illustrated by a picture of a handsome young man in a *kepi* gazing idealistically into the future, over the slogan *Voir la vie autrement*. Perhaps this was the sentiment that had inspired Artur Kuper to one day get on a train and disappear. Or perhaps he had simply fallen drunk into the canal and was decomposing in the sludge. Judging by his picture, the latter scenario seemed more likely.

A policeman emerged from the entrance to the station. Raymond instinctively turned his face away. The *gendarme* passed so close to him that he brushed his shoulder, but he did not so much as glance at him. Raymond walked off. His stomach was churning and he thought he might be about to vomit. He turned into the little park in front of the Protestant temple, where he had sat so often with Yvette. He took a seat on the bench nearest the church. The chestnut trees around the perimeter of the park had begun to shed their leaves. He placed his hand over his eyes and took a few slow breaths. His queasiness subsided a little. An old woman had sat down on the bench opposite and was watching him. Raymond returned her gaze. Her expression was one of mild curiosity, disapproval perhaps. She did not appear in the least afraid of him. There was no reason that she should be. She had no way of knowing that he had a knife in his satchel and could, if he chose, step across the gravel walkway and demand the purse she no doubt kept in the large leather handbag by her side.

Raymond creased his mouth into a smile and said: 'Good afternoon, Madame.'

The woman's expression did not change. Raymond wondered if she was deaf or gone in the head. He directed his gaze towards the trees behind her. After a few minutes, she gathered up her bag and slowly walked off in the direction of the *gendarmerie*.

A cleric in black robes arrived and opened up the heavy wooden door of the church. He stood on the step for a few moments surveying his domain and then went inside. It had never occurred to Raymond that the temple might actually be in use; that it might function as a place of worship, rather than being merely a convenient landmark by which to orient oneself in the town. A few minutes later, the cleric reappeared and stood on the step, awaiting his congregation. He greeted Raymond with a cordial nod, perhaps thinking that he was waiting for the service to commence. He did not appear unduly concerned about the lack of worshippers. An old couple arrived and he greeted them with a handshake, before they went inside. The cleric glanced at his watch. It struck Raymond that were the clergyman stripped of his title and his outlandish attire, his actions would be recognised in all their absurdity. It was only on account of his position that people did not point him out in the street and laugh.

Raymond sat for a few more minutes before getting up and continuing through the town. He felt the heft of his knife in his satchel. He could not imagine that he had once been without it. He had no intention of ever using it, but knowing it was there conferred a feeling of well-being.

Yvette and Stéphane were in the back booth of the Café des Vosges. They were deep in conversation, their heads almost touching across the table. The café had the atmosphere, as it always did on Sundays, of not really being open. There were two other customers, sitting by the window staring blankly out at the empty street, like extras in a film waiting for 'Action' to be called. The waitress with the harelip was cleaning the glass cabinet where the cakes and tarts were kept. When Raymond appeared at the table, Stéphane leaned back and stretched his arms along the back of the banquette. Yvette stared at the empty cup on the table in front of her.

'Hello, old man,' said Stéphane.

'Monsieur, mademoiselle,' said Raymond, nodding to each in turn. He slid onto the banquette next to Yvette. They exchanged a perfunctory kiss on the cheeks.

'So, what's happening?' Stéphane asked. He seemed determined to generate a convivial atmosphere.

'Nothing much,' Raymond replied.

Stéphane had moved to Saint-Louis two years previously. When he had been introduced to the class, Raymond had immediately recognised a kindred spirit. He wore wire-framed oval spectacles and his hair was cut too neatly, as if his mother still took him to the barber's. Nevertheless, he projected an air of indifference: if he was an outcast, it was because he chose to be. A few days later, Raymond spotted him in the canteen. He was hunched over a book. It was Yvette who had insisted that they join him. 'He doesn't know anyone,' she had said.

'Maybe he doesn't want to know anyone,' Raymond replied.

When they sat down, Stéphane closed his book as if he had been awaiting their arrival. He shook hands in an exaggeratedly formal way.

'Stéphane Prudhomme,' he said.

Yvette and Raymond introduced themselves.

'I appreciate you joining me,' Stéphane said. His father's work—he did not specify what he did—obliged his family to re-locate frequently and as a consequence he was quite used to moving schools. 'My policy is never to try to make friends. People are afraid of the unknown. They don't want to get lumbered with someone they know nothing about. So I wait until someone approaches me. Sometimes people do this out of pity, but in other cases it's because they have seen something in me that attracts them. I sense that in this instance the latter is true, and, if I may say so, the sentiment is reciprocated.'

Then he fixed Yvette with a broad smile. Raymond did not feel at all aggrieved that Stéphane's eyes lingered on Yvette. On the contrary, he wanted him to admire her, as if Yvette's fine features somehow reflected well on him. He tried to think of something clever to say in response to Stéphane's little speech, but the moment passed.

A conversation ensued about the book Stéphane was reading, *La Bête Humaine*. Stéphane was dismissive: 'It's entertaining, but if Zola wanted to be a scientist,' he declared, 'he should have taken up a scalpel rather than a pen.' Raymond, who at that time had never read a word of Zola, was captivated. Within weeks, the three of them had become inseparable. Yvette and Raymond seemed to take equal pleasure in their new friend's company. Raymond did not mind that he could not always follow his companions' conversation. The fact that Yvette now had someone with whom she could discuss things on an equal footing only filled a lack in their own relationship.

But now, as the threesome sat in awkward silence around the Formica table in the Café des Vosges, something had changed. Raymond looked at his two friends: Stéphane with his stupid fuzzy moustache, Yvette with the childish Alice band that held her hair behind her ears. They seemed no more than children. Only a week ago, it would never have occurred to Raymond not to share everything with them. Now such a thing seemed inconceivable.

The waitress approached the table. 'A tea?' she asked without preamble.

If Raymond ordered a beer, it was not because he wanted one—he did not—but rather to illustrate the fissure that had opened between them. The waitress nodded disinterestedly and shuffled back to the counter in the battered leather slippers she always wore.

It was, in a sense, Stéphane's fault that they frequented the Café des Vosges. The first time they left school together, he had asked: 'Is there anywhere to get a coffee round here?' Until then, if Raymond and Yvette wished to postpone returning home, they would pause at one of the benches in the little park in front of the Protestant temple. Neither of them divulged this to Stéphane, however. Instead, it was Yvette who had said, for no reason other than that they happened to be passing: 'We sometimes go in here.'

When they had settled themselves in the booth at the back of the café, Stéphane surveyed the place with interest. Raymond, embarrassed by the outmoded surroundings they found themselves in, felt obliged to remark that were was nowhere any better in the vicinity. 'I think it's splendid,' Stéphane declared. Two old women who had not taken off their winter coats—Raymond remembered it clearly—fed lumps of cake to a poodle with rheumy eyes on the floor beneath their table. In time, he was to become familiar with their routine. The women came to the Café des Vosges once a week, on Tuesdays, shared a pot of tea and each had a cake. They varied their choice of cake and this formed the greater part of their conversation. At a certain point the poodle must have died, and from that time Raymond experienced the space on the floor between the women's ankles as a kind of void.

When the waitress approached their table, Stéphane had ordered a café crème. Yvette followed suit. In order to assert his individuality, Raymond asked for a tea. They sat in silence until the drinks arrived. There were other, less dreary, cafés in Saint-Louis, but Raymond and Yvette had conspired in the pretence that the Café des Vosges was their regular haunt. It was not Stéphane's place to suggest going elsewhere. In this way, they were condemned to frequent the Café des Vosges. Raymond often wondered if they would become like the old women in their winter coats, endlessly replaying the same conversation.

The waitress returned with Raymond's beer. Neither Yvette nor Stéphane made any comment on this change in his drinking habits. Raymond took a sip of his beer then licked the foam off his upper lip. It tasted foul.

Stéphane said with affected casualness: 'I called for you last night.'

Raymond could not prevent himself from glancing towards Yvette. She was looking at him questioningly with her chin cupped in the palm of her hand. They must have discussed this before he arrived.

'Oh, yeah?' Raymond said with a little shrug.

'It's just that your mother told me you had gone to Yvette's.'

'Yes,' said Raymond, 'I did tell her that.'

'But I went to Yvette's and you weren't there.' It wasn't clear whether he had gone to Yvette's because Raymond's mother had told him he was there, or if he had been going there in any case.

'Don't tell me you've never lied to your mother,' said Raymond.

'You lied to me as well,' said Yvette. 'You told me that you had to spend the evening at home.'

Raymond looked from one to the other. Far from being ashamed of being caught out, he felt a sense of outrage towards them. Until this point, there had been a tacit agreement between the three of them that while Raymond might see Yvette or Stéphane separately, Stéphane and Yvette never saw each other in Raymond's absence. He was the nucleus around which the threesome revolved. They had violated the norms of the group. Raymond felt that they had conspired against him.

He took a swallow of beer. 'So now I have to account for my movements to you, do I?' he said.

'Of course not,' said Yvette. 'But I'm upset that you lied to me.'

'And I'm upset that you two got together behind my back,' said Raymond.

'You can hardly say that, old man,' said Stéphane. 'I called in for you.'

Raymond ignored him. 'And did you open your legs for him as well?' he said to Yvette.

Yvette had tears in her eyes. 'Why are you being such a shit?' she said.

Stéphane was staring at the table. Yvette shoved Raymond on the arm. He stood up to let her out of the booth. To his surprise, Stéphane also stood up to go. He shook his head at Raymond and the pair left together. Raymond resumed his seat in the booth. The waitress had been watching the little scene from behind the counter. Raymond felt bad. Yvette was right. He was a shit. He should go after her and apologise. She would understand. Yvette always understood. Then he remembered Delph unbuttoning her shirt on the crates in the backroom of Johnny's and the moment passed.

The waitress was looking at him disapprovingly. In order to demonstrate that he was not embarrassed by what had taken place, he ordered a second beer. It was only when he came to pay that he remembered tossing the banknotes he had stolen onto the table at Johnny's.

Sixteen

IF THERE WAS ONE POINT ON which Gorski was in agreement with his predecessor, it was on the usefulness of funerals. 'Always go to the funeral,' Ribéry liked to say. 'Weddings are a waste of time. You learn more from five minutes at a funeral than in a whole day at a wedding.' And so Gorski had found it. Perhaps it was the proximity of death, but it never took people long to loosen up at a funeral. There was always some wag who took it upon himself to be the first to lighten the atmosphere with a joke or a disparaging comment about the deceased. The guests would then breathe a collective sigh of relief and get properly stuck into the liquor. And no one ever looked askance at a cop at a funeral. At a wedding, the presence of a cop cast a pall over proceedings; at a funeral it seemed perfectly apt.

The reception for the funeral of Bertrand Barthelme took place in the house on Rue des Bois. Trestle tables covered with crisp white tablecloths had been set out in the hallway with a selection of hors d'oeuvres and beverages. Uniformed staff had been hired for the occasion and new arrivals were immediately provided with a glass of sherry. A fire had been set in the drawing room where Gorski had had his interview with Lucette Barthelme. All the available seating was taken. Other guests stood around in huddles, as if wary that their conversation would be overheard. Two waitresses circled the room with trays of drinks. The housekeeper, Thérèse, flitted between the two rooms, keeping a watchful eye on the operation.

Lucette was sitting on the chaise longue. She was dressed in a black skirt and jacket, with a pillbox hat and veil. The dark clothing had the effect of making her complexion appear even paler than usual. A grey-haired woman was sitting next to her and talking animatedly, but Lucette did not appear to be listening. Her gaze was directed towards her son, who was loitering in the corner of the room. He had been fitted with a suit for the occasion. The collar and tie made him seem more masculine than before. Despite the delicacy of his features, he was quite handsome. He sipped a glass of sherry. His eyes followed a pretty, dark-haired waitress as she made her way around the room. When he saw Gorski, he wandered over to the casement and gazed fixedly out at the rain.

Nobody spoke to Gorski, but he did not feel ill at ease. That was another good thing about funerals: it was perfectly acceptable to hover on the edge of things. When the waitress reached Gorski, he took a third glass of sherry. Lucette glanced around to see where Thérèse was, anxious that the reception was meeting with her guests' approval. She caught Gorski's eye and smiled in a way that made it clear she would be happy when the gathering was over. He could not help feeling that a moment of intimacy had passed between them.

Gorski's father-in-law was warming his rump by the fire. He had donned his mayoral sash for the occasion. He greeted Gorski with a cordial wave before returning to his conversation with a group of the town's worthies. Maître Corbeil was among them. A sour-faced woman Gorski assumed to be Mme Corbeil stood at his side. It did not surprise him that the great and good of Saint-Louis had turned out for Bertrand Barthelme. Nor did it surprise him that no one seemed particularly concerned to affect sorrow at the old man's demise.

Bertrand Barthelme was a prominent enough figure to merit a slim file of cuttings in the archive of *L'Alsace* newspaper, and in a town like Saint-Louis the inhabitants have little better to do than to repeat and embellish rumours about their betters. Gorski was shrewd enough to treat much of what he heard with a degree of scepticism. Nevertheless, the Barthelme that emerged did not entirely conform to the austere image he had presented to the world. There had been no need for Gorski to be explicit in his enquiries. He needed only to mention, as if in passing, how unfortunate the accident had been in order to elicit a response. Even the cheerful Mme Beck, who kept the florist's beneath his mother's apartment, had made a face suggesting distaste. When Gorski asked whether she had known Barthelme, she replied: 'Only by reputation.' Gorski had gently prompted her, but she busied herself with the wrapping of a bouquet and said that she had taken a little soup to his mother.

Lemerre was less reticent. Gorski had his haircut at the shop on Avenue Général de Gaulle once a month. Céline had often urged him to use one of the town's smarter establishments, but it would not have gone unnoticed, or unremarked upon, if Gorski were to take his trade elsewhere. In any case, Lemerre was one of those people who made it his business to know what was going on in the town. It was expedient to maintain good relations.

Despite the less than hygienic nature of Lemerre's shop, it did not surprise Gorski to discover that Barthelme was a regular customer. Not only were the solicitor's offices only a short walk away, but it was a repeated assertion that he was not a man who liked to spend more money than necessary.

'A stuck-up bugger,' was Lemerre's verdict. 'Never uttered a word. And never tipped neither.'

Gorski tutted his contempt for such behaviour.

Bertrand was born to Honoré and Anaïs Barthelme in April 1923, the second of three brothers. Honoré had established the firm of Barthelme & Barthelme with his brother, Jacques, in 1920 and quickly gained a reputation for competence and discretion. Portraits of the two brothers still adorned the walls of the company's offices. Bertrand's elder brother—also Honoré— was run over by a motor car in 1942, and the expectation to carry on the family business fell upon the middle son. Bertrand's younger brother, Alain, was arrested during the war for black-marketeering, a transgression for which his father never forgave him. Bertrand joined the firm in 1950 having completed his national service and graduated at the top of his class from the University of Strasbourg.

Photographs of Bertrand Barthelme as a student in Strasbourg showed a handsome, fashionably dressed young man, clean-shaven and without the stern demeanour of his later years. He acquired, at this time, the reputation as something of a dandy. He was never short of female company and seemed to have no difficulty combining his studies with nights spent carousing in the city's most disreputable drinking dens. It was at this time that he made the acquaintance of Camille Masson, the daughter of a well-to-do Strasbourg banker, Guy Masson. Camille was a wild child and aspiring dancer, always attired in the latest fashions. Bertrand met her in the Lapin Rouge cabaret, a well-known haunt of artists and musicians. Camille was immediately taken with the well-dressed student, who impressed her on their first meeting with an impromptu recitation of Baudelaire's *Hymn to Beauty*. It was not so much his performance that captivated her, but the way he fixed her with his narrow, flickering eyes. Bertrand refused to join her on the dance floor, but he watched her intently when she danced with others. The couple were soon established as a fixture in the city's cafés and nightclubs. Their courtship was uneventful, aside from an incident in which Bertrand punched a young painter named Marcel Daru, when his dancing with Camille became too earthy. Daru was left with a broken jaw, but no charges were ever laid. Such incidents were commonplace in the nightclubs of the time and it would have been vulgar to involve the authorities. The episode probably did no harm either to Barthelme or Daru's reputations.

Bertrand was introduced to Camille's family and was more than capable of playing the role of respectable future son-in-law. His prospects were good, and neither his manners nor speech betrayed his provincial roots. Guy Masson must have thought he was just the fellow to tame his daughter's wilder tendencies. Camille longed to move to Paris to pursue a career in dance and frequent the cafés of Montparnasse. It is not known whether she had any talent. Certainly she took part in a number of semi-professional revues, but the likelihood is that it was the lifestyle that attracted her more than any desire to express herself artistically. In any case, a month after Bertrand graduated in 1949, the couple were married at a lavish ceremony in Strasbourg town hall. Until then, Bertrand had not introduced Camille to his parents, presumably calculating that a trip to a backwater like Saint-Louis would do little for the image he had carefully constructed for himself. Honoré and Anaïs Barthelme were charmed by Camille, but the provincial lawyer was heard to voice his disapproval of the extravagance of the reception.

The newlyweds set off on a month's tour of Italy, paid for by the father of the bride. It was during their honeymoon that Bertrand informed his wife that he intended to take up a position in his father's firm, and that they were going to live with his parents in the house on Rue des Bois. Camille was devastated. This was not at all what she had envisioned, but she had little idea of just how dreary her new home would be. Maître and Madame Barthelme did their best to make their exotic new daughter-in-law welcome, but their provincial ways—they retired to bed at ten in the evening—appalled her. A soirée was arranged to introduce her to what passed for society in Saint-Louis, but Camille made no secret of how tedious she found the company of the lawyers, merchants and, worst of all, clergymen that were invited. In a letter to a girlfriend in Strasbourg, she wrote that she felt that she had been imprisoned. Bertrand did his best to amuse her in the evenings and at weekends, but there was little he could do. Honoré's health began to deteriorate and Bertrand was forced to take greater responsibility for the family business and work ever longer hours. He grew out his beard, believing it added gravitas to his still-youthful features, and joined the town's various professional guilds. He did not involve himself in local politics, but made sure that he attended events where influential people would be present. Evenings spent reading in the draughty parlour of the house on Rue des Bois, or making polite conversation with petit-bourgeois councillors, were not at all what Camille had in mind when she married the rakish student of Strasbourg. She grew depressed. When a first miscarriage was followed by a second, Bertrand suspected that she had sabotaged the pregnancies. The relationship became characterised by mutual resentment. Camille's death from an overdose of barbiturates in 1955 was recorded as accidental, but the verdict probably had less to do with the truth than with the desire of an influential family to avoid the stigma of suicide.

Honoré Barthelme died of pancreatic cancer two years later in 1957, and the following year Bertrand persuaded Gustav Corbeil, then the head of another Saint-Louis firm, to join the business, arguing that it would be mutually beneficial to join forces rather than compete with each other. Having secured a virtual monopoly on the town's legal business, it only remained for Bertrand to produce an heir. His second marriage was arranged by his mother. Lucette Fischer was the daughter of a local insurance broker, whose wife played bridge with Anaïs. A dinner party was held, ostensibly in honour of Anaïs's sixty-fifth birthday, and the unwitting Lucette was strategically seated next to Bertrand, who mustered some of his old charm, entertaining her with stories from his student days (though tactfully omitting any mention of Camille). Lucette, then twenty-two, was a pretty girl, but shy and unworldly. She had suffered from childhood polio and, as a result of her repeated absences from school, had difficulty making friends. She must have been quite bowled over by the attentions of the handsome and sophisticated Bertrand. On account of her illness, she had spent a good deal of her youth immersed in books, but unlike the first Mme Barthelme she had no creative impulses of her own. After dinner, Bertrand invited her to view the collection of books in his father's study.

Whether he repeated his recital of Baudelaire is not known, but by the end of the evening it had been noted with satisfaction that the pair were wholly absorbed in each other's company. Courting Lucette did not unduly impinge on Bertrand's work schedule. The following Sunday, he took her on a drive to Ferrette, where they took a walk around the ruins of the château and enjoyed a rustic lunch at a local inn. Lucette was smitten, and when Bertrand proposed three months later, she immediately accepted.

Bertrand's second wedding was a modest affair, with a reception at the family home attended by the town's dignitaries. Anaïs, who had never taken to the moody Camille, was delighted both by her son's timid new wife and by her own role in engineering the union. Married life was dull, but Lucette seemed quite content. The drives to country inns soon ceased, and Lucette adapted to her role, which was as much as companion to her mother-in-law than as a wife. In 1963, when Lucette finally produced a son, she had fulfilled her purpose and Bertrand lost all interest in her.

Gorski made his way from the drawing room into the hall. Here, perhaps because they were not in the immediate vicinity of the widow, the guests' conversation was more animated. As he moved through the gathering, Gorski heard little mention of Bertrand Barthelme. Marc Tarrou arrived. Gorski had not spotted him at the funeral itself, though he would certainly have done so given that Tarrou was wearing a royal blue suit with a heavy sheen to the fabric. His hair was wet and he ran both hands through it, before shaking them onto the floor. His shoes were caked with the pale clay mud from the car park of his factory. He accepted a glass of sherry, knocked it back and took a second, not omitting to give a wink to the girl standing behind the trestle table. He spotted Gorski standing at the foot of the stairs.

'Ah, my favourite cop, still sniffing around?' he bellowed. 'Unearthed any of the old rogue's secrets yet?' He wiped his wet hands on the rump of his trousers. 'Couldn't get parked near the place,' he said. 'Who'd have thought the old bastard was so popular, ha ha.'

A few heads turned towards them. Tarrou leaned in close to Gorski's ear. 'Thought I should pay my respects to the merry widow,' he whispered.

Gorski indicated where Lucette could be found. Tarrou slapped him on the shoulder and strode off towards the drawing room. Gorski took the opportunity to slip up the stairs. The housekeeper observed him from the kitchen doorway, but did not intervene. The door to Barthelme's study was ajar. Gorski hesitated for a moment, his head inclined towards the door. When it was clear that there was no one inside, he entered and closed the door softly behind him. He would prefer not to have to explain his presence there—even to the housekeeper. The air was stale with the smell of pipe tobacco. He ran his fingers along the cracked leather of the armchair at the window. Next to it, on a small table, was a copy of *Eugénie Grandet*, a bookmark about two-thirds of the way through. Gorski picked it up and absent-mindedly turned it over in his hands. He had never read Balzac. He replaced the book on the table and stepped towards the desk, all this performed in a casual manner, as if to suggest to anyone observing him that he had no real purpose in mind. He sat down in the swivel chair. It was a handsome desk, with a few precisely positioned objects arranged on the green leather surface. Gorski opened each of the drawers in turn. Aside from a few miscellaneous items of stationery in one, they were empty. Just as he slid the last drawer closed, the door clicked open. Gorski started. He expected to see Mme Thérèse, but instead it was his father-in-law.

'Thought I might find you in here, Georges,' he said. 'I saw you sneak off up the stairs.'

Gorski was about to protest that he had not been 'sneaking off' anywhere, but instead only said, 'Paul,' by way of greeting. He stood up behind the desk. He assumed M. Keller had come to discuss his marital situation; perhaps even to reprimand him for standing up to Céline. Gorski had never been sure to what extent he owed his position as Chief of Police to his father-in-law's influence. The matter had never been explicitly discussed, but over the years certain comments had been made from which Gorski understood that he was expected to feel indebted to the mayor. Now and again after Sunday lunch, Keller had invited Gorski to smoke a cigar with him in the gardens of the family home and quizzed him about ongoing investigations. It was never clear where Keller got his information, but he no doubt had his sources inside the police station; Schmitt, most likely. Gorski resented these intrusions, but he never had the mettle to rebuff Keller's enquiries, and their exchanges never failed to make him feel sullied.

Keller pulled off his sash and tossed it onto the chair by the window. 'Ridiculous piece of tat,' he said. 'But got to put on a bit of a show for the citizenry, eh?'

He pointed to the cabinet behind Gorski and strode across the room. He retrieved a decanter of sherry, removed the stopper and sniffed it. 'Who knows how long this has been in here,' he said.

Gorski had the impression that he was familiar with the layout of the room. Perhaps he and Barthelme had spent evenings here discussing the affairs of the town.

He poured two good-sized measures and handed one to Gorski. They touched glasses. Keller took a couple of steps back and leant against the desk.

'So I hear you've been looking into old Barthelme's affairs,' he said.

The phrase *I hear* was, of course, quite calculated. Gorski did not say anything. Keller raised his eyebrows questioningly. Gorski felt resentful, as if he had been summoned to the headmaster's study and accused of a misdemeanour he had not committed.

'Obviously I'm obliged to investigate the circumstances of his death,' he said eventually.

Keller feigned surprise. 'Are you?' he said. 'I was given to understand that it was no more than an accident.' He made it sound as though he was expressing no more than innocent curiosity.

Gorski said nothing.

'Of course, I know you, Georges,' he continued cheerily. 'You can't discuss an ongoing investigation and all that. Fair enough. It's merely that certain people are concerned that'—he measured his words—'that you might be over-reaching yourself.'

'I don't know what you mean,' said Gorski flatly.

'Oh, I think you do, Georges,' said Keller, his breezy manner suddenly gone. He drained his glass and smacked his lips together. He shrugged his shoulders. He had said what he had come to say. 'Best get back to the party,' he said.

As he reached the door, he realised he had forgotten his sash. He folded it up and stuffed it into the pocket of his jacket. 'Oh and do try and sort things out with Céline,' he said from the doorway. 'She's driving Hélène and me up the wall.'

When he had gone, Gorski exhaled slowly. He put his hand to his forehead and massaged his temples. He refilled his glass and stood listening to the murmur of the reception below. He would have liked to pass a few minutes alone with Lucette, but there was no indication that the party was going to end imminently. If he was honest with himself, it was this, rather than any expectation that he would discover anything new about Barthelme that had motivated him to attend the funeral.

Seventeen

As soon as Raymond stepped out of the limousine with his mother, he realised that the central character in the funeral was not his father, but himself. The coffin was little more than a prop around which the performance was enacted. Lucette took his hand as they walked up the path to the little chapel. She looked rather fetching in her mourning outfit. Raymond had never seen her dressed in black before. The little cop was standing by the roadside smoking a cigarette. By the low wall bounding the churchyard, a labourer was leaning on his shovel next to a freshly dug grave. He removed his cap as Raymond and his mother passed. It was beginning to rain in fat, heavy drops. Those waiting by the entrance to the chapel bowed their heads solemnly. Raymond mimicked the gesture. He felt ludicrous. But his new suit helped. He had tried it on the previous night in front of the mirror on the inside of his wardrobe door. His mother insisted that he come down to the drawing room to show it off. She had wiped a tear from her eye and told him that he looked very handsome. Even Thérèse looked impressed. He felt like an actor donning his costume for opening night.

The priest greeted them. Lucette, who as far as Raymond knew had no religious beliefs, made a little curtsey. Inside, he was surprised to see that every pew was occupied. This for his father, who rarely socialised, never had a good word for anyone, and whom no one liked. Even the town's mayor was there, bedecked in a silly ceremonial sash. As the official stepped forward to offer his condolences, Raymond noticed that the flies of his trousers were not properly closed.

During the service, Raymond made no effort to listen to the priest's words. Lucette kept his hand clasped in her lap, but she did not appear particularly upset. She seemed to have forgiven him for lying about the 200 francs. The incident had not been mentioned again. Raymond gazed at the coffin containing his father's remains. He was aware of the gravity of the occasion, but he felt little other than the cold draught emanating from the back of the building. From an early age, Raymond had learned to expect little from his father. If he had given up trying to please him, it was to protect himself from the disappointment he felt when his approval was not forthcoming. Once, when he was seven or eight years old, the family had driven to Ferrette for lunch. It was a Sunday in spring, Easter perhaps. It was a warm afternoon and they had eaten on the terrace of an inn, overlooking some gardens. Raymond's father was in an unusually expansive mood. He took off his jacket and ordered a second carafe of white wine. Raymond noticed the droplets of water that formed on the cold glass, and Bertrand explained the process of condensation. After lunch, his parents remained at the table and Raymond had been allowed to go and play. At the foot of the gardens was a large pond. Raymond was delighted to find that it was populated by frogs and newts. Forgetting that he was in his smartest outfit, he lay on his belly at the edge of the water with his hand outstretched. Eventually, a bullfrog alighted it on it. Raymond observed the pulsing of its throat and the slow blink of it eyes. Its skin was no thicker than membrane. Seized by an idea, he ran to the kitchens of the inn and asked for a jar, which he filled with pond water and a globule of spawn. There was a stagnant pool at the foot of the garden. He would turn it into his own colony of frogs. When the time came to leave, his father asked what he had behind his back. He took the jar from Raymond and poured the contents onto the verge at the side of the car park. He then instructed his son to return the jar to the kitchens. Raymond howled all the way home. By the time they reached the house, his throat hurt and his breath came to him in fitful gasps. Later, his father came to his room. He sat down on the edge of the bed and explained that the tadpoles would only have died and he had not wanted Raymond to become attached to them. He then placed his hand on his son's forehead and said he was sorry.

The following day, Maître Barthelme returned home from work later than usual. He presented Raymond with a jar of frogspawn, which he must have returned to the inn to collect. Raymond looked at him uncertainly. He did not want this jar of spawn. It was not the spawn that he had collected. The frogs that grew from it would not be his frogs. Nevertheless, he understood that his father was making a gesture of atonement. He thanked him and accepted the jar. When he held it up to his face, he saw that it contained not only spawn, but also some hatched tadpoles. After the evening meal, his father helped him clear some of the slime from the pond at the foot of the garden and filled it with fresh water. Finally, Raymond tipped the contents of the jar into the pool and watched the tadpoles weave their way into their new home. For the next week, Raymond spent every hour after school crouched over the pond, observing his charges. The spawn melted away and was replaced by more tadpoles. A few days later, however, the tadpoles were all dead, eaten by birds or floating on the surface of the water.

As Raymond stared at the coffin, he felt a sob rise in his chest. He swallowed hard to suppress it. His throat convulsed as if he was about to vomit. His eyes stung. He clenched his jaw shut. It was as though, even at the final moment, his father was besting him. He realised he was gripping his mother's hand more tightly. A tear rolled down his cheek. He closed his eyes. Lucette drew him towards her. Raymond was furious with himself. He imagined his father mocking him. Lucette handed him a little embroidered handkerchief, which she produced from her purse and which she herself had not required.

It was easier back at the house. As his parents had not been in the habit of entertaining, Raymond had never seen the house so full. Thérèse made a great display of overseeing the staff that had been hired for the occasion. After an initial period during which various mourners had shaken his hand and offered their condolences, no one paid any attention to him. He could drink as much sherry as he liked. The atmosphere grew less sombre as the guests forgot the reason for the gathering. Raymond wandered from the hall into the drawing room. He was quite taken with one of the waitresses. She was a dark-haired girl with brown eyes. She went about her business efficiently but without any hint of subservience. Raymond observed her increasingly openly, but she was oblivious to him, or pretended to be. He became convinced that she was wilfully ignoring him. He followed her into the hall when she went to replenish her tray. She disappeared into the kitchen and, as Thérèse was guarding the doorway, he did not have the nerve to follow her. He drifted among the guests in the hall, waiting for her to come back out. He was surprised to see the mayor emerge from his father's study onto the landing on the first floor. He could not imagine what he might have been doing there. The official paused at the foot of the staircase to shake hands with a group of guests. No one paid any attention to Raymond as he ascended the stairs.

He pushed open the door to the study. The little cop was standing behind the desk drinking a glass of sherry.

'What are you doing in here?' Raymond was emboldened by the alcohol he had consumed.

Gorski ignored his question, replying instead that he had been impressed by the way Raymond had conducted himself at the funeral. He made no reply. Gorski walked across the room and closed the door.

'Since you're here, this is as good a time as any to have a little chat,' he said.

He guided Raymond to the armchair by the window. Raymond was reluctant to comply. He did not like the fact that

Gorski had been at his father's desk and was now behaving with a proprietorial air. Nevertheless, he sat down as directed. Gorski leaned against the wood panelling by the window. Raymond felt that he was going to be subjected to an interrogation. Gorski took out a packet of cigarettes and lit one, before offering the packet to Raymond, who shook his head.

'You don't smoke?'

'No,' said Raymond.

'The stains on your fingers contradict you,' said Gorski.

Raymond could not prevent himself from glancing down at his hands to verify the detective's observation. Gorski said nothing for a few moments. He let the ash from his cigarette fall onto the exposed floorboards where the carpet did not reach the wall.

'I thought you might be able to shed some light on your father's movements on the night of the accident,' he said eventually.

Raymond looked at him. The cop wore a placid expression that he found quite irritating. 'Why should I?' he said.

Gorski pushed himself off the wall and stood facing Raymond.

'You know, of course, that your father was not where he claimed to be on the night of the accident; that this little club of his was no more than a fiction.' He rotated the hand holding his cigarette as he spoke. 'You must have given some thought as to where he might have been.'

Raymond shrugged. 'I haven't.'

Gorski tipped his head to the side to suggest that he was surprised by Raymond's answer; or that he did not believe him. 'You'll forgive me if I say I find that a little implausible,' he said.

It then struck Raymond—of course!—that the detective had just then been going through the drawers of his father's desk and had found the scrap of paper he had so carefully replaced. Perhaps he knew everything about his trips to Rue Saint-Fiacre; about the theft of the 200 francs; and about the stolen knife now stashed in his satchel at the foot of the wardrobe in his bedroom next door. If Gorski did not confront him, it was to give him the opportunity to come clean of his own accord.

'My father and I were not close,' he said. He resented making even this admission to the cop, who, to his mind, had no business delving into his father's affairs.

'Be that as it may,' said Gorski, 'I would have thought you'd be curious about where he must have been all these evenings.'

'Even if I did, I know no more about it than you.'

'I haven't said anything about what I know or don't know,' said Gorski mildly. 'We're talking about what you know.'

'Well, I don't know anything.'

Was there any real reason he did not mention his trips to Mulhouse? Except that it amounted to nothing. So what if he had found an address on a scrap of paper in his father's desk? There was no evidence that he had ever been there. But there was something else: if his father had chosen to keep a part of his life secret, was that not his right? Despite everything, Raymond felt a certain loyalty to him. And, certainly, he felt no compunction to divulge anything to this wheedling cop.

Gorski was watching him closely. 'You never had any conversation that made you suspect that your father was not being truthful about his whereabouts on Tuesday evenings?'

'No.'

'You never suspected that he might have a mistress or anything of that sort?'

Raymond gave a little laugh through his nose, in order to give the impression that he thought the idea ridiculous.

'He never let slip anything about having been to Strasbourg?'

'To Strasbourg? No.'

Gorski pounced. 'Somewhere else then?'

Raymond felt his cheeks colouring. He was being cornered. 'Do you think if my father had had a mistress somewhere, he would have told me about it?'

Gorski shook his head. 'No,' he said, 'but when three people live under the same roof, it's very difficult to hide things from each other. Tell me, for example, does your mother know you smoke?'

'I don't know,' said Raymond.

'Let me put it another way: do you conceal the fact that you smoke from her?'

Raymond said nothing.

Gorski nodded in acknowledgement of this tacit admission. 'But your mother will have noticed those stains on your fingers. If she has never mentioned it, it's because the two of you choose to conspire in a lie. It's perfectly normal. People like to avoid confrontation. Without ever having spoken about it, she knows you smoke and you know she knows you smoke, but you choose not to acknowledge it. In a similar way, I believe that you know where your father was on the night of his death.'

'I don't,' said Raymond, a little too forcefully. He made to get up from his seat, but Gorski gave a little shake of his head and held out the palm of his hand. He took a step closer to Raymond, so that their feet were almost touching.

'I've been a detective since before you were born,' he said. 'I've spent twenty-five years being lied to. And when you make a living being lied to, you get pretty good at reading the signs. For example, a few moments ago, when I asked if your father had ever let anything slip about being in Strasbourg, you cast your eyes upwards to the left. Of course, you were not aware of it. It's a reflex. And you know what it told me? It told me that you were lying; that you were recalling something you then declined to share with me. Now, that's fine. Strictly speaking, you're not obliged to tell me anything. But don't think I don't know you're hiding something.'

He took a step back to indicate that Raymond could leave.

'I don't care what you think.'

'If you didn't care what I thought, you wouldn't lie to me.' He gave a tight little smile. 'I'll be keeping my eye on you,' he said as Raymond departed.

Raymond leant on the balustrade of the landing. His forehead was pulsing. The guests below continued to enjoy the hospitality. The atmosphere had grown quite convivial. A man in a blue suit was telling a lewd joke to a group of men gathered around the trestle table where the food had been set out. It was clear that no one was in the least bit concerned that his father was dead. The pretty waitress was standing in the doorway of the drawing room with a bored expression on her face.

Eighteen

SCHMITT DID NOT LOOK UP from his paper. 'Your boyfriend rang again,' he said. Gorski did not have to ask whom he was referring to. Lambert had been trying to get hold of him for three days. If Gorski had not returned his calls, it was partly out of a desire to demonstrate that he was not at his beck and call, but also because he did not want to admit that he had so far failed to examine Bertrand Barthelme's financial records. Gorski nodded curtly in response to Schmitt's remark, then instructed him to have Roland sent to his office.

'You mean the Foal?' Schmitt replied.

Gorski looked at him blankly. 'The Foal?' he repeated.

'That's what everyone calls him.'

'Ah, yes, the Foal. Of course,' Gorski said, not wishing to appear that he was not in on the joke.

In his office, Gorski dialled the number of the Strasbourg station even before he had sat down. He could not plausibly postpone calling him any longer. The receptionist put his call through to the detective division. As he waited, Gorski held the receiver in the crook of his neck and struggled out of his raincoat. He threw it over the back of his chair and took out a cigarette and lit it. Eventually a voice informed him that Lambert was out of the office. It was the ideal outcome. Gorski replaced the receiver in its trestle and sat down. The reports into Barthelme's death were still on his desk. Gorski pondered going over their pages again. Sometimes a salient detail only revealed itself on a third or fourth reading.

Someone gave a little cough in the doorway. Gorski looked up. It was Roland.

'I didn't know if I should just—' he began. 'I didn't want to interrupt your call.' He was nervous, no doubt anticipating that he was to be reprimanded for some misdemeanour. He did indeed look like a foal. He had a narrow, equine face, eyes too far apart. His legs were long and gangly and looked as though they might give way beneath him at any moment. His distinctive features were not ideal for the task Gorski had in mind, but that couldn't be helped.

Gorski told him to close the door and have a seat. He offered the young *gendarme* a cigarette, which he declined. Roland seemed reluctant to sit in the presence of his superior, but he eventually did so. His uniform was immaculate. Gorski was aware of how easy it would be to intimidate him. He had the twitchy demeanour of one eager to please. Whenever Gorski saw him in the communal areas of the station, he looked ill at ease. He liked him.

'You recall the errand you ran for me recently?' Gorski began.

'Yes.' Roland spoke tentatively.

'During the drive, did you speak to Madame Barthelme or her son?'

Roland shook his head. 'Barely a word. I didn't think—' He still appeared to assume he had done something wrong.

Gorski stubbed out his cigarette. He asked how old Roland was.

'Twenty-three.'

'I expect you'd like to be a detective some day.'

Roland replied that he would.

'Have you had much training in surveillance?' Gorski asked.

'A little.'

Gorski then asked him to describe Raymond Barthelme. This he did with great accuracy, even down to the colour of his eyes and the clothes he had been wearing.

'That's very impressive,' said Gorski.

Roland looked down at his hands. 'I always imagine that I might be called to give evidence in a trial, so I try to commit as much as I can to memory.'

Gorski smiled. He recognised himself in the earnest young cop. He instructed Roland to go home and change into an inconspicuous outfit. Until otherwise instructed he was to shadow Raymond Barthelme.

'Call the station every three or four hours. If I'm not here, you can report to Schmitt, but don't mention Barthelme by name. Refer to him as "the subject".'

Roland was clearly delighted at this elevation in his duties. He nodded vigorously and assured Gorski of his discretion.

With Roland dismissed, Gorski remained seated at his desk. He ran his fingers over the manila cover of Bertrand Barthelme's post-mortem. He was intrigued by what he had learned of Barthelme's previous life. There was no denying that his colourful past in the city where the murder of Veronique Marchal had taken place made him a more plausible suspect. The coldness—cruelty even—that characterised his relations with his wife also made it easier to conceive of him engaging in the arcane sexual practices indicated by the ties on Mlle Marchal's bed. And he was, furthermore, clearly a man capable of deceit. None of this, however, constituted evidence, and if Gorski was reluctant to share his information with Lambert, it was because he was all too aware that his Strasbourg colleague would not be so chary. As things stood, the only evidence came from Weismann's claim to have seen Barthelme in the stairwell. Lambert might have no reservations about the manner in which he had extracted this information, but Gorski could imagine the ease with which even the most mediocre advocate would demolish the historian's testimony. And yet, Gorski could hardly place the blame at Lambert's door. It had been he, after all, who had first posited Barthelme as a suspect. On one point, however, Lambert was correct. If Barthelme had been a client of Veronique Marchal, it was likely that there would be some evidence among his financial records. By the same logic, however, if his accounts showed no unexplained transactions, it would constitute a blow to Lambert's flimsy edifice.

It was clear that, without the necessary paperwork, Maître Corbeil would never permit access to his former partner's records. Instead, Gorski made a tour of the town's banks. It was the sort of methodical task he relished, and in a certain way he would have been disappointed if he had been successful at the first attempt. The Société Générale on Rue de Mulhouse was the third establishment he visited. Gorski explained the nature of his visit to the teller. She was a plain girl with a skin complaint, barely out of her teens. She appeared quite flustered by the sight of Gorski's police ID, as if it was she that was being accused of something. She obediently consulted a set of box files arrayed along the wall behind her, before confirming that the bank did indeed hold Bertrand Barthelme's accounts.

'But I'm not sure I'm allowed to—' She looked embarrassed.

Her name was written on a badge pinned to her blouse.

'Why don't you let me speak to the manager, Carolyn?' Gorski said.

'Yes, of course,' she said, relieved to have the matter taken out of her hands. A few moments later, the girl showed Gorski into the office behind the counter. A sharp-faced woman in her forties was standing behind the desk. A pair of spectacles hung on a chain around her neck. Gorski recalled her from a previous case.

'Mademoiselle Givskov,' he said. 'I must congratulate you on your promotion.'

'It's merely an interim position,' she replied curtly.

'Ah,' said Gorski. Although she had not invited him to do so, he sat down in the chair opposite the desk. Mlle Givskov remained standing.

'I'm afraid your request is quite irregular, Inspector,' she said.

'Yes, it is,' he replied cheerfully. 'Are you in a hurry to leave?'

Mlle Givskov sat down warily, as though the chair was set

above a trap door. She was not an easy woman to charm.

'I suppose you must have known Maître Barthelme,' Gorski said.

'As a client only,' she replied, as if he had insinuated that she had been his mistress.

'Nevertheless, you'll be aware that he was a prominent figure in Saint-Louis. Perhaps you also know his wife, Lucette?'

'I don't.'

'A charming woman,' said Gorski. 'Devastated by her husband's death, of course.' He then—aware of the theatricality of the act—drew his chair a little closer to Mlle Givskov's desk and explained in hushed tones that there were certain circumstances surrounding the solicitor's death that required investigation. Lucette Barthelme was anxious that these enquiries be made as discreetly as possible, and Gorski did not wish to add to the distress of her bereavement.

'Of course,' he said, 'it would be perfectly straightforward to obtain the necessary paperwork, but that would entail bringing things into the public domain, which is precisely what Madame Barthelme wishes to avoid.'

Mlle Givskov looked at him for a few moments. She was wearing a light blue cardigan over her blouse. The wool was frayed at the cuff of the left sleeve. Gorski gave her his most encouraging smile.

'Perhaps if I knew something of these circumstances you have alluded to,' she said.

Gorski smiled apologetically. 'I'd be only too happy to tell you, were it not for the need to avoid unnecessary scandal.'

The word 'scandal' sparked a quickly suppressed flicker of excitement in Mlle's Givskov's eyes. The fingers of her right hand began to worry at the sleeve of her cardigan.

'Such a request would require the approval of head office,' she said. Gorski was familiar with the formal tone people adopted when they did not wish to take responsibility for their own actions. She reached towards the telephone on the desk.

Gorski pursed his lips and shook his head slowly.

'I think this is something best kept between the two of us,' he said. 'I can assure you that you will have the gratitude of Lucette Barthelme, and I'm sure you would wish to retain her family's business. I don't imagine head office would look favourably on the loss of such a valuable account should you wish to make your current position permanent.'

Gorski clasped his hands on his lap. There was no need to say anything further. Mlle Givskov stood up and walked across to a filing cabinet on the left of the room. She put on her reading glasses and retrieved a file from the top drawer. She turned her head away as she handed it to Gorski, as if disavowing any knowledge of what she was doing.

'Thank you,' he said. He would like to have been left alone to peruse its contents, but he did not want to further test Mlle Givskov's patience. She flitted around the office, occupying herself with non-existent tasks. It did not take more than a few seconds for Gorski to find what he hoped he would not. At half past eleven on the day of the accident, Bertrand Barthelme had made a sizeable withdrawal from his account. Gorski turned the pages of the document. Similar amounts, increasing slightly over the years, had been withdrawn for as long as the records went back.

Mlle Givskov was watching him from the corner of her eye.

'I see that Maître Barthelme made a regular withdrawal every Tuesday,' he said. 'Did he make these in person?'

Mlle Givskov did not look at him as she spoke. 'No one else was authorised to access the account.'

Gorski thanked her and stood up. As she showed him out, he said, loudly enough to be heard by the other members of staff: 'Of course, I understand your need to protect your client's privacy, mademoiselle.'

A look of gratitude passed across her face.

Outside on the pavement, Gorski exhaled slowly and walked the short distance back to the *gendarmerie*. In his office he sat staring at the telephone, the fingers of his right hand beating a rhythm on the surface of his desk. He lit a cigarette and stood at the window smoking. The old woman with the battered shopping trolley was walking slowly past on the opposite pavement. She paused for a moment, as if utterly exhausted. Then she continued on her way. Gorski watched her until she was out of sight. He reminded himself that it had been some days since he had called in on his mother.

He resumed his seat. He had no choice but to share his findings with Lambert. Not to do so would constitute withholding evidence from an investigation. Why then did he feel a certain reticence? Only a week or so ago, nothing would have pleased him more than to furnish his city colleague with information about a murder case. Yet the feeling that he was setting in motion a chain of events over which he could exert no control gnawed at him. It was important to think through the implications of what he had discovered. He himself had leapt to the conclusion that Barthelme had made the withdrawals to pay Veronique Marchal for her services. But this was no more than a supposition. The money might have been used for any number of purposes. Lambert would be untroubled by such scepticism, however.

Gorski stubbed out his cigarette. While there was no question of keeping the information to himself, he was under no obligation to call Lambert immediately. He would pay a visit to his mother first. It would give him a little time to settle his thoughts.

As he exited the station, a dark blue BMW pulled into a reserved parking space in front of the building. Gorski paused at the top of the steps. Lambert got out of the car.

'Georges!' he exclaimed. 'I didn't expect a welcoming committee. So this is the kingdom of Saint-Louis.'

Gorski glanced around. There was something incongruous about seeing Lambert in the drab surroundings of Rue de Mulhouse, as if an exotic animal had escaped from a zoo and was prowling the streets. Gorski stepped onto the pavement and the two men shook hands.

'I hadn't heard from you, so I thought I'd drive down and get a feel for the place. You on your way somewhere?'

Gorski did not have the wherewithal to invent something. 'I was just going to visit my mother,' he said, immediately regretting his words. 'She hasn't been so well,' he added, as if this would somehow make it an acceptable mid-afternoon activity for a chief of police.

'Well, I'm sure Old Mother Gorski can wait, eh? Where's good for a tête-à-tête around here?'

Gorski had no desire to explain to Schmitt or anyone else what a Strasbourg detective was doing in Saint-Louis. He quickly led Lambert off in the direction of Le Pot. He took out a cigarette and lit it.

Lambert did the same. Everything about the Strasbourg cop had the effect of accentuating the drabness of Saint-Louis. His face was too handsome, his suit too well cut, his hair too blonde and well groomed. Even his confident gait contributed to the effect that he was an actor striding through a badly painted backdrop. In Saint-Louis, it is frowned upon to have good posture, or to walk purposefully along the street as if one is in control of one's own destiny. If asked how one's business is doing, the customary response is: 'Could be worse,' or 'Just about surviving.' Anything more upbeat is reckoned insufferable boasting. Personal achievements should be dismissed as flukery and mentioned only after an extended period of arm-twisting. It is regarded as a great misfortune for one's daughter to be too pretty or one's son to be too bright. In Saint-Louis, as in all provincial backwaters, the inhabitants are most comfortable with failure. Success serves only to remind the citizenry of their own shortcomings and is thus to be enthusiastically resented. So, as Gorski struggled to keep up with the striding figure of Lambert, he suffered a two-fold embarrassment: first, because he did not wish to be seen with someone who blatantly did not subscribe to the local ideology of mediocrity; and, second, because it was humbling to have Lambert behold the modest nature of his dominion.

So it was a relief to enter Le Pot, a place that made a virtue of its shabbiness. Lambert did not, of course, enter with the customary meekness of the establishment's habitués, and the eyes of all those present were immediately drawn to him. The company consisted of three people: the proprietor, Yves, who was dressed with his customary disregard for the norms of hygiene; Lemerre, whose shop was a few doors down the street and who regularly dropped in for a snifter between customers; and a middle-aged former schoolteacher who never ordinarily raised his eyes from his copy of *L'Alsace*.

'Afternoon, gentlemen,' Lambert declared in jovial fashion, recklessly laying waste to the code of silence that existed between them. The schoolteacher lowered his eyes to his newspaper. Lemerre turned to Yves and muttered something under his breath. Yves returned Lambert's greeting with an impassive upward nod of his head and asked what they would have.

'Two beers,' Gorski replied, in an attempt to gain some control of the situation.

'Splendid place, Georges,' said Lambert as they took a seat at Gorski's regular table. 'I bet you never have to pay for a drink in here.'

Gorski put his hand to his forehead, as if shielding his eyes from the sun. He lit another cigarette and offered the packet to Lambert. Yves placed two glasses of beer on the table between them.

'Give me one of these hotdogs while you're at it,' Lambert said, gesturing towards the boiler on the counter from which Le Pot derived its characteristic aroma. 'And be a good fellow and turn the radio on, will you? We're hoping to have a private conversation here.'

Yves looked at him implacably, before responding with a single word: 'Mustard?'

'Plenty of it,' said Lambert. 'And one for my friend here as well. He looks hungry.'

To Gorski's surprise, Yves did as he was asked and the tinny sound of pop music did a little to alleviate the atmosphere in the bar.

Gorski leant over the table. 'So what brings you down here?' he asked.

Lambert took a slug of his beer. 'You didn't return my calls,' he said. 'I was beginning to think you were avoiding me.'

'Not at all,' said Gorski. 'I've been busy.'

'Busy visiting your mother?' said Lambert.

The hotdogs arrived on paper plates. Lambert took a large bite. Mustard spilled down his chin. He wiped it off with the back of his hand.

'How's the case?' Gorski asked.

Lambert gave a long, slow nod. His mouth was full.

'I paid another visit to our friend the professor,' he said.

'Oh, yes?' Gorski wondered aloud if Weismann had had second thoughts about seeing Barthelme.

Lambert swallowed the remains of his hotdog and wiped his mouth with the paper napkin provided. He leaned in close over the table and for the first time lowered his voice. Over his shoulder, Gorski could see Lemerre and Yves straining to hear what he was saying.

'Quite the contrary, Georges. I got him hook, line and sinker. Reeled the old onanist in like a fat carp. You ever do any fishing, Georges? We should do that sometime.' He drained the contents of his glass and gestured to Yves for two more. 'I told him straight out. "Prof," I said, "We've got someone else in the frame. You can forget about the guy you saw on the stairs." And, of course, you could see he was devastated. He got me by the sleeve and dragged me into his apartment. "But Inspector," he told me, "since you were here last, it's all come back. I saw him several times. I even spoke to him in the stairwell now and again." So I asked him what they talked about. "Just good day, nothing more than that," he said. "But it was certainly the man in the photograph. A tall man with a beard." I told him that it didn't matter, that we had someone else, but he wouldn't let it go. Then he told me he'd seen Barthelme on the night of the murder. He couldn't swear to the time, but he had happened to be looking out of his window and saw him enter the building. Even then I insisted that it didn't matter, so he told me that he had gone to his front door and looked through the peephole and seen Barthelme go into Mlle Marchal's apartment. Hook, line and sinker, ha ha.'

Gorski forced a laugh.

'And'—Lambert gave Gorski a theatrical wink—'it turns out that the good lawyer stopped by in our favourite bar after the deed for a quick snifter to calm his nerves. My friend Bob recognised him straightaway when I showed him his picture. Knocked back two brandies at the counter. Apparently he appeared to be in a state of some agitation.'

Gorski felt nauseous.

'So that's my news. How about you give me yours. How's the money trail?'

Gorski related in some detail how Barthelme's papers had been gathered up by his business partner and how he had, for the sake of discretion, thought it wise to keep matters off the record for the time being.

'I like your thinking,' put in Lambert.

Gorski took his time relating how he had traced Barthelme's accounts to the Société Général, hoping that by burying the solicitor's withdrawals in a mass of irrelevant detail, he might somehow lessen their significance. He eventually delivered the salient piece of information with a dismissive shrug.

Lambert looked at him with a grin. 'You're a character, Georges, I'll give you that.'

Gorski shrugged. 'There's no evidence to suggest that this money ended up in Mademoiselle Marchal's hands,' he said.

'No evidence?' Lambert laughed. 'So, what do you think he was doing with it? He wasn't donating it to the local orphanage, was he?'

Gorski spread his hands. 'I just can't help thinking—' he began.

'That's your problem right there, Georges,' said Lambert. 'Too much of this.' He tapped the side of his forehead exactly the way Ribéry used to. 'You think police work is all about brainwork. It's not. It's about telling a story. A judge is no different from a child. He wants to hear a good story, and when you tell him one he'll fit the evidence to suit it. I've see it a hundred times.' He raised his index finger. 'Let's take an example: a man—upstanding pillar of the community—has been married for twenty years. But if you scratch the surface, you find that all is not as it seems. He and his wife keep separate rooms. Once a week he withdraws a large sum of money, tells his wife he is dining with business associates, and drives to a neighbouring city where he indulges his more exotic desires with an accommodating mistress. But then something goes wrong. Perhaps the accommodating mistress gets greedy, or perhaps their activities simply get out of hand, but in any case, our pillar of the community strangles her and makes his escape. As he drives home, he's overcome with remorse and steers his car off the road. Or, perhaps, in his state of agitation, he loses control of his vehicle. It doesn't much matter. But you cannot tell me, Georges, that that is not a compelling story.' He spread his large hands across the table to suggest that his version of events was indisputable.

'It might be a compelling story,' said Gorski, 'but that doesn't make it true.'

Lambert gave a dismissive laugh through his nose. He raised his glass and took a good swallow, leaving a caterpillar of foam on his top lip. A few minutes later, he scraped back his chair. He went into the WC and urinated noisily. In his absence, Gorski hastily paid Yves for the beers. He walked Lambert back to his car and the two men parted on the street. Gorski waited until he had driven off, before continuing along Rue de Mulhouse.

It was perfectly obvious why the proprietor of Lambert's little bar would do whatever was asked of him. What Gorski found harder to understand was why Weismann would do the same. Of course, Gorski had come across his share of busybodies over the years, the sort who felt that involvement in a police investigation endowed them with a certain status; a status that increased in relation to the gravity of the crime in question. But Gorski had never known a witness to so enthusiastically fabricate evidence in a murder case. Perhaps Weismann was simply a highly suggestible individual, who, in his eagerness to curry favour with Lambert, had come to believe the truth of what he was saying. Or perhaps—and if one was dispassionate, the idea could not be entirely dismissed—Weismann really had seen Barthelme on the night in question. Gorski, however, remained unconvinced and was left gloomily pondering the historian's motives.

Nineteen

Two days after his father's funeral, Raymond stood at the counter in the kitchen, eating his breakfast. Since the theft of the banknotes, he and Thérèse had ceased to exchange even the most rudimentary pleasantries. Thérèse no longer kept the housekeeping money in the jar on the counter. The silence between them was uncomfortable. Raymond could easily have taken his breakfast elsewhere, but to do so would be an admission of defeat. Instead he deliberately lingered over his bread and jam, while Thérèse made it clear from her movements and the little snorting noises she made through her nose that he was in her way. Perhaps tomorrow, Raymond thought, he would test her resolve by passing some remarks about the weather or some similarly banal topic.

It was not clear, even to Raymond himself, at what point he abandoned the pretence that he was going to attend school. He had checked his timetable for the day and had packed the relevant books in his satchel, piling them on top of the knife without which he could no longer imagine leaving the house. Before he left, he looked in on his mother, who was sitting up against a pile of pillows, her breakfast tray on her lap. He had not explicitly stated that he was going to school, but the act of putting his head around the door at that time in the morning was enough to suggest that he was. She seemed pleased that they were returning to their normal routine. She asked him to sit with her for a moment, which he did, before looking at his watch and saying that he had better be going. She wished him a good day. As he left the room, she suggested that he invite Yvette to join them for an evening meal sometime soon. Raymond assured her that he would.

Raymond kept up his charade as far as the corner of Rue des Trois Rois. He had walked there purposefully, so that no one who observed him would have any doubt about his intentions. Normally when he called on Yvette, she would arrive at the door stuffing books into her bag, or brushing her teeth. She was never ready and sometimes she invited him to wait in the tiny hallway of the house. The Arnaud household was in a perpetual state of good-humoured disorder. Members of the family were constantly demanding where such-and-such an item had got to. Yvette's father often squeezed past Raymond, stuffing a croissant in his mouth on his way out to work. Her mother would sit on the narrow stairway to fasten her shoes or quickly run a comb through her hair. Raymond had always enjoyed these moments. The contrast with his own home, where everything was in its proper place and no voices were ever raised, could not have been greater.

Raymond wondered whether, now that the formalities of his father's death were over, Yvette would be expecting him to call for her. Given his recent conduct, however, there was no reason why she should. He loitered at the end of the street. It would be a simple matter to walk the hundred metres or so and press the Arnaud's doorbell. Raymond was sure that Yvette would forgive his shabby behaviour: it could all be explained away by the shock of his father's death. Wasn't it only natural that he had gone off the rails a bit? Raymond was struck by a yearning for everything to be as it had been before; for the two of them to set off together for school, him stepping off the kerb as they passed Mme Beck, the florist, who even at that early hour would be arranging her wares on the pavement outside her shop. He knew that this was impossible, however.

The idea that he could return to school and sit meekly at the back of the class while his teachers scratched their lessons on the blackboard was laughable. Such things belonged to a world he had left behind. Still, it took an effort of will not to follow his old routine and call at the Arnaud's.

After a few minutes, Yvette emerged. She looked as she always did, both slightly harassed and utterly self-possessed. She had her satchel over one shoulder and a linen bag of books in her left hand. Her hair was tousled. Raymond half-hoped that she would look in his direction—he had made no attempt to conceal himself—and he would raise his arm in greeting and trot along the pavement to where she was waiting. But she did not do so. Instead, she set off in the direction of school, giving every appearance of having forgotten that he existed.

Raymond recalled the first time he and Yvette had walked to school together. The previous afternoon he had lingered at the corner of Rue des Trois Rois, before following at a safe distance to see exactly where she lived. He was aware that he could simply have asked her address, but he had already hatched a plan to make his presence outside her house the following day appear to be a matter of chance. It was a plan that protected him both from potential rejection and from the necessity to reveal the longing he felt to spend every possible moment in her company. He was thirteen years old. Thus, the following day, he concealed himself in a doorway a few metres from the Arnaud's house. When Yvette emerged, he called out to her as if he just happened to be passing. She seemed pleased to see him. Raymond suspected that she had seen through his subterfuge, but she kept her thoughts to herself. From that point, it had been a natural progression to actually calling for her. Was he not in any case passing her house?

So it was with a melancholic feeling that Raymond followed Yvette along Rue des Trois Rois. Mme Beck was setting out her blooms and Yvette paused for a moment to exchange a few words with her. Once she had turned onto Rue de Mulhouse, it was busy enough for Raymond to gain a little ground on her. There was a light drizzle in the air. Yvette was wearing her green plastic mac with the tear in the right shoulder, but she did not bother to put up the hood. Raymond wondered if, even now, he might catch up with her and accompany her to school. Then, as they approached Avenue Général de Gaulle, he saw Stéphane waiting at the corner. Stéphane spotted Yvette and raised his hand in greeting. Raymond stepped into the doorway of a travel agent's. He watched as they greeted each other before continuing towards school. Stéphane took the linen bag of books from Yvette's hand and slung it over his shoulder. Raymond and Yvette had often bumped into Stéphane on the way to school, but until now it had never been an arrangement between them. Raymond followed them as far as the corner of Rue des Vosges and watched them recede into the distance.

It was when he turned back towards Rue de Mulhouse that he saw the young man with the long face for the first time. Or rather, it was not for the first time, because he recognised him from somewhere. In a town like Saint-Louis, there was nothing unusual in this. In all likelihood, the young man was simply on his way to work, and Raymond would have seen him as he made his way to school. This did not, however, explain why he appeared startled and immediately became absorbed in the advertisements in the travel agency that Raymond had passed a few moments before. As Raymond retraced his steps, the young man kept his gaze fixed on the window. He had a distinctive profile and large, protruding eyes. After he passed, Raymond glanced over his shoulder several times. Eventually, the young man moved off in the opposite direction.

There was no question of returning home and explaining to his mother that he had, after all, decided not to go to school. So Raymond spent the day wandering the streets of his home town. This was not as straightforward an activity as it might be in a larger town or city. Raymond had never been to Paris, but he imagined that one could, if one so desired, stroll endlessly through the city without ever passing down the same street twice, and without ever attracting a curious glance. In a town like Saint-Louis, one could not simply roam the streets without drawing suspicious looks from residents and shopkeepers. How, Raymond wondered, would he reply if someone were to stop him and demand to know where he was going? In a town devoid of points of interest, to say that one is merely drifting is entirely implausible and likely to attract the attention of the police.

So Raymond kept up a good pace. He glanced regularly at his watch to suggest to anyone observing him that he was late for an appointment. As he did not wish to run into the little cop, he took a detour to avoid passing the *gendarmerie*. He re-joined Rue de Mulhouse and walked as far as the roundabout before turning into Rue de Village-Neuf. Unless one was a postman or a resident, there could be no possible reason for walking along such a street, but he could hardly abruptly turn back without engaging in an elaborate pantomime for the benefit of those he imagined were observing him from behind the shutters of the fake-beamed houses that lined the street. He would continue as far as the canal and then take the route he had so often walked with Yvette.

He felt less conspicuous on the canal path. It was a common route for dog walkers or those simply out for a leisurely stroll. There was a bench a short distance ahead. He would pause there for a while. He enjoyed staring at the still green water of the canal. As he neared the bench, however, a man of about forty approached from the opposite direction. He did not appear to be walking a dog and Raymond wondered what reason he could have for being there. The canal was rumoured locally to be the haunt of homosexuals. Raymond never imagined that any such activities actually took place there—certainly he had never seen anything of that nature—but he and Yvette had often passed remarks about single men they had seen frequenting the path.

On account of his feminine features, boys at school often taunted Raymond with certain epithets. He never responded to their insults. They could think what they liked. And he had, in case, learned from experience that engaging in such arguments quickly escalated into fisticuffs. He decided against stopping at the bench. The man might take it as an invitation to engage him in conversation. The drizzle was in any case turning to rain. When they were about thirty metres apart, the man turned his back on Raymond and gave a short whistle. A spaniel emerged from the undergrowth, its undercarriage wet with mud. As he passed, the man bid Raymond good day.

By the time Raymond completed his circuit of the town, it was only a little after eleven o'clock. He found himself back at the junction where Yvette had met Stéphane. Inasmuch as Saint-Louis could be said to have a centre, this was it. The young man he had seen earlier was sheltering under the awning of a shop. He was smoking a cigarette, holding it between his thumb and middle finger in a way that suggested he had only recently acquired the habit.

Raymond could not go on aimlessly pacing the streets. Nor did he want to face the recriminating looks of the waitress in Café des Vosges. He continued walking. Not wishing to loiter at the junction advertising his indecision, he turned into a side street, and for the second time that day walked in the direction of the railway station. There was a little bar in the street. It had no windows and held the promise of anonymity. Raymond passed it on the opposite pavement. It was not even clear if it was open, and he did not have the courage to try the door. Instead, he remembered the café on Rue de la Gare. He walked directly there and entered with a purposeful air. It was a place where travellers killed a little time before catching their trains. It was larger than it appeared from the outside. An old woman sat near the door, a glass of brandy or rum on the table in front of her. Her head sat low on her shoulders, as if she had fallen asleep or died. Raymond imagined that she had chosen that table because she did not have the strength to venture any further into the café. There were no other customers. The proprietor was leaning on the counter, reading a newspaper. Raymond took a seat in the corner furthest from the door. He was glad to sit down. And he was pleased with his choice of establishment. No one knew him here. After some moments, the proprietor approached. He appeared wholly uninterested in his new customer. When Raymond ordered a tea, he gave the briefest nod and retreated to the counter. The lace of his left shoe was loose and he scuffed his feet on the linoleum, as though he was aware of the fact, but was too lazy to bend down and tie it. When the man returned, carrying a tray with a smoked glass cup and a pot of boiling water, Raymond was sure he was going to trip up and scald them both. The untied lace was shorter than the distance the man covered with each step, so it was unlikely that in the normal course of things he would step on it. Even so, Raymond felt that he would find such a discrepancy in the tightness of his shoes vexatious. His own shoes had become quite soggy during the walk along the canal. The cuffs of his trousers were spattered with mud. Later, when the café had become a little busier, he thought that one of the regular customers might draw the proprietor's attention to the offending lace, but no one did. He tried to divert his attention elsewhere, but Raymond became increasingly agitated by the scuffing of the man's shoes on the floor. It caused a tightening in his throat, so that it became impossible to enjoy his tea. Each time the man brought a drink to a customer's table, Raymond felt a tension build in his chest. He had planned to linger in the café for as long as possible, but in the end he could not stand it any longer. He placed some coins on the table and left.

At precisely half past three, Raymond found himself outside the school gates. The rain had stopped. Raymond's shoes had almost dried. He stood among the trees on the opposite side of the road. He did not want any of his teachers to see him. He only wanted to see Yvette. He had not formulated any kind of plan, but when he saw her everything would fall into place. Even if she was with Stéphane, he was sure that she would understand that he wanted to be alone with her. Perhaps they would go to the Café des Vosges together. Or perhaps they would proceed directly to her home. Yvette's parents rarely disturbed them and never entered Yvette's tiny bedroom without first knocking.

Twenty minutes passed, then thirty. The schoolyard was empty before Yvette emerged from the direction of the school library. She was with Stéphane. She no longer had the linen bag of books she had been carrying earlier. Stéphane was circling his hands in the way that he did when he was telling a story or had embarked on one of his speeches. Although they were still a good hundred metres away, Raymond could see that Yvette was listening intently. Then, when Stéphane finished speaking, Yvette reached her left hand across her body and grasped Stéphane's hand. Her right hand gripped the crook of his elbow. Stéphane inclined his head so that his cheek nestled in Yvette's hair. They proceeded across the schoolyard in this manner for several paces. Raymond stepped back behind the trunk of the tree he had been leaning on. Then Stéphane released his arm from Yvette's grip and put it round her shoulders. They exited the schoolyard and crossed the road, passing only metres from where Raymond had concealed himself. Yvette had slipped her right hand into the back pocket of Stéphane's jeans. Raymond suppressed a convulsion in his stomach.

He waited a few moments before following them as they walked towards Avenue Général de Gaulle. They were sure to go into the Café des Vosges and, after allowing a suitable amount of time to elapse, Raymond could join them. But to say what? To do what? He and Yvette had never walked along the street in such a manner. Their relationship had been a private affair; it was not something to be paraded for the entertainment of all and sundry. Or perhaps there had been nothing to parade. Perhaps the special understanding he had with Yvette—an understanding he had never felt the need to articulate—existed only in his own head.

Yvette and Stéphane did not enter the Café des Vosges. Nor did they part, as Raymond expected them to, at the corner of Avenue Général de Gaulle and Rue de Mulhouse. Instead they continued, still locked in their ridiculous embrace, to the corner of Rue des Trois Rois. They turned into Yvette's street. Raymond was no more than twenty or thirty metres behind. Then, just beyond Mme Beck's shop, Yvette halted and gently pushed Stéphane against the wall of the house next door to her own. She pushed herself onto tiptoes and kissed him on the mouth. Raymond could see that her legs were parted slightly. With her left hand she gripped Stéphane's buttock, drawing his groin towards hers.

Neither of them had so much as glanced in his direction, but Raymond was sure that they knew he was there, and that their lewd performance was entirely for his benefit. He thought briefly of the knife that still nestled beneath the books in his satchel. He saw himself pacing towards the couple and silently pushing the blade into Stéphane's midriff. But he did no such thing. Instead, he turned and ran in the opposite direction, almost colliding with the long-faced young man as he did so.

Twenty

IT HAD COME AS SOMETHING of a surprise to Gorski that Céline had suggested meeting in the Restaurant de la Cloche. As far as he knew, she had never set foot in the place. The restaurant did the greater part of its trade during the day, so in the evenings it was frequented mostly by widowers, bachelors and the itinerant salesmen for whom it was more economical to spend the night in Saint-Louis than across the border in Switzerland. Members of this latter group generally bolted their meals before creeping off to find a more dimly lit refuge in which to get sozzled. A few brought paperback Westerns or detective novels, which they propped against their carafes of house wine. Gorski envied these men. They could eat and drink what they wanted. They were not obliged to inform anyone of their whereabouts. They were answerable to no one. Yet Gorski knew he would not survive a month of such an existence. He was wedded to Saint-Louis; to the little patch of unremarkable streets where his position as chief of police accorded him a status he barely merited.

Marie greeted him warmly.

'Will you be dining with us tonight, Inspector?' she asked.

She showed him to the table in the corner: Ribéry's table. Gorski did not object. It placed him furthest from the other patrons and was thus best suited to a private conversation. Pasteur was engaged in a game of cards with Lemerre and his cronies at the table by the door. He acknowledged Gorski's arrival with an upward motion of his head.

Gorski removed his raincoat and folded it on the banquette next to him. He had been sure to arrive a few minutes early. Marie lingered by his table. There were no menus in the Restaurant de la Cloche. The dishes on offer were displayed on a pair of large blackboards attached to the wall opposite the door. It was Pasteur's first order of business each morning to climb the rickety stepladder kept behind the door of the WC to chalk up the day's specials.

Gorski explained that as he was expecting someone, he would wait a little before ordering. Marie adopted an enquiring expression.

'My wife,' said Gorski. For some reason he lowered his voice.

Marie made no attempt to conceal her delight. She bustled off to the hulking dresser in which the crockery and napkins were kept, returning with a linen tablecloth, which she expertly spread over the waxcloth deemed adequate for less worthy guests. She set two places with various glasses, holding them to the light to verify their spotlessness. When she finished she stood back and surveyed her handiwork with satisfaction.

Gorski leaned back on the banquette, embarrassed by this special treatment. The other customers watched resentfully. A man in his mid-thirties, sitting at the table next to the WC, looked up from his newspaper. He was wearing a dark suit. His tie was loosened at the collar. Gorski made an apologetic face, but the man merely returned his gaze to his paper. The Restaurant de la Cloche was not the sort of place where one fell into conversation with one's neighbours. Marie did her best to foster a convivial atmosphere, pausing now and again to pass a few pleasantries with regulars and strangers alike, but conversations were generally held in hushed tones. It would not have been Gorski's venue of choice to discuss his marital difficulties, but he had been in no position to demur.

Marie suggested an aperitif.

Gorski had already drunk three beers in Le Pot and he was about to order another, but he thought better of it. Céline did not approve of beer at the dinner table. There was no point unnecessarily provoking her. He asked for a glass of wine.

Marie proposed a bottle. 'We have a lovely Riesling,' she said.

Gorski acquiesced. Marie returned with the wine and displayed the label to Gorski before opening it. She poured a drop into the green-stemmed glass on the table and waited for Gorski's approval.

'I'm sure it will be to Madame Gorski's liking,' she said.

It was curious to hear his wife referred to in this way. Céline generally used her maiden name. It was, she had frequently explained, nothing personal. It was simply that 'Gorski' did not strike the right note for someone in the fashion business. Nonetheless, it never failed to irk Gorski to hear his wife refer to herself as Mme Keller.

The wine was dreadfully sweet. Céline would pull a face when she tried it.

'Perfect,' he said with a tight smile. Marie filled his glass.

She appeared eager to continue the conversation, but as Gorski said nothing more she retreated to the counter. Lemerre placed his cards face down on the table and made his way across the room towards the WC. He paused at Gorski's table and offered him a limp handshake.

'Are we expecting Cleopatra herself?' he said, gesturing towards the table.

Gorski forced a little laugh.

'Ah, a clandestine rendezvous. Don't worry, Inspector,' he said, tapping the side of his nose, 'your secret's safe with me.'

Gorski was about to respond to the effect that if he were planning a tryst, he would hardly conduct it in the Restaurant de la Cloche, but he checked himself. It was never wise to allow oneself to be drawn into conversation with Lemerre.

'And keep an eye on these shysters over there, will you?' he went on, jabbing his thumb towards his cronies. 'You should join us for a game sometime.'

'Thanks,' said Gorski, 'but I'm not much of a player.'

'Doesn't stop these jokers,' the hairdresser responded, before waddling off, his left hand clamped to his belt as if holding in a hernia.

Gorski sipped his wine. He glanced at his watch beneath the table. It was only ten past eight. It did not greatly concern Gorski that Céline was late. She had never been greatly concerned by punctuality, and if she chose to make him wait for a few minutes she would be quite justified. Nevertheless, he began to feel self-conscious. The salesman by the WC ordered coffee. The other remaining diners were already eating dessert. The card players by the door glanced over regularly and leant across their table to exchange whispered comments. Were it not for the fact that it would hurt Marie's feelings, he would suggest going somewhere else as soon as Céline arrived. He poured himself a second glass of wine.

In any case, perhaps his wife's tardiness was no bad thing. Gorski had barely even thought about what he wanted to say. Despite the fact that it had been Céline who had walked out, he was the one expected to make a show of contrition. The problem was that he did not feel contrite. He simply did not know what he had done wrong. Of course, he was not successful or ambitious enough for Céline. But that was hardly a failing on his part. He was who he was. He was not overly concerned with what car he drove or where his suits were made. He was more comfortable scoffing a hotdog at a Formica table in Le Pot than he was in the fashionable eateries of Strasbourg. The fact was, he and Céline had little in common, yet it was his role to implore her to come back and undertake to change his ways. But he did not want to change his ways. Nor did he want to Céline to change hers. For all her snobbishness and silly pretensions, he liked her. He missed her when she was not there. Then there was Clémence to consider, although she gave no indication of being anything other than indifferent to her parents' squabbles. In any case, she would be off to college in a couple of years and would barely give them a passing thought.

Gorski poured himself a third glass. From behind the counter, Marie glanced up at the clock and gave him a concerned look. Gorski found himself thinking about Lucette Barthelme. If he had declined her invitation to lunch, it was not on account of any investigative protocol. It was because he still thought of himself as married. He *was* still married, and the attraction he felt for the widow discomfited him, as if it already constituted a betrayal. Prior to his marriage, Gorski had not had a great deal of experience with women. He was not well versed in the dumb-show of flirtation. Nevertheless, there was something in the way Lucette looked at him—in her girlish giggling and the nervous way she smoked—which suggested the attraction was mutual. He swilled down more wine; what did it matter if Céline thought he was drunk? It was her fault for being late. Perhaps he *would* have lunch with Lucette Barthelme. He recalled the way in which her nightdress had been disarrayed around her breasts.

His thoughts were interrupted by Marie. She was too tactful to imply that Mme Gorski might not be coming, but she did remind him that the kitchen would soon be closing. It was only then that Gorski understood Céline's ruse. Why else would she have suggested meeting at the Restaurant de la Cloche? It was the most public place in which to humiliate him. He almost admired her guile. He admitted defeat and ordered *steak-frites*.

'Will you order for madame?'

'She must have been delayed,' he said weakly.

Gorski did not begrudge Céline her little act of vengeance, but he was sorry that Marie had been disappointed. She would have enjoyed dropping into conversation that the mayor's daughter was now patronising her establishment.

She returned a few minutes later and placed his food in front of him. The steak was smothered in a thick pepper sauce. Gorski thanked her. He had almost finished the bottle of Riesling. He told Marie to bring him a glass of beer. The card players were watching the unfolding drama with amusement.

'Is a guy supposed to go hungry?' Gorski said with a theatrical shrug.

'More trouble than they're worth,' replied Lemerre, before adding a crude generalisation about the female sex. Marie fixed him with a stern look.

Gorski turned his attention to his steak. It was good. He finished it in a few minutes and mopped up the sauce with his *frites*. Afterwards he would go to Le Pot for a couple more beers to settle his stomach. To hell with Céline. He was better off without her. Had he not lived his whole life doing what other people expected him to do? Maybe now it was time he did what *he* wanted. If he wanted to drink himself senseless, he would. And if he wanted to jump into bed with the widow, who was to stop him? Perhaps he would call on her that very night.

Gorski was wiping the remains of the pepper sauce from the corners of his mouth when Céline made her appearance. It was nine o'clock. She was wearing an ankle-length fur coat that her father had recently bought her. She pushed through the velvet drapes that protected the restaurant from draughts in the winter months and surveyed the room. She did not see Gorski—or pretended not to—obliging him to raise his hand to attract her attention. She strode across to his table, the heels of her shoes clacking on the floor. This exotic sound caused those who had not witnessed her entrance to look up from their drinks. Lemerre tipped his head to the side to better observe her progress, then pursing his lips, slowly nodded his approval.

She looked at the bottle on the table and then at Gorski's empty plate.

'How good of you to wait for me,' she said.

Gorski got up, knocking the table with his thigh. The wine bottle teetered for a moment, before Céline reached out and settled it. She allowed him to kiss her on both cheeks. In her heels, she was half a head taller than him.

He mumbled an apology. 'I assumed you weren't coming. The kitchen was closing.'

215

Céline looked at him. 'You're drunk,' she said.

Gorski shook his head, but he could not deny the evidence of the bottle in front of them. Marie arrived at the table. She greeted Céline effusively and took her coat. She was wearing a grey knitted dress, which clung to her austere figure. Gorski felt a twinge of desire.

'How nice to see you, madame,' said Marie. 'I hope everything will be to your satisfaction.' Marie beamed at her, then turned to Gorski with an approving look. It was a look he had seen countless times over the years, a look that plainly stated: *You've done well for yourself, haven't you?*

'I'm sure it will be,' said Céline graciously. 'I'm only sorry I'm too late to sample your cooking.'

Marie looked aghast. 'Not at all, madame,' she said. 'My husband will be happy to prepare whatever you want.'

Céline said sweetly that she did not want to be any trouble.

'It will be no trouble at all,' said Marie.

Gorski resumed his seat. Céline ordered a vodka tonic and sat down opposite him. Marie took Céline's coat to the stand by the door, pausing for a moment to admire it, before returning to the table. Céline asked Gorski what he had had and said she would have the same. Marie conveyed her order to Pasteur, who glanced up at the large clock on the wall. A whispered conversation ensued, which ended with the proprietor throwing his cards on the table and disappearing into the kitchen.

Céline watched the little scene with amusement, before turning back to Gorski.

'So this is the famous Restaurant de la Cloche,' she said. 'I must say I find it rather charming.'

She went on to pass comment on the various fixtures and fittings in a voice loud enough for everyone to hear. Her hair was disarrayed, as if she had left the house in a hurry. Perhaps her lateness had merely been an oversight. She seemed in high spirits. Gorski wondered if she had forgiven him for standing her up. Maybe there was not really so much wrong with their relationship. Had there ever been a couple who did not aggravate each other after twenty years of marriage? Perhaps, after all, the faults were on his side. As time had gone on, he had made less and less effort to accommodate Céline's wishes. His reluctance to attend social events meant that she had long since ceased asking him. When they were first married, they had often gone to the cinema and sometimes even to the theatre in Strasbourg. Gorski had never enjoyed the theatre—he could not get over the essential absurdity of watching people pretend to be someone they were not—but that was not the point. The point was that they had done things together. Gorski recalled an occasion ten or more years ago. He had been reading a newspaper at the kitchen table after their evening meal.

'There's a new production of *The Misanthrope* at the Théâtre National,' Céline had said. 'I thought we might go.'

Gorski recalled that he had not even looked up from his paper. 'Do we have to?' he had replied wearily.

'Of course we don't have to,' Céline had said angrily.

And that had been that. They had not been to the theatre since. And so it had been with all their social activities. Maybe all that was required was a little effort on his part.

Marie arrived with Céline's steak. Gorski wished her *bon appétit* and she tucked in with gusto. Despite her slim figure, Céline had never been picky about food.

What can I say? she liked to declare. *I have a high metabolism.* And if there were any men within earshot, she would add saucily: *For everything!*

Gorski watched her eat. She had a wide mouth and prominent high cheekbones. She flashed her eyes towards him.

'I'm starved,' she said through a mouthful of steak. Good table manners—along with punctuality—were, she maintained, the preserve of the lower classes.

'How is it?' Gorski asked.

She nodded, a little surprised perhaps. 'Not bad.'

Gorski felt encouraged by this amicable little exchange.

'Perhaps we should do this more often.' He was aware that he was slurring.

Céline stopped eating for a moment. She looked at him. 'Don't you think it's a little late for that, my dear?' she said.

He took a swallow of beer.

Aside from Lemerre and his cronies and the salesman, the restaurant was now empty. Céline speared a number of *frites* on her fork and stuffed them into her mouth.

Gorski was too drunk to care that everyone was now listening to their conversation.

'Perhaps we just need to make a little more effort,' he said. Céline glanced up from her food. 'What I mean is that *I* need to make a little more effort. I've been neglectful, I know,' he said.

'Oh, Georges,' she said in a tone that suggested she was addressing a silly schoolboy.

He leaned across the table. 'I'm serious,' he said.

Céline looked at him. She appeared to be weighing up what he had said. Marie cleared her plate. It had not taken Céline more than five minutes to polish it off. She ordered a slice of Black Forest gâteau.

'And for you?' Marie asked.

Gorski shook his head. He had never had a sweet tooth, but he immediately regretted his decision. Of course he should have dessert. They should eat dessert together like a functioning married couple. Nevertheless, he had the feeling that everything was going to be all right, and that from now on it would become their custom to visit the Restaurant de la Cloche every Thursday evening. They would eat *steak-frites* and Black Forest gâteau and reminisce about the time they had almost separated.

Céline lit a cigarette and leaned back in her rickety chair. Gorski castigated himself for not offering her the banquette; what a buffoon he was! Marie brought a large slice of gâteau topped with whipped cream and a preserved cherry.

'How delightful!' Céline proclaimed.

Marie suggested a glass of kirsch to accompany it. 'An excellent idea,' said Céline merrily. Gorski was beginning to suspect that she too was drunk. He had a strong urge to fuck her.

Pasteur had emerged from the kitchen and re-joined the men at the table by the door. They did not take up their cards, however, preferring instead to watch the spectacle in the corner of the restaurant. Céline put out her cigarette and started on the gâteau. For the sake of something to say, Gorski enquired after her parents.

Céline rolled her eyes. She swallowed a mouthful of cake.

'Maman's driving me up the wall. Papa, too,' she said. 'In fact, it's partly that I wanted to talk to you about.'

'Oh, yes?' Gorski felt a twinge of hope.

Céline took another spoonful of cake then turned to Marie, who was loitering by the dresser sorting cutlery. 'It's delicious, madame,' she said. Marie bowed her head in acknowledgement.

She turned back to Gorski, then said in an offhand manner: 'I've decided to move back to the house.'

Gorski could not help glancing round the restaurant to make sure everyone had heard. He stood up and, leaning across the table, put his arms around her shoulders. His tie dangled into her gâteau. 'That's wonderful,' he said. 'I'm very pleased.'

Céline put a hand on his chest and pushed him firmly back across the table. Gorski felt embarrassed by his drunken display of affection. Céline indicated that he had cream on his tie. He wiped it with his hand. Céline shook her head despairingly. When he had finished attending to his tie, he asked when she planned to return.

'As soon as practicable, I suppose,' she replied.

Gorski nodded vigorously. He reached across the table and placed his hand on hers.

She took another mouthful of dessert. 'Of course, I'll expect you to have made alternative arrangements by then.'

'Alternative arrangements?'

Céline gave a little shrug. 'To find somewhere else to live.'

Gorski cast his eyes towards the table. He withdrew his hand.

He felt nauseous.

'Of course,' he said.

Céline nodded, satisfied that agreement had been reached. She pushed away the remains of her dessert and stood up. Gorski looked at her helplessly.

'I do hope we can be amicable about this,' she said.

He nodded sadly. 'What about Clémence?' he said.

Céline looked him at quizzically, as though it was the first time she had considered the issue. 'You can see her whenever you want, of course. Assuming she wants to see you.'

Behind her, the card players had taken up their hands and were playing with studied concentration, affecting to have witnessed nothing of what had occurred. Gorski swallowed hard to prevent himself from vomiting.

Marie hurried over with Céline's fur and helped her on with it. It was only when Céline strode out the door that Gorski noticed pale clay mud spattered on her shoes and the hem of her coat.

Later, Gorski sat in Le Pot until Yves pulled down the shutter on the door. The salesman from the table next to the WC in the Restaurant de la Cloche was drinking whisky at the counter. Neither acknowledged the other's presence.

Twenty-one

RAYMOND PUSHED OPEN THE heavy wooden door of 13 Rue Saint-Fiacre. Inside, it was cool and dark. A little sunlight filtered through the filthy window on the first-floor landing. There was an aroma of simmering stock. It reminded him of the smell that often greeted him from the kitchen when he returned home from school. Raymond mounted the stairs, his right hand on the worn banister. As he climbed, the stairwell became lighter and warmer. He could not imagine his father's heavy tread on these steps. Nor could he imagine that he had ever entered any of the apartments behind the shabby doors that he now passed. He pressed the buzzer of the apartment on the second floor: Duval. For no particular reason he had decided that this was where Delph lived. *Delphine Duval* had a ring to it that none of the other names did. He had recited it under his breath on the train. His heart was beating quickly. Raymond passed his hand through his hair, pushing it back from his forehead. After a few moments, a woman spoke through the door: 'Who is it?' She had an attractive, low voice. Perhaps it was the woman with the green belted raincoat.

'I'm looking for Delph,' Raymond replied. There was a nervousness in his voice. He had not thought about what he was going to do or say. Only that he needed to see her.

'Delphine? She lives upstairs.'

'Thank you,' said Raymond. 'Which apartment?'

But the woman's footsteps were already retreating.

There was a large skylight above the top landing and several plastic basins had been positioned to catch dripping water. He knocked on the door to the left. There was silence and the sound of a shuffling walk, then the skittering sound of claws on floorboards. This was the apartment of the old woman with the wheezing pug who went out daily to buy her vegetables.

Raymond called an apology through the door. 'I'm looking for Delphine,' he said.

'Opposite,' the old woman replied through the door. Her steps receded. The dog barked half-heartedly. So it was Comte. Delphine Comte. He smiled at the notion that he had so convinced himself that her name was Duval. The woman he had spoken to on the telephone must be her mother. He knocked on the door. A few moments silence then, just as next door, the sound of footsteps. He recognised the voice of the woman immediately. 'One moment.' she called. 'Who is it?'

He heard the sound of a chain being slid into place. Raymond did not know how to reply. The door opened a few centimetres. The first thing Raymond noticed was how small the woman was. Her eyeline was only just above the door chain. He instinctively stepped back a pace, so as not to intimidate her.

'I'm sorry to disturb you,' said Raymond. 'I'm looking for Delph. For Delphine.'

Even before he finished his little speech, the woman's face had broken into a wide smile.

'You must be Raymond,' she said.

The door clicked closed and he heard the sound of the chain being unfastened. Raymond was confused, then pleased: Delph must have mentioned him to her mother. And not only that, she must have done so in favourable terms. The door opened and the woman was still smiling at him. She was around forty. Her eyes were blue and twinkling. A brightly coloured kimono was fastened around her waist. Around her neck was a pendant with some kind of Eastern symbol.

She held out a firm hand and said: 'I'm Irene. But, of course, you know that already.'

Raymond shook hands with her. Then she appeared to think better of this formal greeting and clasped his shoulders and kissed him on both cheeks. Her hair smelt of cinnamon or some other spice. She released him and invited him inside.

The tiny hallway was chaotic. Coats and jackets bulged from hooks. An overflowing shoe-rack prevented the door from opening fully. Raymond recognised the boots Delph had been wearing at Johnny's. The walls were crammed with Chinese and Indian prints in mismatched frames, some of an erotic nature. As soon as he entered, Raymond had had a strong sense of déjà vu. Perhaps it was the sound of the voice he had heard on the telephone.

Irene saw Raymond looking at a print on the wall. A couple were engaged in an acrobatic sexual act. Irene stood beside him.

'Are you interested in Oriental art?' she asked. 'We've so much to learn from each other, don't you think?'

Raymond did not know whether she meant the East and West or she and him. But he nodded earnestly. She led him through a beaded curtain into the kitchen. This room was every bit as cramped and cluttered as the hallway. Two large rubber plants stood sentry at the door. Along the window sill, herbs grew in a wooden box. Every surface was piled with magazines, sketch-books and letters. Above the stove, a shelf was stacked with boxes of tea. A small wooden table was set against the wall with three mismatched chairs. A cat was asleep on one. Raymond congratu-lated himself on correctly imagining this one detail. On the wall above the table was a large corkboard pinned with photographs, postcards and various notes.

The woman shooed away the cat and told Raymond to sit, which he did, placing his satchel on the floor by his feet. She put some water on the hob to boil. On the ceiling above her head was a brown tidemark, where at some point there must have been an ingress of water from the roof.

'You'll have some tea, won't you, Raymond?'

The situation was puzzling. Even if Delph had mentioned him, it hardly explained the warmth of the welcome he had received. The heel of his left foot was trembling, making the coins in the pocket of his trousers jangle. He put his hand on his knee to stop it. Despite his bewilderment, he could not help but find the woman charming.

'Yes,' he replied. When she gestured towards the array of boxes, he said that he would have whatever she was having. She pondered the assortment.

'I think this calls for ginseng,' she declared eventually.

Raymond watched her prepare the tea. She had a slender figure. Her robe was of black silk, with a pattern of dragons embroidered in red and gold. It was secured beneath her neat bosom with a silk tie. She flitted around the tiny space with precise, efficient movements.

'Is Delphine here?' It was perfectly obvious that she wasn't, but he wanted to remind her of the reason for his visit.

'Delphine? Oh, no.'

Raymond asked if she would be back soon.

Irene glanced at a clock on the wall. 'I don't imagine so. She'll be starting work.'

She placed the teapot on a cork mat on the table and fetched two cups from the drainer. She sat down and gazed fondly at Raymond.

She shook her head. 'You're so like him,' she said. She brushed a tear from her eye with the back of her index finger. Then it struck him: amid the rising aroma of ginseng and the herbs on the window sill, there was the dark tang of pipe tobacco.

Raymond got to his feet, knocking his chair against the wall behind him.

'He was here, wasn't he?'

'Of course,' said Irene. She smiled sympathetically. 'Isn't that why you've come?

'He was here the night of the accident?'

Irene glanced down at the table, nodded sadly. She began to pour out the tea, as if all this was no more than small talk. Her composure had a soothing effect on Raymond. He resumed his seat. The apartment now seemed pervaded by the aroma of his father's tobacco. And yet it was impossible to picture him—so stiff and formal—in this cosy, cluttered apartment. He couldn't stand disorder. Raymond looked at Irene Comte: his father's mistress. She did not seem in the least disconcerted by the situation. She sipped her tea, holding her cup in both hands, and sat back in her chair. Raymond gave a little shake of his head. Questions flitted through his mind, but he did not know if it was appropriate to ask them.

Instead, it was Irene who spoke: 'I knew as soon as you called that you'd come.'

'How did you know it was me?' said Raymond. He was embarrassed to recollect the stupid telephone call he had made.

Irene laughed. 'Raymond, you sound exactly like him. You look like him. You act like him.'

She reached across the table and, gripping him gently by the chin, turned his face to profile. 'That nose,' she said. Raymond jerked his head away, as if there was a fly on his face.

Irene laughed again. 'That's exactly what your father would have done.'

'Why didn't you say anything?' said Raymond. 'Why didn't you say who you were?'

Irene pursed her lips. She adopted a more serious tone. 'As I recall, you didn't give me much chance. And, in any case, your father never wanted you or your mother to know about me. It wasn't my place to tell you.'

'So he came here every Tuesday?'

'Every Tuesday.'

'And at other times?'

Irene shook her head sadly. 'Bertrand liked to keep things in their compartments. Even me.'

There was an ashtray on the table. Raymond took his cigarettes from his jacket pocket.

'May I?' he said.

'Of course.' When he had put the packet on the table, she took one and lit it. They looked at each other through the rising smoke. When it came down to it, it did not seem to matter much. Raymond rather liked the idea that his father had spent time with this agreeable woman. It was pleasant to be in this funny little apartment, with its curious smells and mishmash of junk. It could barely be more different from the house on Rue des Bois. He asked how long his father had been coming there.

Irene smiled her pleasant smile. 'A long time,' she said. 'Since before you were born.'

Raymond indicated that he would like to hear more. Irene blew out a long stream of smoke. He had the impression that she was not in the habit of smoking. She crossed her legs, rested her bare foot on Raymond's shin, and began talking.

She had been well aware of Bertrand's reputation when she started working for Barthelme & Corbeil. It was shortly after he remarried. For the first few months, he behaved very correctly. Then one afternoon, when Maître Corbeil had gone out to meet a client, Bertrand invited her for a drink. It was about time they got to know each other better, he had said.

'You have to remember, Raymond, that I was barely twenty. Your father was a very handsome man. And he had a certain way of looking at you. I was under no illusions about what he meant by a drink and in the event we went straight to the Hôtel Berlioz. There was no discussion. We both understood what we were doing.' Raymond walked past the Berlioz every day on the way to school.

After that, their liaisons became a more or less regular thing. If he sent her out on a certain errand, it was their code that she should go to the Berlioz and wait for him there. Afterwards, they might drink a bottle of wine on the tiny balcony of the room. It surprised her how unconcerned he was about the possibility of being seen, but passers-by never raised their eyes from the street below. 'He had,' she said, 'an air of invincibility about him.'

Irene told her story without a hint of bitterness, and as if it was all perfectly conventional.

'Of course, things changed when Delphine came along,' she continued. 'That was when he started coming here.'

Raymond felt a coldness creep over his skin.

'But what about her father, Delphine's father?' he said. 'Didn't he object?'

'Her father?' she repeated.

'Yes,' said Raymond.

It was Irene's turn to look confused.

'Bertrand is her father,' she said. '*Was* her father.'

Raymond stared at her. A sad expression passed across her face and she lowered her head. Raymond said nothing. Once, when he was ten or eleven years old, he had been cycling around the Petite Camargue when a low-hanging branch had struck him on the head and knocked him off his bicycle. He now felt a similar sensation. He had difficulty drawing breath. Irene took a paper handkerchief from a box on the table and blew her nose. When she looked up, she had tears in her eyes. Raymond gazed past her to the brightly coloured boxes of tea on the shelf. He had never seen so many varieties of tea. His father hated tea.

'I always wanted you and Delphine to meet,' Irene was saying. 'I suppose the one good thing about this, about the accident, is that you will.'

She seemed shocked when Raymond got to his feet. She asked him what the matter was. Raymond batted his mug across the table. The sudden movement sent the cat scurrying from the kitchen. Raymond snatched up his satchel and followed the cat from the room. He became tangled in the beaded curtain. Some of the cords came away in his flailing arms. Wooden beads scattered across the floor. Raymond freed himself and kicked over one of the rubber plants.

Irene stood in the middle of the kitchenette repeating his name in a soothing voice. He fumbled with the locks on the inside of the front door and then threw it open. He lost his footing on the first flight of stairs and landed on all fours on the landing below. The right knee of his corduroy trousers ripped. Irene called out to him from the doorway of the apartment, imploring him to come back. He put his fingers to where his forehead had struck the concrete. It was grazed, but there was no blood. He picked himself up and looked back at Irene. She extended an arm towards him and again appealed for him to come back inside. Raymond shouted an obscenity at her.

He careered down the remaining flights of stairs, threw open the main door and emerged from the darkness of the stairwell into Rue Saint-Fiacre. He came to a halt, confused, as if he had alighted on the platform of the wrong station. The philatelist was pulling down the metal shutters of his shop. He starting coughing and a cylinder of ash dropped from the cigarette that was hanging from his mouth. The young man with the long face who had followed him onto the train in Saint-Louis was standing in the arched entrance opposite, smoking a cigarette.

Twenty-two

GORSKI PARKED IN A SPACE A FEW streets to the west of Quai
Kellermann and got out of his car. He kept an even pace, not
wishing to draw attention to himself. In order to reduce the
possibility of running into Lambert, he approached Veronique
Marchal's building from the opposite side of the police station
in Rue de la Nuée-Bleue. Nevertheless, he was uneasy about
encroaching on Big Phil's turf. He reassured himself, however,
with the thought that a chance encounter was far less likely in a
city the size of Strasbourg than in his home town.

He paused at a kiosk to call the station in Saint-Louis. Earlier
that morning, Roland had called him to report—almost tear-
fully—that he had lost Raymond Barthelme. Gorski had been
dismayed, but he suppressed the urge to rebuke him, instructing
him only to do his best to find him.

Schmitt answered Gorski's call in his usual irritable tone and
went on to wearily relate that Roland had called in again to say
that the 'so-called subject' had been relocated and had gone to
the railway station.

'And do we know where he went?' Gorski asked.

'He didn't say.'

'When was this?'

'When was what?' Schmitt replied.

'That Roland called.'

'I don't know. Half an hour ago, maybe more. Do you expect

229

me to write everything down?'

Gorski hung up. He resisted the temptation to stop off for a snifter in the bar with the zinc counter, calculating that his presence there might well be reported back to Lambert, and proceeded directly to Mlle Marchal's block.

Even though he must have put his eye to the peephole— Gorski had seen it darken— Weismann opened the door on the chain. Gorski creased his face into a smile. The historian looked at him suspiciously.

'Inspector Lambert told me that I was not to discuss the case with anyone,' he said.

'Absolutely,' said Gorski. 'And I hope you haven't done so. However, given your great importance to the case, he asked me to go over the details of your evidence before you make your statement to the examining magistrate.'

His words had the desired effect and Weismann unfastened the chain. Gorski stepped inside. There was the usual powerful odour of cologne.

'You must forgive my circumspection, Monsieur—'

'Gorski,' he reminded him. 'Chief Inspector Gorski.'

'Ah, yes, Gorski,' he repeated, as if the name failed to meet with his approval.

Weismann led him into the study. The air there was stale. Gorski had the feeling that the windows had not been opened in years.

'I'm surprised you haven't had any journalists knocking on your door,' said Gorski.

'I have,' replied Weismann proudly. 'But I didn't utter a word to them.'

'Good man.'

As on the first occasion that Gorski was here, the two men stood awkwardly in the middle of the floor. Apart from the chair behind Weismann's desk, all the available seating was piled with books and papers.

'Of course, I understand that you're a busy man,' said Gorski. He picked up a book from the top of a pile and turned it over.

'An interesting period, I understand,' he said. 'I'm afraid I don't know a great deal about it.'

'It's quite fascinating,' said Weismann. 'But somewhat neglected. I assure you, Inspector, you are not alone in your ignorance.'

Weismann then embarked on a lecture on the history of the Alsace during the Reformation. The historian became quite lost in his monologue, retrieving books and papers as he spoke to illustrate his points. His enthusiasm for his subject was endearing. His initial wariness gave way to something approaching charm. After ten minutes or so, Gorski interrupted.

'I can certainly see why you are so renowned in your field,' he said.

Weismann smiled sadly. 'I'm afraid your colleague somewhat exaggerated my status,' he said. 'And vanity prevented me from correcting him. My work is published in monograph only.'

He tore open a box and handed Gorski a stapled pamphlet entitled *The Bundschuh Conspiracy*. 'No publisher has ever been interested in my work,' he said. 'My ideas are too controversial. It is my contention that the so-called Twelve Articles were in fact written by the Catholic hierarchy in order to legitimise the suppression of the peasantry.'

Gorski nodded seriously. He handed the pamphlet back to Weismann, but he waved it away. 'Please keep it,' he said. Then added sadly: 'I have boxes of them.'

Gorski thanked him. He took his notebook from the pocket of his jacket.

'My apologies, Inspector, I must have been boring you.'

Gorski assured him that he had not. 'Nevertheless—' he said. He turned the pages of his notebook. They contained no more than the notes he had made at the scene of the accident. Weismann now hastily cleared some papers from two chairs.

'I must apologise. I have forgotten my manners. I'm not used to entertaining guests.'

Gorski accepted the seat he was offered.

'And I must offer you a drink, Inspector.'

Gorski thanked him. Weismann produced a bottle of schnapps from the floor behind the desk. A pair of mismatched glasses were located on the window sill. Weismann gave them a cursory wipe with his shirtsleeve. He poured two measures and handed one to Gorski. Gorski took it and carefully set it on the floor by his feet. Weismann sat down. He knocked back his drink and appeared visibly revived.

'I wanted to go back to the first time you saw Maître Barthelme,' Gorski said.

'The first time?' said Weismann. His left leg was twitching and he placed his hand on his thigh to calm it.

'Yes,' said Gorski. 'It's important to establish how long he had been visiting Mademoiselle Marchal.'

Weismann wrung his hands and cast his eyes towards the ceiling. 'I'm not sure I could say with any certainty,' he said. 'Inspector Lambert was very clear that I shouldn't testify to anything I was unsure of. That I should stick to the facts.'

'That is sound advice,' said Gorski. 'But even if you can't recall the precise occasion when you first saw Maître Barthelme, perhaps you could say how long ago it was.'

Weismann looked troubled. Clearly he did not want to give an answer that might discredit his evidence. 'I saw him on the night of the murder. Isn't that all that matters? Inspector Lambert did not seem concerned with these details.'

Gorski smiled patiently. 'Which is precisely why he has asked me to go over them with you. My colleague would be the first to admit that he's sometimes guilty of taking a rather gung-ho attitude, but as these are questions the examining magistrate will put to you, it's important that we're prepared for them.' He used the first person plural advisedly. 'I'm sure, as a historian, you understand the need to build a case from a solid evidential base.'

Weismann seemed pleased with this comparison. 'Yes, of course,' he replied. 'But even so, it's hard to recall.'

'Nevertheless,' Gorski said, adopting a breezy tone, 'would

you say it was a matter of months or a matter of years?'

'Some years, I suppose,' Weismann said vaguely.

Gorski nodded and made a little note in his book. 'It's just a question of building up as full a picture of their relationship as possible.'

'Their relationship?'

'If, as you say, Maître Barthelme was a frequent visitor, then that would constitute a relationship, wouldn't you say?'

Weismann made a face. It seemed likely that he did not have much expertise in the sphere of human relationships. He decided it was time to refill his glass. Gorski had not as yet touched his drink.

'Of course, Mademoiselle Marchal had so many visitors I couldn't be sure. In any case, it's possible that he'd been visiting her long before I ever saw him.'

'Indeed,' said Gorski. He smiled reassuringly. 'Please understand, Monsieur Weismann, I'm not trying to trip you up. It's simply a question of making sure that you're clear in your own mind about what you saw.'

He tapped the page of his notebook with his pen.

'Now, this might be important,' he said thoughtfully. 'In any case, you're sure to be asked about it: on the night in question, when you saw Maître Barthelme enter Mademoiselle Marchal's apartment, what led you to go to your front door? You can't just have happened to be there.'

Weismann screwed up his face. 'As I explained before, I often mistook the sound of Mademoiselle Marchal's buzzer for my own.'

'Ah, yes,' said Gorski, as if he had forgotten this detail. 'And did you open the door or just look through the peephole?'

'I looked through the peephole,' he replied, as if this was somehow shameful. 'As I could see that the visitor was not for me, there was no need to open the door.'

'So before I came up, you must have heard me press your neighbour's buzzer?'

'As a matter of fact, I did,' he said.

Gorski nodded. He had done no such thing.

'I also need to ask about your own relationship with Mademoiselle Marchal.'

'I had no relationship with her,' Weismann said sharply. He had already finished his second measure of schnapps.

'You must have encountered one another in the stairwell now and then.'

'Now and again, perhaps,' said Weismann, 'but I would hardly describe that as a relationship.'

'Surely you must have exchanged a few pleasantries?'

'In passing only.'

'So you would not describe her as a friend?'

'I would not.'

'You never, say, invited her to your apartment?'

'Of course not. Why should I?'

'She was an attractive woman. What could be more natural for a bachelor like yourself than to invite her in for a cup of coffee or a little glass of schnapps? I daresay, if I was in your position, I might have tried my luck.'

'Well, I didn't,' said Weismann.

Gorski nodded placidly. 'And you are a handsome fellow yourself. Did she never invite you across the landing?'

'Certainly not.'

Gorski sighed, as if the truth had suddenly dawned on him. 'Ah,' he said, 'perhaps you are not that way inclined?'

'I'm not sure I understand what you mean,' said Weismann.

'Monsieur Weismann, I can assure you that your sexual inclinations are of no consequence to me.'

Weismann stood up. 'I'm not sure I see any purpose in continuing this conversation,' he said.

Gorski remained in his seat. 'My only interest is in understanding why an eligible fellow like yourself would have no interest in such an attractive neighbour.'

'I'm not a pansy,' he said. He had grown quite agitated.

Gorski nodded slowly. 'Of course not,' he said. 'Forgive me.' He suggested that Weismann sit down.

The historian filled his glass for a third time. His hands were shaking. Gorski didn't say anything for some moments.

'You must excuse me for putting these questions to you,' he said. 'I assure you that it's only to ensure your evidence is completely watertight. We don't want to let any discrepancies get in the way of a successful prosecution.'

Weismann resumed his seat. 'Of course not,' he muttered.

'So, just to be absolutely clear, you have never set foot in Veronique Marchal's apartment?'

'Never.'

Gorski nodded as if he was now satisfied. He took his own glass of schnapps from the floor and, holding it delicately between his thumb and middle finger, drained the contents. He then took a plastic evidence bag from the pocket of his raincoat and dropped the glass inside. Weismann watched him.

'I hope you don't mind if I keep hold of this,' he said. 'It's a mere formality. There is an unidentified print on a glass in Mademoiselle Marchal's apartment. This will help us to eliminate you from our enquiries.'

'But that's impossible,' Weismann blurted out, 'I—' He clamped his hand over his mouth.

'Yes, I know,' said Gorski, nodding slowly. He stood up and pushed the glass into the pocket of his coat. Weismann sat forward in his seat with his head in his hands. Gorski felt a little sorry for him. He wondered if the historian might be tempted to take his own life. He showed himself out of the apartment.

Outside in the street, he took the glass from his pocket and dropped it into a litter bin. On the way back to his car, he went into a bar, ordered a beer and put in a second call to Schmitt from the old-fashioned cabin in which the telephone was located.

Twenty-three

RAYMOND SET OFF IN THE direction of Le Convivial. His walk
quickly turned into a run. He felt unsteady on his feet, as if he
had been drinking. His head hurt. It was getting dark and he
had to shield his eyes from the headlights of passing cars. He had
no idea what he was going to do. He felt murderous. They had
conspired against him, the lot of them: his father, Irene, Gorski,
Yvette, Delph. Delph most of all. He felt a sudden fury towards
her. How could she not have known? What an idiot he had been
to allow himself to be drawn in!

He reached the junction where Delph had ambled so noncha-
lantly across the road. It was busy with late afternoon traffic.
He recalled the grubby scene in the backroom of Johnny's, his
risible attempts to thrust his limp penis between his sister's legs.
He rested his hand against a lamp post and doubled over. His
stomach convulsed, but nothing came up. He wiped his mouth
with the back of his hand. It would be a simple matter to step
off the kerb in front of a passing truck. Raymond imagined the
sound of brakes, the impact of the cab on his ribcage, his skull
cracking against the radiator. Then an easeful slump to the
ground. The texture of tarmac on his cheek, a pool of dark blood
forming around his head. Voices in a gathering crowd shouting
for an ambulance to be called. The driver protesting that there
was nothing he could do: the kid had just stepped out in front
of him.

The motion of the passing vehicles made him dizzy. He turned away from the road. The young man who had followed him onto the train was twenty metres or so behind, lingering outside a shop on the corner of Rue de Manège. As soon as Raymond had seen him making an inept attempt to conceal himself on the platform at Saint-Louis, he recalled Gorski's promise to keep an eye on him. Then he remembered the young cop who had driven his mother and him to the mortuary. He looked quite different in his civilian clothes, but Raymond was sure it was him. Raymond had waited until the very last moment to board the train. The young cop had followed suit, abandoning all pretence that he was not trailing him. Once in Mulhouse, Raymond had not looked over his shoulder again. So what if he was followed? If anything, it only heightened his sense that things were coming to a head.

He stepped off the kerb. A car braked sharply. The driver mouthed an expletive through the windscreen. Raymond gazed blankly at him and continued across the carriageway. He looked back across the road. The young cop was nowhere to be seen. Raymond paused on the opposite kerb, then spotted him tentatively picking his way through the cars. When he was sure that he had seen him, Raymond turned and ran along Rue de la Sinne until he came to a halt on the opposite side of the street to Le Convivial. He paced the pavement. What exactly did he intend to do? He wished he had never found the scrap of paper in his father's desk, never come to Mulhouse, never set eyes on Delph. He realised that he could—if he chose—continue along Rue de la Sinne, get on a train to Saint-Louis and return to the house on Rue des Bois as if nothing had happened. But that was out of the question. Something *had* happened. And it had happened without any exertion of will on his part. One thing had simply followed from another. And now here he was, pacing the pavement outside a bar that, until a few days ago, he would never have had the nerve to enter.

It was impossible to see beyond the reflections on the

plate-glass windows of the bar. Raymond patted the pockets of his jacket and realised he had left his cigarettes on Irene's kitchen table. He checked his satchel. It contained only his book and the knife. The young cop was only a short distance behind.

Raymond crossed the street and pushed open the glass door of the bar. The regulars were congregated around the tables by the door, just as they had been on his previous visit. Delph was nowhere to be seen. Raymond approached the counter. Dédé welcomed him with the curt upward nod of his head with which he greeted all his customers.

Raymond asked for a packet of Gitanes.

Dédé fetched the cigarettes and placed the box on the counter. He eyed Raymond impassively. 'Been in the wars?' he said.

Raymond looked blankly at him. Dédé gestured towards the graze on his forehead. Raymond instinctively raised his fingers to his brow.

'I fell down some stairs,' he said.

'That's what they all say,' said Dédé drily.

Raymond climbed onto a stool with some difficulty. He was swaying slightly. He could not just pay for the cigarettes and leave. He asked for a beer. Dédé weighed up whether to serve him. Then he shrugged to himself—what did he care if the kid was drunk?—and poured the drink. Raymond attempted to remove the cellophane from the packet of cigarettes, but his hands were shaking too violently to complete the task. When Dédé placed his beer on the counter, he took the packet and wordlessly unwrapped it. Raymond thanked him. He took one out and managed to light it. He swivelled on his stool and looked outside. The young cop was standing on the pavement. It pleased Raymond that whatever was going to happen would be witnessed; that there would be an official record which he was sure would absolve him of all responsibility.

He made a mental effort to properly take in his surroundings: the torn corners of the playbills plastered to the two pillars that informally divided the room; the singes on the floorboards by the bar where customers had ground out decades of cigarettes; Dédé's habit of stroking his little beard between his thumb and forefinger; the slow movement of the clock on the wall. The old man with the wattle entered the bar and shuffled to the counter. His slippers made a sound on the floor like wood being sanded. Raymond could hear the wheeze of his shallow breathing. Dédé placed a glass of rum on the bar. The old coot stared at it for some moments, both hands gripping the brass railing of the bar as if summoning a reserve of strength, then knocked it back. He delved in his trouser pocket for a coin and slapped it noisily down on the counter. He turned to Raymond and looked him up and down with a disdainful expression, then left without a word. Raymond's gaze followed him out of the bar. The regulars resembled an audience awaiting the curtain of a play. The pockmarked man who had given Raymond directions was among them. He nodded a greeting. Only the two chess players, intent on their game, seemed oblivious to Raymond's presence. The clock ticked towards the hour.

Delph emerged from the door marked *WC Femmes*.

'Hello, Raymond,' she said. 'What brings you here?' She did not seem disconcerted to see him.

Despite everything, Raymond felt a pang of desire in his groin. 'I need to talk to you,' he said.

She glanced at the beer on the counter.

'So you've recovered from the *tomates*?' she said. 'You were very drunk.' She tutted slowly, shaking her head in mock disapproval.

Raymond stared at her uncomprehendingly. How could she behave as if nothing untoward had occurred? But there it was: she was the consummate actress. Perhaps the whole thing was an elaborate charade. Her address had been planted in his father's desk for Raymond to find. Delph—perfectly cast—had been cued to exit the apartment building at exactly the right moment. And the knife: of course the knife had been set out where he would see it. The philatelist's shop was likely no more than a set. Raymond half expected his father to emerge from behind the bar, still in the make-up he had been wearing on the slab in the mortuary, and the participants would laughingly take their curtain call. What a lark it had all been! But, of course, that was nonsense. Everything that had occurred was all too real. Raymond became more and more agitated.

Delph was looking at him with a perplexed expression. 'What have you done to your head?' she asked.

'I fell down the stairs outside your apartment,' said Raymond. There did not seem any point in hiding the truth. 'I paid a visit to your mother.'

Delph widened her eyes, making her squint more pronounced than ever. 'You did what?' she said.

'I wanted to see you, so I went to your apartment,' he said.

At this point, Dédé gave a theatrical cough. 'Much as I hate to interrupt the course of true love,' he said, 'but our patients require their prescriptions.' He gestured towards the customers by the door.

Delph seemed relieved by the distraction. She took up her tray and began to clear the tables. Raymond turned back to the counter. He observed Delph in the mirror behind the bar as she exchanged her usual greetings with the regulars. He drank his beer. Delph returned and recited the orders to Dédé as she unloaded the empties onto the counter. He, in turn, removed the glasses and cups to the sink and started setting out the drinks. Delph placed these on her tray. This was their little routine. Delph was close enough for Raymond to smell the peppery aroma of her sweat. He felt a sudden desire to kneel in front of her and bury his face in her sex. He leaned back on his stool, inhaling deeply. Delph moved off with her tray of drinks, pointedly ignoring him.

Raymond asked for another beer.

Dédé looked at him impassively. 'I think you've had enough already. Time to clear off.'

Raymond stared at him defiantly, but he simply returned

to his chores. When Delph returned to the counter, Raymond reiterated his desire to speak to her.

'If you're so desperate to talk to me, come back at ten,' she said.

'I need to talk to you now,' he said with greater urgency.

Dédé looked up from the drink he was preparing. 'Did you not hear what I said, kid? Time to pay up and shove off.'

Raymond slid off the stool and took a step towards Delph. A look of what might have been fear passed across her eyes, but she stood her ground, her right hand resting on the counter. In his peripheral vision, Raymond was aware of the regulars by the door shifting in their seats to get a proper view of what was going on. Even the chess players looked up from their game. Raymond glanced at the clock on the wall. Barely ten minutes had passed since Delph's appearance.

'Do you not know who I am?' said Raymond.

'Of course, I do,' she said, glancing towards Dédé. 'You're a dumb kid from Saint-Louis who can't get it up.'

Raymond rummaged in his satchel and brought out his knife. He pulled off the leather sheath and held the blade out in front of him. Dédé breathed a weary sigh. He had witnessed many such incidents. He stepped through the hatch and placed himself between the two protagonists.

'Now, what are you planning to do with that?' he said.

He took a step towards Raymond. Raymond took a step back, knocking over the stool he had been sitting on.

'I need to speak to Delph,' he said. He pronounced each word as if it was a complete sentence. His eyes were smarting.

Someone shouted: 'Give him a smack, Dédé.'

To general laughter, a second voice yelled: 'Go for him, kid!'

Raymond glanced at the faces around the room, eager for a bit of action. The young cop was peering through the door. If they wanted a performance, they were going to get it.

Dédé approached Raymond with an outstretched arm, ready to shepherd him to the door. But the bartender did not appear unduly troubled by what was happening.

Raymond was unable to retreat any further. He took a step forward and flapped the knife unconvincingly in front of him. Quite by chance he caught the bartender's hand at the root of his thumb. Dédé recoiled. He examined the wound on his hand. There were half-hearted cheers from the onlookers. Raymond was horrified by what he'd done. Delph placed her hand on her forehead. Her tray of drinks fell to the floor. Dédé grabbed a cloth from the counter and wrapped it round his wounded hand. It was quickly soaked with blood.

'I'm sorry,' said Raymond, but he continued to hold out the knife.

Dédé threatened to break his arm.

There was a lull, of no more than a few seconds, while those involved assessed their positions. Raymond, for his part, would happily have dropped the knife and walked out of the bar. Had it not been for the expectant crowd, and for the fact that he had not yet paid for his beer and cigarettes, he might have done so. He imagined their jeers as he left. Dédé would no doubt shout some abusive remarks at his back. Perhaps he would even pursue him to the door and give him a good beating. But, as it was, events had already escalated beyond his control.

Delph stepped past Dédé. 'You need to get out of here,' she said. Then it struck Raymond. Her nose, jutting sharply outwards at the bridge then continuing down at an angle, was his father's nose. The high cheekbones were his father's cheekbones. Even her sardonic manner was a mirror of his father's. It was astonishing that he had not seen it before.

Raymond recalled her opening her shirt—his own father's shirt—to display her chest in the backroom of Johnny's. He now felt intoxicated by her scent. He raised his knife hand at a right angle to his body, his arm fully extended. Then, with a firm jerk of his elbow, he thrust it into the side of his neck. He felt the blade penetrate his skin, make some progress through the muscle, before his hand instinctively loosened its grip. The knife lodged there for a few seconds—no more than that—before dropping to the floor. Raymond was pleased the effect of his action. Delph stifled a scream. There were gasps from the onlookers. Chairs were scraped back as people rose to get a better view. Even Dédé appeared taken aback. Raymond imagined a great arc of blood spraying across the floor, but in reality only a small glug emerged from the wound. He grinned stupidly at Delph. Then his legs gave way beneath him. He fell face first to the floor, his arms hanging limply at his sides. After a moment, he was aware of the rough texture of the floorboards against his cheek. He suddenly felt tremendously foolish. What an idiotic thing to do! He wondered whether these were to be his final moments of consciousness. And if his final thought was to be that, he was an idiot. But it was not. He became aware of an assortment of footwear around where he lay on the floor. He recognised the black slip-ons of the pockmarked man. The toe of another man's shoe was splayed open, and Raymond could see a patch of dried glue where he had attempted to repair it. He looked for Delph's boots but they were not to be seen. He was hauled to his feet and deposited on a stool. Someone suggested calling an ambulance, but it was decided there was no need. Various derogatory words circulated. Someone asserted, with a hint of admiration, that he could have properly hurt himself. At a certain point, the young cop entered. He declared that he was a policeman, but in such an unauthoritative voice that no one paid him any heed.

Once it was decided that Raymond was not seriously hurt, the regulars drifted back to their tables. The chess players reset their clock and resumed their game. The young cop enquired if there was a telephone on the premises and was directed to the kiosk in the street outside.

Dédé pulled a stool up in front of Raymond and instructed him to tilt his head to the side. He deftly cleaned the wound on Raymond's neck. Delph appeared from behind the counter and silently handed him a roll of gauze and some sticking plaster. She did not look at or speak to Raymond. Dédé applied a dressing with some dexterity and stuck it down. Then he got up and brought Raymond a shot of brandy and indicated that he should drink it.

Raymond thanked him and apologised for the trouble he had caused. Dédé shrugged. 'No harm done,' he said. He made Raymond empty his pockets and took what money he had to cover the cigarettes and the beer he had drunk.

Raymond felt weary. He was ready for home. He drank the brandy he had been given. It was as if nothing had happened. Someone must have picked up his knife and Raymond did not ask for it back. The blood that had been spilled on the floor had been mopped up. At the table adjacent to the door, a pack of cards had been produced. A fat man in braces slowly dealt out the hands. The chess players finished their game and packed up the pieces in their usual fashion. The pockmarked man finished up his drink and left, bidding good evening to Dédé. Delph reappeared from somewhere behind the counter and collected a few glasses. No one made any comment about what had occurred. She did not look at Raymond. He had no desire to speak to her. Perhaps none of it even mattered. He looked up at the clock on the wall. Barely half an hour had passed since he entered the bar.

Outside, he stopped and looked at his reflection in the darkened window of a butcher's shop. He put his fingers to the dressing of his wound. A little blood oozed through the gauze. He pushed his hair back behind his ears. He now had a bluish lump on his forehead from where his head had struck the floor. This to add to the graze and torn trousers from falling down the stairs. Behind him, the young cop followed on the opposite side of the street. Raymond walked to the station. A train arrived as soon as he reached the platform. He boarded without buying a ticket. What was the worst that could happen? If a conductor came along, he would only put him off at Bartenheim.

Twenty-four

GORSKI HAD TO ASK DIRECTIONS several times before he found Rue Saint-Fiacre. It was an unremarkable street, a little run-down, but respectable. Gorski parked and walked from one end to the other. Roland was nowhere to be seen. He walked back along the opposite pavement, pausing to look in the window of a philatelist's. The cluttered array of goods reminded him of his father's pawnshop.

He went into the little café on the corner. It was the sort of place that depended on a clientele too idle to walk more than the most minimal distance from their homes. The floor was polished concrete, an arc etched into it where the metal door opened and closed. Next to the door was a refrigerator bearing illustrations of various ice creams. There were four round plastic-topped tables, each with a single cone-shaped metal leg, these arranged along the wall to the right of the door. A metal rack held the day's newspapers. Behind the counter was the usual assortment of cigarettes and lottery tickets. On the far wall next to a door to the WC, a series of yellowed clippings from *L'Alsace* were pinned. A small television was attached to the wall above the door by an ugly metal stanchion. It was not switched on. There were no other customers.

The proprietor was a mild-looking man of around sixty. The sleeves of his shirt were rolled up and fastened with clasps above the elbow. His tie was neatly knotted and secured with a silver clip. Gorski asked if a young man had been in to make a telephone call. The proprietor confirmed that he had. Gorski asked in which direction he had left. The man looked at him questioningly. If he did not answer immediately, it was not because he wished to be unhelpful, but rather because he was the type that respected the privacy of his customers. Gorski showed him his ID.

The man looked at it carefully and inclined his head in apology for his reticence. 'I'm afraid I did not pay sufficient attention,' he said.

A fat man with a terrier was sitting at one of the two metal tables on the pavement outside. There was no drink on the table and it appeared that he had merely stopped for a breather. Gorski went outside and repeated his enquiry about Roland. The man mulled over the question then shook his head slowly. He bent to tickle the back of his dog's ear. Gorski went back inside and asked for a *jeton*. He called the station. Schmitt answered. Roland had not called again.

'If he does,' said Gorski, 'tell him I'm in the café he called from earlier.'

'Boyfriend stood you up, has he?' said Schmitt. He started to say something else, but Gorski hung up. He approached the counter and perched on one of the three stools there. He lit a cigarette and asked for a beer.

The proprietor carefully placed a bottle on a paper doily in front of him. Then he lit a cigarette himself. Usually in such a situation, the proprietor of a bar will busy himself with some menial task—polishing glasses or wiping down surfaces—so that his customer does not feel self-conscious about drinking alone. Or he will feel the need to make some banal remarks. But the proprietor of the café on the corner of Rue Saint-Fiacre did neither of these things. He simply stood behind the counter, watching Gorski with a placid expression. Once in a while he stepped forward to tap his cigarette into the ashtray on the counter. Gorski felt quite comfortable. There was no point chasing round the streets of Mulhouse looking for Roland. It was well over an hour since he had called from the kiosk outside Weismann's apartment.

An old woman with a pug entered the bar. She was carrying a canvas bag of vegetables. The dog struggled to climb the single step into the bar. The woman sat down at the table nearest the door. The proprietor greeted her by name and brought her a measure of brandy. The woman gazed fixedly at the drink for some minutes, as if to demonstrate the extent of her willpower. Then she raised the glass to her lips and took a tentative sip as though testing to see if it was poisoned. She set the glass back on the table and waited. Then, seemingly satisfied that the drink was uncontaminated, she picked up the glass for a second time and knocked back the remaining contents with a sharp twist of her wrist. She remained there for some minutes more, as if the brandy was merely incidental to the purpose of her visit. Then she placed a coin on the table and left. The proprietor collected her glass and, though it was quite unnecessary, wiped down the table. When he returned to his post behind the counter, Gorski ordered another beer.

Outside, there was a scraping of metal on concrete. The fat man with the dog was getting to his feet. He gave a little salute to the proprietor through the window and ambled off. Gorski liked it here. It was the sort of place he could happily get used to.

LATER THAT EVENING, GORSKI put his suitcase gently down in the vestibule. He had not told his mother he was coming, but there were two places set at the table by the window.

'Ah, good, you're here. I was just going to call you again,' she said as he pushed open the door.

'It's me, Georges,' he said.

She looked towards the door.

'Ah,' she said with a smile. 'I'll have to set another place.'

She made her way ponderously across to the sideboard where the placemats and napkins were kept.

'There's no need, Maman,' said Gorski. 'It will just be the two of us.'

A confused expression clouded his mother's face, but it quickly passed and she took herself off to the kitchen, where a pot of bouillon was simmering. Gorski sat down at the place Mme Gorski had set for her husband. It took her an age to ladle out two bowls of soup and carry them to the table, but Gorski did not intervene.

When she sat down, Gorski asked if there was any wine. He already knew there were a number of bottles in the cupboard beneath the sink. Mme Gorski replied that she rarely bothered with wine now, but he was welcome to look. Gorski fetched a bottle and uncorked it. He poured a little for his mother.

'It's good for you,' he said. 'Keeps the blood clean.' This had been one of his father's sayings. He filled his own glass to the brim. Gorski broke up the bread that his mother had placed in the centre of the table. He buttered a piece and put it on his mother's side plate, but she did not eat it. They ate their soup in silence. When they were finished, Gorski cleared away the bowls and washed up, taking his time in the kitchenette. When he returned, his mother was back in her chair by the fire. Gorski poured himself another glass of wine. The silence was oppressive. He did not know how to bring up that he intended to stay the night. He went out into the vestibule and took his suitcase into his old bedroom, carefully leaving the door ajar.

He had not set foot in this room for twenty years or more. It was tiny. There was space only for the small desk at which he had once sat doing his homework, the oversized wardrobe and the narrow divan. The room smelt of old books. He opened the small window. Gorski laid his suitcase on the bed. Above, there were two shelves of the detective novels he had been fond of reading as a teenager.

When he returned to the living room, he paused in the doorway. His mother smiled sadly at him from her chair. There was no need to explain anything. Gorski raised his fingers to the mezuzah attached to the jamb.

'You know, Maman, I've often wondered about this little box,' he said.

Mme Gorski appeared surprised by the question. Gorski pointed more clearly to the decorative casing.

'It's pretty, isn't it?' she said.

'Yes,' said Gorski. 'But I wondered how it came to be here.'

Mme Gorski gave a little shake of her head. 'It was there when your father and I moved in,' she said. 'Either that or your father put it there. I can't remember. He was always bringing knick-knacks up from the shop.'

Gorski nodded. He sat down at the table, facing his mother. Her eyes were beginning to close. After a few minutes, she announced that she was going to bed. She would leave Gorski to turn off the lights. He bid her good night. He sat at the table for some time. It felt strange to be alone in his parents' apartment. He found himself picturing Lucette Barthelme sitting in his mother's chair. The fact that there now was nothing to prevent him from calling on her saddened him. Perhaps he should go down to the Restaurant de la Cloche for a beer or two. What could be more natural than that? Maybe one evening he would even take up Lemerre's offer to join his cronies for a game of cards. But he did not want his mother to hear him go out, and she might be alarmed if he returned late at night. Instead, he waited until he was sure she was asleep before fetching a second bottle from the cupboard beneath the sink.

Translator's afterword

WHEN *L'ACCIDENT SUR L'A35* appeared in France in the spring of 2016, the press coverage focused less on the merits of the book than on the question of to what extent it was a work of fiction. Raymond Brunet himself invited this response, teasing the reader with the novel's epigraph—*What I have just written is false. True. Neither true nor false*—itself taken from Jean-Paul Sartre's notoriously unreliable memoir. In their shrewd marketing of the book, Éditions Gaspard-Moreau also encouraged readers to see the work as thinly veiled autobiography. Rather than issue a conventional press release, rumours of the existence of the new Brunet manuscripts were leaked in late-night conversations in bars around the Latin Quarter where the publisher is based. Gossip began to appear on Twitter and in a number of obscure blogs, but Gaspard-Moreau refused to make any official comment. Eventually, an article entitled *Le retour de l'étranger?* appeared in the weekend edition of *Le Monde*, which in turn generated further coverage. Aside from the free publicity, these articles served to return Raymond Brunet to the consciousness of a reading public that had largely forgotten him. No review copies were sent out in advance of publication. This naturally gave rise to speculation that the novel was substandard, but paradoxically increased the level of interest in the book among the French literati. Gaspard-Moreau, often regarded as one of France's most conservative publishing houses, then released the book in a modest first edition of a few hundred copies. Not surprisingly, this sold out in a few days and the demand for the book was such that Gaspard-Moreau then felt confident enough to undertake a considerably larger print run. Within a few months, *L'Accident sur l'A35* had clocked up as many sales as Brunet's previous novel had in thirty-four years.

So to what extent is *The Accident on the A35* 'true'? Raymond Brunet, it will be recalled, was born in Saint-Louis in 1953. Aside from a short stay in Paris following the release of the successful film of *La Disparition d'Adèle Bedeau* in 1989, he lived a life of obscurity in his home town until his suicide in 1992. He was by all accounts a likeable but withdrawn man, who, like many of his characters, seems to have found the everyday interactions of life unduly traumatising. He was a misfit.

A great deal of *The Accident on the A35* is clearly autobio-graphical. Raymond Brunet, like his fictional surrogate, Raymond Barthelme, was the son of an austere lawyer, also named Bertrand. He was brought up in an imposing house on the leafy outskirts of Saint-Louis, although in what was perhaps a rather half-hearted attempt to protect his mother's privacy, there is no such street as Rue des Bois. Most of the locations in both Saint-Louis and Mulhouse were, however, closely based on real places. Saint-Louis, it should be said, is by no means as dismal as it is described in the novel. Unremarkable, perhaps, but neither the town nor its inhabitants deserve Brunet's venomous portrayal; a portrayal that undoubtedly says more about the author's self-loathing than about the town itself. Crucially, however, the central event of the novel occurred almost exactly in real life as it does in the novel. On the night of the 9th of October 1970—a week before Brunet's seventeenth birthday—Bertrand Brunet's Mercedes left the southbound carriageway of the A35, a few miles north of Saint-Louis. He was killed instantly. His whereabouts on the evening of the accident were, noted *L'Alsace*, a 'minor mystery'.

So the premise and central characters of the novel were clearly rooted in reality, but what of the narrative? Certainly, the somewhat gaudy subplot involving the murder of Veronique Marchal is pure fiction. No such murder occurred in Strasbourg at the time, and the description of the crime owes a great deal to the opening of Claude Chabrol's 1971 film *Juste avant le nuit*, in which a middle-aged businessman strangles his mistress in circumstances much like those in the book. Chabrol had directed the screen version of *La Disparition d'Adèle Bedeau*, and there can be little doubt that Brunet, who was in any case something of a cinephile, would have seen his earlier work.

Far greater uncertainty surrounds the adventures of Raymond Barthelme in Mulhouse, however. Much to the glee of the board of Gaspard-Moreau, a handful of journalists made it their business to uncover the 'true story' behind *The Accident on the A35*. It helped that there was (and still is) a bar on Rue de la Sinne named Le Convivial, and although it bears only a passing resemblance to the establishment in the book, for a while it became the unofficial base camp of these literary detectives. None of the regulars or staff in the bar remembered an event like the one that forms the climax of the novel; nor did they remember a young man like Raymond Barthelme visiting the premises. But why should they? If the incidents had actually taken place, they would have done so over forty years before. One regular, by then in his seventies, did vaguely recall a bartender named Dédé, but he was never traced.

The journalists' activities centred on Rue Saint-Fiacre. The street is a few minutes' walk from Rue de la Sinne, but while it is broadly as described in the novel, it boasts neither a philatelist's shop nor a corner café. Had Rue Saint-Fiacre been the location of actual events in Raymond Brunet's life, these differences may simply have been due to the vagaries of memory. Or they may have been inventions to allow the author to introduce certain elements of his story; in particular, the theft of the knife, which closely mirrors an incident in Sartre's *The Age of Reason*, in

253

which the character of Boris buys a knife from a similar shop before stealing a thesaurus. On the other hand, and given that Brunet invented a name for the street where his own home was located in Saint-Louis, any actual events may have taken place in another street entirely. It's possible that the choice of Rue Saint-Fiacre was simply a nod towards Brunet's literary hero, Georges Simenon, one of whose earliest novels was entitled *L'Affaire Saint-Fiacre*.

Neither this, nor the fact that Irene Comte—had she existed—would have been well into her eighties, prevented the journalists from knocking on the doors of every apartment in the street. An ageing spinster, Isabelle Cabot, living in an apartment at 10 Rue Saint-Fiacre (diagonally opposite No.13), denied ever having met Bertrand or Raymond Brunet. She did, however, have a daughter—coincidentally or not—called Delphine, who was tracked down to her home in Lyons. Delphine Cabot inadvertently fuelled the speculation by refusing to talk to any journalists. Some claimed that Isabelle Cabot was only remaining loyal to a promise she had made to Bertrand Brunet to keep their relationship secret. And had the events of the novel taken place as described, it would be quite understandable for Delphine not to wish to have them publicly raked over. It was more commonly held, however, that the attention focussed on the two women was nothing more than the unseemly harassment of individuals entirely unconnected to what were most likely fictional events.

Whether Isabelle and Delphine Cabot were the prototypes for Irene and Delph will never be known (Isabelle has since died). It does, however, seem valid to ask why, if the events portrayed in the novel had no basis in truth, Brunet would have been so anxious for it not to be published in his mother's lifetime. And, if we allow ourselves to speculate further, had some sexual relations occurred between Brunet and a half-sister, the trauma of this might account for the difficulties he experienced with the opposite sex later in life. During his spell in Paris publicising the film of *La Disparition d'Adèle Bedeau*, Emmanuelle Durie, the actress who played the role of the title character, developed something of a fondness for the author. During the few weeks Brunet spent in Paris, the two discreetly dined together and accompanied one another to the city's art galleries. In an interview conducted many years after Brunet's death, Durie described him as a softly spoken, intelligent man with a self-deprecating sense of humour. He liked nothing more than to sit in the Jardin du Luxembourg speculating about the lives of those who walked past. She had, she admitted, been quite smitten with him. But, she said, 'He seemed to have a kind of horror of any sexual contact.' At the time she had concluded that he was a 'suppressed homosexual'.

However, while such speculation might make for fine entertainment, it is, at the end of the day, no more than tittle-tattle. What matters is not whether *The Accident on the A35* is 'true', but whether it is any good. The real measure of 'truth' in any novel is not whether the characters, places and events portrayed exist beyond the pages of the book, but, rather, whether they seem authentic to us as readers. When we open the pages of a novel, we enter into a pact with it. We want to immerse ourselves in its milieu. We want to engage with the characters, to find their actions psychologically plausible. We invest a little bit of ourselves in the narrative and, while never quite forgetting that it is fiction, experience the disappointments, humiliations and petty successes of the characters as if they were our own. A novel is, in Sartre's phrase, 'neither true nor false'; but it must feel *real*.

Certainly, it must have felt real to Raymond Brunet. As both a novelist and an individual, he was entirely trapped in his home town. Natives of Saint-Louis, disgruntled by his earlier portrayal of their municipality, found little to placate them in *The Accident on the A35*. Similarly, the characters have stepped from the same playbook, and whether directly autobiographical or not, they undoubtedly reflect the preoccupations of an individual who appears to have grown increasingly neurotic as his life went on. His brush with celebrity, and the all too brief time he spent in the cosmopolitan environment of Paris, can only have thrown the monotonous nature of his life in Saint-Louis into relief. The fact that Brunet was, in effect, waiting for his mother to die so that he might continue to publish his work, must have been an insufferable torment. In the end, he chose to bring about his own death rather than wait for hers.

While Gaspard-Moreau's astute marketing ensured that the book outsold *La Disparition d'Adèle Bedeau,* critical reception was mixed. One reviewer, while snootily noting the 'unseemly circus' surrounding the publication of the novel, observed that it was perfectly obvious why Brunet had killed himself rather than see the book published. It was the work, she averred, of a writer who 'had only one idea, and not even a good one at that'. On the other hand, Jean Martineau, writing in *Lire,* was relieved to find a novel that 'eschews the gimmickry of so much contemporary fiction and relies instead on the time-honoured virtues of character and story'. It was, he said, 'hopelessly and agreeably old-fashioned'.

It is, of course, for readers of this, the first English language edition, to decide for themselves who is right. A translator is first and foremost a reader, and it is my hope that others will share my pleasure in returning to the non-descript streets of Saint-Louis.

GMB, April 2017